Axe-ing For Trouble

The Maine Lumberjacks

Book 5

Daphne Elliot

Published by Melody Publishing, LLC

Editing by Beth Lawton at VB Edits

Cover by 50's Vintage Dame

 Created with Vellum

Dedication

To My Imposter Syndrome.
You are a shit stirring little troll who lives rent-free in my
brain. I see you. I hear you. And yet I still wrote this book. So
please choke on it and then kindly fuck off into the void.

Prologue

Mila

The last thing I expected was to get shot at today.

In fact, I'd woken up feeling pretty optimistic. After months of patience, I'd finally had a breakthrough. I'd been allowed into the back room with the power players.

Yes, I was serving drinks and getting leered at, but I'd seen him. The boss. The guy I'd spent a year tracking down.

The plan I'd been carefully constructing for months was coming together. Using the Velcro tape I'd stashed for this occasion, I stuck my phone to the underside of my tray. Then I strolled among the power players, offering drinks while secretly recording as much of the conversation as I could.

There was no way I could have taken photos undetected, so I prayed the microphone I'd bought on Amazon would do the trick and committed all the faces to memory, doing my best to track ages, heights, and identifying marks for those I didn't know.

Mapping out the organization had taken a lot of time, especially since everyone involved used aliases and code words that had taken me months to decipher. But I had photos and audio of most of them, along with details and dates.

To them, I was a ditzy bartender. Eye candy. A hanger-on.

I smiled and flirted and then conveniently left the tray on the stand near the poker table before I left the room. Being underestimated certainly had its perks.

It was after one a.m. when the game finally broke up. I'd delivered several rounds of drinks by then, but I'd left the tray in place, hoping with all I had that I could pick up all the important details.

I volunteered to clean up, then pretended to be concerned with counting my tips. While I puttered around, I slyly grabbed the phone and shoved it into my bra. I'd upload all these goodies to the cloud later, and then it was lights out for these fuckers.

I was determined to take them down. Every one of them. Because this was personal.

They'd come for my family. So I'd make them pay.

I WAS CERTAIN I'D GOTTEN AWAY WITH IT UNTIL RAZOR came banging on the door of my trailer this morning. I hadn't left the bar until almost three, so more than anything, I wanted to pull the covers back over my head. But when he started spewing threats, I bolted up in bed.

Heart pounding, I threw on somewhat clean clothing and a pair of sneakers. Then I peeked out the window.

It appeared that he was alone, thank God, and his bike was parked on the side of the street in front of my patio.

He wore his usual leathers and sunglasses, so I couldn't see his eyes, but the rage was evident in his voice. Normally an easygoing guy, I could tell he was furious this morning.

"Who are you? Amy? Or is it really Mila? Are you a journalist? What the fuck do you think you're playing at?"

My heart lurched. Aw, fuck. How the hell did he know my real name?

Had I gotten sloppy? Had my actions last night been sniffed out? I'd covered my tracks so thoroughly, fake passport and all, so I couldn't fathom what had tipped them off. I'd been living as Amy for so long I barely remembered my real name.

And Razor, of all people?

Shit. It was time to get out of here. I'd put on a pair of sweats and an old sports bra, but there was no time to change. So I tugged a T-shirt over my head, then shoved my phone, license, and a wad of cash into my bra.

I was contemplating climbing up onto a chair to fetch the go bag I'd stashed above the loose ceiling tiles when the sound of tires on gravel caught my attention.

Heart racing, I peered out the crack between the curtains again.

A blacked-out SUV had joined Razor's bike. It was parked mere feet from the door of my trailer.

It was official. I was fucked.

So I did what any person would in my situation.

I stole my ex-boyfriend's motorcycle and took off.

As stealthily as I could, I climbed out the back window and jogged around the other side of the trailer.

Razor was still banging and shouting, unwittingly drowning out any sound I made.

Since he'd so stupidly parked on the street, I snuck around my neighbor's trailer and crouched low. At the front corner, I peeked out, then pulled back quickly again. A couple of big guys in sunglasses were climbing out of the SUV. The minute the driver slammed the door behind him, I made my move, sprinting toward Razor's bike as fast as I could. Idiot left the keys in it. So I revved the engine and took off. I wished I could have seen his face, but I was too busy trying to keep the damn thing upright.

The dirt roads helped, and I'd been jogging around here for the last six months, so I was familiar with the trails. Keeping off main roads, I sped toward the bar. I'd talk to Otter. He was the peacekeeper, the mediator of all disputes within the club. And he'd taken me under his wing.

As I crossed the bridge over the river, two more SUVs appeared. And when they started shooting at me, I knew there was no coming back from this.

I guess I hadn't been as stealthy as I thought. If I had to bet, someone had sold me out. Probably Razor. When I'd broken up with him, he'd taken it hard. I didn't know why. It had been a casual thing. I was bored and lonely, and he was dumb and hot. But after a few weeks, I couldn't even pretend to be interested in anything he said, and by then, I'd gained access to the inner circle, so he'd outlived his usefulness.

Pulling back the throttle, I headed for the forest. Dammit. I should have stopped to grab my go bag. I'd made it over the river, navigating toward Lovewell, when I realized I was running on fumes. The cheap fucker hadn't filled up his tank before coming over to threaten me. Typical.

Continuing on foot was my only option. I'd lie low for a bit and work through my options. Then, when it was safe, I'd go to law enforcement. Thank God I'd slipped into my sneakers on autopilot. And at least I had my phone.

Given that these guys had sent the cavalry, they must have been discussing legitimately incriminating shit last night. While I jogged through the woods, I couldn't help but grin. These idiots had likely knotted their own noose. With any luck, they'd just made my job easier.

All I had to do was stay alive. Though at the moment, that seemed difficult.

Thankfully, I knew my way around these woods, and I'd kept up with running and martial arts training on my own.

As boring as I'd found rural life, I couldn't deny that the lack of nights out at clubs and good restaurants had given me ample time for exercise.

I tripped on tree roots and slipped on pine needles that were wet from last night's rain, but I stayed on my feet. My thigh was bleeding, but I couldn't stop to assess the injury. When I'd made it to the far side of the state park, I slowed a bit, sucking in lungfuls of air. I was almost certain I was in the clear until the roar of ATV engines bounced off the trees around me.

The sound was commonplace in Maine, but ATVs were banned in this part of the state park.

I stilled, eyes narrowed, trying to pinpoint which direction they were coming from. Fucking Razor knew I loved to jog in this park.

With one more deep inhale, I took off in the opposite direction. The cuts and scrapes I'd amassed during my escape stung in the cold air, but I pushed forward.

Just as I crested a small hill, I caught sight of a figure ahead of me. Before I could change direction, a gunshot rang out, and wood splintered in all directions from the tree behind me.

As panic flooded my system, I pivoted, heading off the trail into the thick forest.

I kept my head down and forced myself forward, but the forest floor was thick with vegetation and rocks. I climbed over a large boulder in an effort to put something solid between me and the men with the guns, but as I reached the top, I slipped.

Losing my footing, I scrambled for the nearest tree limb, worried I was going to crack my skull. As I clutched the branch, my shoulder popped, and agonizing pain shot from my neck to my fingertips.

With a stifled groan, I slid down, hitting my tailbone hard and landing on my knees in the brush. Tears streamed down my face as I struggled to get up. I was shaking, maybe from shock, but I kept going, putting one foot in front of the other, struggling not to scream from the pain.

When another shot cracked through the air, I knew I had to get deeper. Crouching, I banked left and ran, putting distance between myself and the place where they'd last spotted me. At a break in the tree line, I got on my hands and knees and crawled to avoid detection. I'd never felt such excruciating pain as I did when I put weight on my left arm.

Twigs and branches scratched my face, but nothing, not even the wound in my thigh, compared to the blinding pain in my arm. Even so, I kept pushing. Though with every step, I got more delirious.

I came across an area where several trees had been

downed and dragged myself over, wedging my body between two of them. Both were large brown pines. They were in pretty serious states of decay, but they provided decent cover.

I pulled pine branches, leaves, and dirt over my body and shimmied as low as I could, focusing on breathing.

My body shook—a mixture of cold and shock, I was sure—as I squeezed my eyes shut and willed my being to remain still and silent. Everything hurt and the gash in my thigh was on fire. With the moldy leaves I'd used to hide myself coming into contact with all of my wounds, I'd probably end up with a staph infection.

My shoulder screamed every time I moved even an inch. My fingertips had gone numb, save for small electric shocks of pain shooting down my arm at regular intervals.

I shimmied my right arm out and reached up to my chest to make sure my phone was secure. When I was met with the give of my body rather than the hard surface of the device, my stomach sank.

Biting back a cry of pain, I shifted and forced my hand up to the neckline of my shirt. I pulled out my license and a wad of cash.

But no phone.

I sat up, risking possible discovery, and scanned the ground around me, my pulse thundering in my ears. It had been there. I'd shoved it straight into my bra. Fuck. Where did it go?

Shouts rang out, voices bouncing off the trees. The sound startled me, sending my heart jumping into my throat. With a sharp breath, I pushed myself down, trying not to hyperventilate.

Where was my phone? How could it have fallen out?

It was probably on the ground nearby. Surely, it'd gotten dislodged when I was dragging leaves and debris over myself. I'd wait it out and then find it once I was in the clear.

There was no other option. That phone had all the evidence I'd collected.

Without it, I couldn't go to the FBI. I couldn't take them down. And if that happened, then this nightmare would never end.

I closed my eyes and exhaled, and that's when it hit me: I was utterly and totally alone.

So I lay there, protected by the cold, damp earth, while I formulated a plan.

"I will not die today." Jaw clenched so I wouldn't cry out in pain, I repeated the mantra over and over. "I will not die today." All the while, my limbs shook and my teeth chattered and my muscles screamed in pain.

Hours later—I thought; I had no concept of time with no watch or phone—the forest was silent but for the rustling of leaves and the occasional bird call. No more engines, no more guns.

The sky was darkening when I poked my head out, and the air was colder. I climbed out, wincing as I pushed up on my good arm. Over the last few hours, the cold earth had numbed a lot of the pain. Being immobile helped too. Now, though, I was stiff from lying in one place for so long, making my injuries more acute. I'd need to get it looked at eventually, but for now, I had to push forward.

Using the fading daylight, I scoured the forest floor around my hiding place, looking for my phone. I skimmed my hands over and under every log and root and picked up handfuls of wet leaves and earth.

It was futile.

So I expanded the perimeter of my search, tracing the path I'd taken back here. I'd opted for a plain black case to avoid detection. That was great for evidence-gathering, but a pink and glittery cover would be much easier to find in the fucking forest.

As the sky darkened almost completely, I began shivering uncontrollably. As my adrenaline subsided, the full extent of my injuries made itself known, making it hard to even stand.

Focusing on breathing, I walked slowly, avoiding the trails, heading to the north entrance of the park. All the while, I cringed at the thought of where I had to go now.

I'd promised myself I wouldn't involve him. That I'd let the quiet, sexy musician live his life in peace. He seemed like the kind of guy who wanted to be left alone, and the poor man had already been through hell with his family.

We'd only had one night together, but that was enough to show me that I'd do all I could to protect him. To keep him and his family far away from this.

And I'd done all I could. Involving him was no longer inescapable. The whole group of them had been dropped into the middle of this war. It was virtually impossible not to hear the gossip at the bar, and when news of a fire had broken out, it was clear they were in danger now too.

I crossed Route 16 and walked along the northbound side, just inside the tree line. It was quiet tonight, but when the occasional car approached, I ducked behind a tree.

Every day, tensions here rose, making this idyllic rural area less safe.

And I was the only one who could stop it. Who could keep the people of Lovewell safe.

It had been far more difficult to stay away from him than I'd anticipated, but I'd made a promise to myself. That someday, after I'd dealt with this, after Hugo had recovered, I'd find him again.

But with every passing day, reality had made staying away from him more difficult and had made the future I hoped for more unlikely. Real life wasn't neat and tidy. It was messy and unpredictable.

So, out of options, I turned onto the secluded mountain road that led to his house.

I had information that could help him.

So it was time to pay a visit to my one-night stand.

Chapter 1
Jude

She was standing in my living room.

Amy.

No, not Amy.

Mila.

If that was even her real name.

My head was spinning. My small house was filled to the brim with my nosy family, and Ripley stood next to me, on high alert.

The hair on the back of my neck stood up. I hadn't seen her in over a year, and now, as she stood in front of me, explaining herself, all I could think was *trouble*.

My pulse pounded in my ears. This was bad. Dangerous.

Gus, who stood nearby, gave me a nod. That gave me a sliver of comfort. I could always depend on my older brother to take charge when things got difficult. He and I had worked together, keeping the family timber business going, for a decade, and we had developed our own shorthand.

Neither of us liked to talk more than necessary. So with

one look, he understood what I needed and gathered up his wife and infant daughter.

"The kids need to get to bed, and we should give Jude some privacy," he said.

Cole followed suit, collecting beer bottles and plates and taking them to the kitchen.

Finn and Noah did the same, clearing out the living room and packing up their kids. We'd been having family pizza night, a recent tradition.

It was one of my favorite pastimes. Cooking for my brothers and their families.

I hadn't anticipated becoming an amateur pizza chef, but I'd loved the challenge. The endless testing and careful preparation soothed me. I thrived on finding the perfect hydration ratio for my dough and getting the wood-burning oven to the precise temperature to bake the pies to perfection.

It suited my need to keep my hands busy. Stretching and kneading dough was therapeutic, and it forced me to slow down a bit.

The company wasn't terrible either. I lived alone up here on the mountain in my little house, just Ripley and me, and most of the time, it was exactly the way I wanted it.

But once in a while, it was nice to be surrounded by my family. When my house was filled with laughter and jokes, it reminded me that healing was possible. That with all the shit our father had put us through, we'd be okay. We could be a family, despite the lies and deceit and the way he tore us all apart.

We were moving forward, creating new bonds, welcoming kids and building lives. Even so, we were still living with our father's crimes hanging over our heads. We'd spent the last year evolving and finding our way.

Now, a bleeding woman had appeared, and she was standing in my living room, telling me we were in more danger.

The woman who had haunted my dreams.

She'd been here more than a year ago, played a role in the best night of my life, and then poof, she'd disappeared, never to be heard from again.

Now she stood, trembling, breathing shallowly, bleeding, in my living room.

Her hair was different. Shorter and darker.

Her black leggings were torn, and the gash on her thigh looked quite deep.

Her T-shirt was streaked with dirt and blood, and her arms and face were covered in fresh bruises.

My gut dropped as every detail registered.

My mind spun and I clenched my fists. Caught unaware like this, by such a chilling sight, I felt out of control. My thoughts spiraled in a way I typically worked hard not to allow. How much danger was she in? Who had hurt her? What could I do to help?

Cole walked out with the rest of my brothers and their families but returned a moment later with a large duffel bag. He'd barely set it on the coffee table before Willa was tearing into it, producing bandages and gauze.

She led Amy... er... Mila to the couch and gently helped her sit on the ottoman. Then she kneeled in front of her and asked a slew of pragmatic medical questions. Thank God for Willa. She was cheery and professional, even while tending to the scared, bleeding woman.

"Jude, can you get a set of clean clothes?" Willa asked over her shoulder.

Wordlessly, I went to my room and collected a T-shirt and a pair of sweats.

When I returned, she was assessing the injuries, gently talking through what she was seeing. The woman was awe-inspiring.

Mila sat on the ottoman, her face totally serene.

She looked like she'd fought a bear, but she was composed and calm.

Still beautiful. Regal, almost.

Tall and slender, with sharp cheekbones, plump lips, and steely gray eyes.

Every detail of the night we'd spent together had been burned into my brain. She'd burrowed its way into my soul in a way no other woman had.

That night, I'd seen her in the crowd, dancing with abandon as I played. I'd met her a few times at the dojo in Heartsborough. She'd come to a few self-defense classes I'd helped teach, and we'd chatted a bit. I thought she was gorgeous then.

But the night she showed up at the Moose, she was luminous. I couldn't take my eyes off her. Every single note I played was for her and her alone.

As a musician, I was used to being ogled by women. I was used to being approached after a set and flirted with while I played.

But I'd never experienced a connection like I had that night.

We had an entire conversation without speaking.

Her smile was electric. I could close my eyes and pull up the memory of it even now, every detail still crystal clear.

A spark had ignited, a tether linking us. So the moment the set ended, I strolled up to her and took the beer bottle from her hand and took a swig. The move was completely out of character for me. I was typically the quiet and let women come to me type.

But with her? I couldn't hold back. As if, subconsciously, I knew we had limited time, so I was determined to make the most of it.

An hour later, we were here, tearing each other's clothes off. Once we'd quelled the need consuming us, we laughed, talked, raided the kitchen, took Ripley out for a late-night walk. Then we fell asleep tangled in one another.

But when I woke, I was alone.

She'd left without a trace.

Without leaving a phone number.

While I still believed her name was Amy.

Cole nudged me, breaking me out of my thought spiral. "You okay?"

Arms crossed, I nodded, unable to look away as Willa shined a flashlight in Mila's eyes.

"You have a concussion," Willa concluded, clicking the light off. "Likely mild, but we need to be careful."

Mila put her head in one hand, that shoulder slumping, while she kept the injured arm cradled to her chest. "That explains the headache."

"What happened?" my sister-in-law asked. "Can you explain? I'd like to take you to the hospital—"

"No hospitals," Mila snapped. Her body tensed like a coiled snake ready to strike. She held her injured arm with the good hand, her eyes flashing with panic. "Hospitals ask questions and make records. Can't risk it."

Willa turned to me, her expression full of all kinds of questions.

My heart constricted painfully. "Can you help her?"

My sister-in-law was a wonderful doctor and an even better person. She made house calls regularly and had braved a snowstorm not all that long ago to help a pregnant woman in distress. And on top of that, she took care of the citizens of Lovewell every day.

"I can try." She turned and patted Mila's thigh. "Let's get you out of these dirty clothes. Then I'll examine you. We need to immobilize that shoulder. Given the bruising on your arms and stomach, I'd also like an X-ray to check for fractured ribs."

Mila shook her head vigorously, letting out a cry of pain that made my heart leap into my throat. Eyes filling with tears, she breathed in sharply. "Please. Can you please examine me here and see if anything's broken?"

Willa let out a big sigh. "Generally I need images to diagnose, but I'll try this way."

"I'll call in a favor," I said. "I've known a couple of the EMTs all my life. They could transport you to another hospital. Take you all the way to Augusta if we need to."

"No." The tears streamed down her cheeks now, leaving tracks in the dirt still covering her.

I squeezed my hands at my sides and inhaled deeply. I'd never felt so helpless or terrified. Her hair was crusted with dirt. Every inch of her was filthy. And the bruises were darkening by the minute. This woman, who'd been so alive, so strong the night we'd spent together, looked so frail.

Every instinct in me screamed to protect her. But how could I do that if I didn't know what was going on?

"Who did this?" I asked, the words coming out deeper than I'd anticipated. "Who hurt you?"

Willa peered over her shoulder, brow arched. "Boys, give us some privacy, please. I need to examine my patient. You may hear noises as I poke around, but please stay in the kitchen. I'll take care of her. Promise."

I couldn't leave, not while she was crying and in so much pain.

But I was too weak to fight off Cole, the biggest of my brothers, when he took the clothes from my hand and set them on the couch, then grabbed my elbow and pulled me into the kitchen.

While I paced the small space, he loaded the dishwasher, studying me every few seconds or so.

He wanted answers. But what he didn't understand was that I didn't have any.

"Boys," Willa called after only a few minutes. "Clean off and sterilize the kitchen island, please."

My heart lurched, and Cole went ramrod straight, looking at me with the same kind of horrified expression I was probably wearing. Sterilize the counter? Fuck. Mila needed a hospital, so why was she refusing to go?

We knew better than to disobey Willa's medical orders, so I choked the questions back and helped my brother clean off the large island. I'd donated the small table and chairs I'd once had set up in here and then installed the island a couple of years ago. I wanted more prep space, and the granite countertop made the tiny kitchen feel more modern.

Cole grabbed the cutting board and plates while I

grabbed bleach wipes from under the sink, and in minutes, we had it all cleared, cleaned, and sanitized.

Willa led Mila in with her hand on the small of her back.

"We need to manipulate her shoulder back into place," she explained, her tone cool and authoritative. "So we'll get her up on the island so she's lying on her stomach with her left arm and shoulder hanging off the side." At the island, she stopped and ensured Mila was still cradling her arm, then looked back at us. "I'll need both of you to help."

Without hesitation, I pulled a chair over and held out a hand, helping Mila step up onto it and then lower herself until she was lying on the cool granite.

"Cole, stand at the end and hold her legs to ensure she doesn't kick in reaction to the pain. Jude, stand on her right side. Keep her stable and make sure that shoulder doesn't move."

Mila lay face down, her head turned my way. Her complexion was pale but her expression was determined.

"You sure you're okay with this?" I asked, tentatively placing a hand on her right shoulder blade.

She nodded. "Yes." She squeezed her eyes shut. "Thanks for helping."

Though there was a layer of stained fabric between my hand and her back, I could feel the heat of her skin underneath my fingertips. She reached out, searching, so I slid my hand into hers and gave it a squeeze.

"Now," Willa explained, "I'm going to apply pressure to the socket joint. Between my pushing and the gravity pulling your arm down, it should slide back into place. I'll go slowly so I don't cause any ligament damage. But this will hurt."

Mila sucked in a shaky breath. "Okay."

"And I want to note that we could be doing this with anesthesia at a hospital."

"I'm fine, Doc," the woman lying prone between us gritted out. "Just do it."

Though her voice was stony, her hand was trembling. I threaded my fingers through hers, trying to offer some comfort.

"Ready?" Willa asked, looking from Mila to me to Cole.

Once we'd all confirmed that we were, she probed Mila's shoulder with her fingers, then pushed down.

When Mila screamed, my blood ran cold. Every instinct was telling me to pick her up and run far away. The thought of anyone being in pain, especially her, made my stomach roil.

"Almost there," Willa said, pulling on her arm while pushing on her shoulder. "Okay. That's it. I felt it pop back into the socket."

Mila was crying now, her whole body shaking with sobs.

Fuck. Wishing I could do something to take the pain away, I lamely rubbed circles around her upper back, still holding her hand.

"Cole, help me get her off the counter. Jude, grab a clean pillowcase." She put a gentle hand on Mila's back. "You were amazing. I'm going to make a sling to immobilize the arm. This will take some time to heal."

I darted away and returned immediately with a pillowcase, holding it out to my sister-in-law.

She took it without a word and used her surgical shears to cut it into triangles, then folded them and tied them together.

I'd never seen Willa in action like this. To me, she was

my baby brother's wife and a friend. I was taken aback by what she could accomplish with only a kitchen counter and a pillowcase.

"You're in shock," she explained to Mila. "The most important thing you can do is rest. We can drive you wherever you need to go."

"She'll stay here," I declared before I'd even considered what I was saying.

Even now, though she was hurt and scared, she was still brave and defiant. I knew in my bones I needed to protect this woman. That she needed to be here. She was clearly in danger, and as much as I did not want my family involved, I couldn't let her leave.

This house was remote and quiet, and I had Ripley. I could take care of her while keeping my family out of it.

"Stay," I said.

Though by the determined look on her face, I was sure she'd argue, she surprised me by giving me a small nod.

Willa stepped back and washed her hands. "For now, the best thing you can do is rest. I'll leave mild painkillers. Get plenty of water. Then sleep for as long as you can. I'll give Jude instructions for checking on you, but don't worry about anything but recovering. Okay?"

Mila, head hung and still teary, nodded.

"I'll be back tomorrow morning before I open the clinic. I'll bring antibiotics then so we can stave off any infection. I'll have real painkillers and a proper sling too. Once I've checked the joint and the swelling, we can decide what to do next."

I led Mila into the living room and guided her onto the couch. She leaned back and closed her eyes. Ripley was immediately by her side, hopping up onto the cushion and resting her head in her lap.

She reached out with her good arm and gently stroked my dog's fur, looking exhausted and worn out.

As I opened the door for Willa and Cole, my brother whipped around and hissed, "Dude, what the fuck? She is not okay."

I shook my head, dread washing over me. "I don't know. I'll figure it out."

Willa swallowed thickly but stood tall—or as tall as she could next to my six-foot-seven brother. "We should get the police involved. Her injuries are serious."

I took off my glasses and pinched the bridge of my nose. "Give me a day or two to figure out what's going on first. She needs rest, and then I'll talk to her."

When they'd reluctantly agreed and Cole, carrying Willa's medical bag, ushered her to his SUV, I closed the door and rested my forehead on the dark wood for a moment. The world was spiraling out of control. What the hell was going on? And if she'd open up about her injuries, could I trust her story? She hadn't even given me her real name.

I headed back to the living room, where I found Mila tentatively adjusting her position on the couch.

"You need to sleep in a bed. I'll sleep on the couch."

She grunted, keeping her gaze averted. "I'm fine here."

"My sister-in-law popped your shoulder back into place on my kitchen counter. You're injured and need rest. Just take the bed."

Finally, she looked at me, her full lips in a tight line. "No. I'll sleep here."

My head throbbed, pounding hard enough to pull my

attention from the madness that had descended. What the hell was going on? Was I harboring a fugitive?

The pain was all it took for me to snap. "Give me one good reason not to call the police," I said. "You show up here injured and filthy, tell me you were shot at, and that a criminal network is chasing you."

She tipped her chin up in defiance.

"But," I gritted out, "why should I believe you when you've lied to me before?"

She let out a sigh, her body deflating. "The police are compromised." Despite the pain she was in, her voice was frosty. "Your police chief is corrupt. He's on the payroll of narcotics traffickers."

"Was corrupt," I corrected, forcing my tone to level out. "He's suspended pending an investigation into misconduct after he went after Cole."

She raised an eyebrow. "He's done a hell of a lot more than that. And he isn't the only one. I can only imagine all this information is hard to process. Please know that I wouldn't have come here, I wouldn't have put you at risk, if I had any other options. Just... please," she begged, her breath hitching, "can I sleep here? I'll leave in the morning."

I wanted to push. My need to be in control of the situation was screaming inside me. But in this moment, she was so helpless, so small, propped up on my couch with her arm in a makeshift sling. Clearly, she'd been through hell. It was unfair to continue to push her.

Yes, I had to keep my family safe, but if I didn't eventually get answers from her, I wasn't sure I could do that. So I'd do everything I could to keep her close until she opened up.

I put my hands up. "Please stay. You're safe here. It's just

Ripley and me. I've got the room, and I spend most of my time at work anyway." With a long exhale, I raked a hand through my hair. "I think you'd be more comfortable in a bed, but if you really want to sleep out here, then I'll grab a couple of pillows and a blanket."

Her only response was a nod.

So, though it went against my every instinct, I dragged myself down the hall to fetch pillows and blankets.

Damn this stubborn woman. And damn my protective hero complex.

My entire world had been turned upside down tonight. And I had the distinct feeling my life would never be the same again.

Chapter 2
Mila

I shifted, and a bolt of pain shot through me. My head was groggy, and my mouth was dry. My left arm was pinned to my chest, and my thigh throbbed. With more effort than it should have taken, I lifted my right arm and touched the left. That movement alone was agonizing.

Eyes still closed, I took a deep breath. Despite the pain, I was warm, and the surface beneath me was soft. There was even some kind of pillow pile keeping my shoulder stable. With my good hand, I grazed the chunky knit blanket covering me, reveling in its plushness, grateful for its comfort.

Though in the back of my mind, a little voice urged me to panic, to move, to hide, my muscles ached too much to allow it. So, taking my chances, I lay still, piecing together where I was and why every inch of my body ached so badly.

Running through the woods.

Losing my phone and the evidence.

My chest tightened at the memories. Fuck.

Jude.

Though there was no relief when I thought of him, the pain was a little more bittersweet.

That pretty doctor who laid me on the kitchen counter and cranked my shoulder back into place.

That may have been the most painful moment of the day, but the almost immediate relief was worth it.

Falling asleep on the couch while patting the giant dog.

Huh.

Slowly, I forced my eyes open, searching for Ripley. But rather than being met with Jude's living room, I found myself propped up by a mountain of pillows in the middle of a massive king-size bed, staring up at a ceiling fan. I scanned the room, noting the thick blanket that in the light peeking in from around the curtains was a deep shade of green and was tucked around my toes to keep them warm.

I was assessing the dark furniture when Ripley padded into the room, followed by her owner.

I winced.

Jude.

He wore a pair of gray sweatpants and a faded T-shirt. His dark hair stood up in every direction, sleep-mussed, and his glasses were askew. I was practically immobile, feeling like I'd been run over by a bus, and the man strolled in wearing fucking sweatpants. Could I not catch a break?

"She is awake. Good girl." He patted the dog's head as he strode to my bedside.

"What am I doing here?" I asked, taking the glass of water he offered me.

"Resting, as the doctor ordered."

"I said I'd sleep on the couch."

"And I said you had to take the bed." His tone was firm, but the corner of his lip quirked.

"But I *was* sleeping on the couch." I remembered that part clearly. He'd been adamant that I sleep in his bed, his tone almost condescending. It rankled me, making it easy to draw a line in the sand. I was an unwanted guest. I would not put him out any more than I had to.

With a hum, he set a bottle of over-the-counter painkillers on the nightstand. "Once you were asleep, I carried you in here."

My heart stuttered. "I don't remember waking up. But I would have had to with the way my shoulder hurts."

He shrugged. "I was careful and you were exhausted." He grasped the blanket but didn't move to pull it back. "Can you sit up?" he asked, genuine concern in his eyes. "I'll make breakfast. Willa said you need to eat."

With his hand on my upper back, he helped me sit up. For a big, rugged guy, he was so gentle.

The dog rested her head on the edge of the bed at his side, her dark eyes surveying me.

Unable to resist the temptation, I scratched her ears.

"Ripley likes you." He worked around me, arranging the pillows to support my back more effectively. "She doesn't like most people."

"I need to go," I said, shifting so I could swing my legs over the side of the mattress.

"No." He leaned closer, and I was hit with a whiff of toothpaste mixed with a scent that was distinctly male. "Willa will be here soon. Rest for now. Your body needs it."

The dog leaned closer, nuzzling my hand. Her affection settled me. I'd always wanted a dog. It was another promise

I'd made myself many times. Maybe when this was all over, I'd get one. If it ever ended. Most days, I wasn't sure it would. Though after yesterday, it was clear it had to, and it would be in one of two ways. I'd either ride off into the sunset with a dog, or I'd be six feet under.

Jude hadn't moved from my side. Though he'd been a little bossy, he was as handsome and caring as I remembered. The burly lumberjack who'd taken me home, rocked my world, and then made me chocolate chip pancakes at three a.m.

I hadn't forgotten a single detail of the night we'd spent together. The weather, the moonlight, the way his strong, calloused hands felt on my body. Or the location of this little house in the middle of the forest.

"I shouldn't have come here," I murmured. "I promised myself I'd keep you out of this."

"Out of what?" he asked, his gaze intent behind his dark-rimmed glasses. "I still have no idea what's going on."

"I need to go." My first order of business was to head back to the woods. I wouldn't rest until I found that damn phone. I'd worked too long and too hard to lose the evidence.

"Stop." He stepped up closer so I couldn't move around him without having to scoot down the mattress. In this much pain, and under his scrutiny, I didn't dare attempt it.

"You're safe here. No one knows where you are except my family. Take some time to recover."

Embarrassingly, a big, fat tear rolled down my cheek.

"I'm sorry." He eased onto the edge of the bed, careful not to disturb my shoulder. "You're in shock. Please let your body recover. We can talk about all of this later."

Overcome by another wave of tears, I slumped back.

Pain shot through my arm, making me grimace. I'd been so close to finishing all of this. And now I'd lost the evidence. I was on the run and injured. All out of sorts in the presence of this large man and his equally giant dog.

I willed the frustration to settle. It was time to lighten the moment. He probably already thought I was a complete headcase, showing up here the way I did and then sobbing in his bed.

"I have a question," I said, keeping my tone easy. "Why Ripley? Is that a family name or something?"

He chuckled, dropping his chin to his chest. "No. Definitely not a family name." With a stroke of the dog's fur, he side-eyed me. "I named her after Ellen Ripley."

"Who's that? A musician?" As I asked, it suddenly hit me how terrible I must look. I was still covered in filth, and I could only imagine how wild my hair was.

He laughed again, the sound echoing off the walls and making my heart stumble a little. "Sorry." He wiped at the smile on his face. "No, Ellen Ripley, the hero of the *Alien* franchise."

I frowned, confused. "Are those movies?"

His eyes bulged. "You've never seen *Alien*? Jesus, we've got to fix that. Screw getting checked by a doctor. Let's have a movie marathon."

A laugh bubbled out of me. I'd forgotten how much I enjoyed his sarcasm. "Should I have seen them?"

"Yes. In addition to being my favorite movies, they're pop culture touchstones. Were you one of those kids who read books instead of watching TV, Trouble?"

After the last twelve hours, the conversation was

anything but appropriate, but I couldn't deny that the levity was welcome.

"No. Not at all. I've seen lots of movies. My favorite is *The Princess Bride*. I've seen it dozens of times and could quote it all day."

"Interesting." He crossed his arms, his biceps rippling.

The move made my mouth go dry. Or maybe it was my morning dragon breath. Either way, he was a sight to behold.

"How about I make breakfast while you get washed up?"

I nodded, suddenly desperate for a mirror. *God, what he must think of me?* "One more question?"

"Sure."

"Do you have any Pop-Tarts?"

His lips tipped up as he shook his head. "Uh, no. You realize they're nothing but cancer and frosting, right?"

Incensed, I stuck my tongue out. "Pop-Tarts are fucking delicious, and they're perfectly capable of being a balanced breakfast."

He cracked a smile. "I've got eggs. How about an omelet? I can put spinach in."

Fighting the instinct to gag, I scrunched my nose.

With a sigh, he stood. "How about chocolate chip pancakes? You're in luck. I keep chocolate chips around for my nieces and nephew."

I grinned. "Coffee too?"

"Of course. Just please rest."

He insisted on helping me out of bed but thankfully left me alone while I attempted to pee. Since the sweats he had given me were so large, it wasn't too terribly difficult to pull them down with one hand. It was hard for me to ask for help in any sense, but in the bathroom? It was an absolute no-go. I did have some dignity left, after all.

He'd left a brand-new toothbrush on the bathroom sink, which I made good use of. My mouth felt like the inside of a dumpster on a hot day.

As I brushed, I made the mistake of assessing myself in the mirror.

Shit.

Bruises bloomed across my face and neck, accompanied by the small scrapes and cuts I'd accumulated while crawling through the forest. My hair was filthy and matted, and my complexion was sallow. My face was so drawn it felt as though my skin was hanging off my skull.

Jeez. There was a time when I would have considered myself hot. I'd worn cute clothes, and I'd dated, living like a normal adult woman. Jude had seen me at my best. Before stress and living a double life had aged me significantly. Before stress had caused me to drop so much weight.

Here and there, I missed that life, that version of myself.

But when I reminded myself of why I was doing this, the sadness over the loss of the woman I used to be faded. I'd given up my life to seek justice. I was on a mission, and I wasn't about to stop now.

WILLA ARRIVED SOON AFTER, WEARING A SMILE AND toting a medical bag. She fussed over me and accepted a massive mug of coffee from Jude.

I'd been eager to see her, anxious to find out what I could do to ensure a quick recovery.

But when she examined me, especially when she prodded my back, my spirits fell.

"We're looking at least one fractured rib," she said, poking around.

Every time she used even a small amount of pressure, the pain that radiated through me brought a wave of nausea with it.

"I'm not sensing anything significant, but the bruising and swelling that developed overnight confirm it."

Jude came into the room, his arms crossed with concern. "How bad?"

Willa turned to him, wearing a sad smile. "She's banged up. I'd love an MRI of that shoulder and an X-ray of these ribs, but if that's not an option, then I can keep an eye on things—"

"Yes." I straightened, only to wince when pain rocketed through me.

"But only"—she eyed me—"if she agrees to take it easy."

I grunted in response. The last thing I wanted was to take it easy. There was too much to do. I was so close, and from what I'd witnessed, something big was coming. I just needed to figure out where and when.

Willa produced antibiotics, anti-inflammatories, and painkillers and rattled off how many and how often I should take each one.

The instructions went in one ear and out the other, but luckily, Jude grabbed a notepad and scribbled them down for me.

She then helped me into a real sling. It was bulky and ugly but better than the pillowcase that had been looped around my neck.

"Wear this all day and night," she explained. "Except while showering."

"Even sleeping?"

"Yes." She dipped her chin. "For the first week. Then I'll examine you again and get a sense of how it's healing. From there, we can reduce the amount of time you keep it immobile and start a regimen of wrist and elbow exercises to keep the blood flowing."

"A week?"

She tipped her head, brow furrowed, her blond waves falling in her face. "Yes. It's dislocated, and I suspect you've torn your rotator cuff. This isn't a scrape on the knee, Mila."

"How long...?" My tone was desperate, unhinged. I couldn't help it. As badly as every cell in my body hurt, I couldn't give up. Not after all the work I'd done. "How long until I'm back to normal?"

"Not sure. No less than a month. Maybe six weeks."

"No," I shouted, my heart lurching. I had work to do. I had to recover my phone and meet with the FBI. I needed to get the rest of my notes from my trailer. I couldn't waste another minute.

They both gaped at me.

"Sorry." I cleared my throat, dropping my gaze. "I just wasn't expecting that."

Willa patted my leg. "You've been through a lot, and your body is still processing. It's important for you to rest, eat, and hydrate. Take the meds and let your body heal."

My stomach twisted painfully. "I can't stay here."

"Sure you can. Jude's not home much anyway. I bet Ripley would love the company."

As if on cue, the dog came over and put her head on my

knee, turning those beautiful dark doggy eyes on me. She got it. She could see how screwed I was.

"But—"

"Please. Stay here," Jude said. "I'll stay out of your way so you can rest. And Ripley takes care of herself."

I studied him, then his sister-in-law. They were relative strangers, but they'd both shown me tremendous kindness. I didn't want to fucking rest. But I closed my eyes and nodded. What other choice did I have?

Willa hopped to her feet and clapped. "Great. I need to get to the clinic. If you're feeling up to it," she said to me, "you can take a shower tonight. Jude can help you change the bandages then."

I nodded. Though I wouldn't let Jude do any such thing, a shower sounded like heaven. And surely I'd do a better job searching if I was clean.

I looked over at the man who was dead set on helping me. His face was stoic, impossible to read.

The awkward shame that consumed me in this moment was worse than the fractured rib and busted shoulder. I was embarrassed. Not only that, but I felt helpless—a sensation I loathed more than just about anything—and exposed.

This man had seen me naked. He'd pinned me against the big picture window in this very room and eaten my pussy until I screamed his name.

Now he was my caretaker, and I was a deranged runaway who'd taken over his bed, forcing him to sleep on the couch.

Jude walked Willa out, and when he returned, he shoved his hands into the pockets of his jeans and rocked back on his heels, giving me a pitying look. "I've got to go to the office for a bit," he explained. "Meetings."

Lips pressed together, I nodded.

"I won't be long."

"It's fine." I waved him off with my good hand. "I'm going to take a painkiller and attempt to sleep."

That was a lie. My real plan was to get out of here and find my phone, but something told me that if I was transparent about that, he'd lose his shit.

"In the bed?" he raised his eyebrows.

"No. On the couch." I patted it for effect.

He huffed, head bowed. When he looked up again, he zeroed in on me. "Ripley will stay with you. Her food and water bowls are filled, and she's got a doggie door."

"Okay."

He headed to the kitchen and came back with a big glass of water and a sleeve of crackers, which he put on the coffee table.

After that, he disappeared down the hall and returned with the green fuzzy blanket I'd been so enamored with when I woke up, as well as an armful of pillows.

I smirked. "So you *can* respect my preference for the couch."

He hovered over me, glaring. "Only because I don't have time to argue. Tonight, you sleep in the bed."

"Good luck with that." I leaned back gently, fussing with the pillows.

"Let me do it." He slid a hand behind my back and angled me forward gently, shifting the pillows around until I was at the perfect angle for my shoulder.

So close like this, it was impossible to avoid soaking in the heat of his body, and I was fully engulfed in his scent.

So much so that I had to hold my breath to keep from burying my nose in his neck as he pulled the blanket up and tucked it around me.

His hands paused on either side of my thighs, and he froze there, his face only inches from mine. His gaze darkened as he looked at me, causing a tiny fizzling sensation in my stomach.

"There you go," he said, straightening. "I'll be back."

Just like that, the moment was over. He snagged his keys from the table by the door and shrugged on a coat, and then he was gone.

When the sound of his truck's engine faded, I fell back and closed my eyes, wishing I was anywhere but here.

A deep exhaustion settled over me, the weight pinning me to the couch. I needed to get up. Find a car or a bike or an ATV and get back out there.

But I was warm, and the painkillers were kicking in. And my limbs were so heavy. I'd close my eyes for a minute, then I'd get up. Yes, that would be fine. Just a few minutes and then I'd head out.

Chapter 3
Jude

The furniture and decor in the big conference room were nothing like what had been here when my dad ran the place. Since Chloe had purchased the timber company, so much had changed. And for the first time in years, the place was bustling.

We'd had to sell some of our land to the Gagnons last year in order to keep the lights on, and most of the furniture and equipment had been sold. Sure, we'd weathered some hard times, but as she promised she would, Chloe kept on every single employee that had remained when she took over. While rebuilding had taken some time, we were well on our way.

Almost every aspect of the business was different. Chloe hired scientists to consult so we could focus on sustainability, and she'd even sent me to a forestry training seminar in Minnesota in the spring.

And she'd insisted on promoting me to management. I'd tried to resist, but there was no winning an argument with that woman. Gus was much more suited than I was in these ranks, but he backed her up, insisting I join them. He'd always wanted to take over for our dad and become the fourth generation of Gagnon men to run the business.

And yeah, he did so temporarily after our dad went to prison, but we'd had to sell. If not, we all would have gone down with it. So he was not, in fact, the figurehead, but he seemed to be doing fine. Chloe owned the company, but he stood by her side when she needed it. Though he spent most of his time doting on their daughter. His life was another reminder that sometimes things work out in ways we don't expect.

Four of my brothers were here, seated around the large table. Chloe was here as well. She fiddled with the fancy space pod in the middle, and suddenly, Owen's voice echoed off the walls.

"Lila and I are here," he declared in his usual business voice. He was calling in from his skyscraper office in downtown Boston, where he was CFO of a construction company. After years of staying far away from Lovewell and anything to do with the business, he'd come back last year to help us sell, and we'd grown closer in the process.

Chloe smiled and sat back in her chair. "Great. Okay, calling this meeting to order. We've got to talk about the woman."

"Mila," Noah said, tone subdued. "She's got a name."

He was seated next to me and clearly uncomfortable. He'd worked as a woodland firefighter out west for the last fifteen years and had only recently come back to Lovewell and been dragged into the disaster our family had been submerged in for years.

I gave him a grateful dip of my chin. Though this wasn't

an ideal way for him to spend his time, I was beyond thankful to have him by my side. Not only because he was my twin, but because, unlike the rest of my brothers, he had a fresh perspective on this mess.

"So she just showed up?" Owen asked, his tone tinny through the speaker. "Out of the blue?"

"Yes." I leaned over, speaking into the microphone, ignoring the pointed looks coming from Gus, Chloe, and Finn. "And it's fine."

"None of this is fine," Chloe said under her breath.

"It's only been a day." I straightened, hands on the armrests of my chair. "And she's badly injured. Willa examined her and got her set up at my place so she can heal."

"She was chased and shot at," Cole added unhelpfully.

I watched as Gus and Chloe exchanged a worried look.

"What happened?" Owen pressed. "Who was she running from and why were they shooting at her?"

Without thought, I took off my glasses and lifted the hem of my shirt, using the soft cotton to clean them.

Noah leaned in a little closer, eyeing me knowingly. Dammit. This little move was a habit I often gave into when I was frustrated.

"She's a journalist," I explained, sliding the frames back onto the bridge of my nose. "Her younger brother was the one who was attacked here last year."

Lila's gasp was amplified by the speaker. She'd found Hugo injured on the property and had called 911.

"She came up here to investigate and managed to get in with a group of traffickers that works out of the Ape Hanger in Heartsborough. Apparently they found out what she was doing and came after her."

"So she ran to your place?"

"We know each other," I hedged.

"You dated her?" Owen asked, his tone firm.

"Not exactly. I met her at the dojo in Heartsborough. She came to some of the self-defense classes I assisted with. She came to the Moose one night while I was playing too."

Every set of eyes in the room widened at me. I was not a monk, but I tended to keep my private life private.

"And she came home with me. Told me her name was Amy. Said she was from New Hampshire and was a bartender in Heartsborough."

And I was a chump. I'd believed every word the beautiful, captivating girl had spoken. She'd enamored me from the moment I saw her swaying to the music. The feeling had only grown as the night went on. She'd been so smart and animated, telling me stories about weird food she'd eaten while traveling and her favorite places to ski. It was easy, being in her presence. So learning that it was all a lie had messed with my head.

"She left before I woke up the next morning. I assumed she'd gone back to New Hampshire and pushed her out of my mind." Or tried to, at least, but I keep that to myself. "Then, months later, the FBI showed up at my door claiming she was a missing person."

"Shit," Finn hissed.

"And now she's here," Gus said. "Do we believe her? What's to say she's not lying again?"

I clenched my fists on the table in front of me as rage boiled in my gut. The urge to defend and protect Mila was so strong, but why? I barely knew her, and the circumstances of her arrival were suspect at best.

Though the doubt was there, I'd seen the pain in her eyes. I'd watched her suffer while Willa put her shoulder back in, and I'd sensed how scared she'd been when she walked through my door.

I couldn't help but want to protect her. Whatever was going on, she was in deep. And she was in no shape to fight this on her own.

"She has the credentials," Chloe said. "I had my guy run a background check. She's legit. Journalism degree from Yale, was a producer for the International News Network, and spent three years writing for the Portland Herald Tribune."

She angled forward and placed a manilla folder in the middle of the table.

"Here are some of her articles. Deep dives into opioids and government corruption. She's got the goods."

"So she can help us?" Finn zeroed in on me.

I had no idea. And honestly, I was more concerned with helping her. But we'd been up against this for years, and with the information Chloe had given us, it was hard not to hope she could.

"Why didn't she go to the police?" Noah asked.

"She says she's seen Souza colluding with various criminals at the bar. Claims he's dirty and so are some of his deputies," I say. "Same with the FBI. And given our own experiences, I think she may be right."

All around the table, my brothers were nodding. We'd learned the hard way that we couldn't always trust law enforcement.

Cole had pulled out knitting needles and yarn at some

point. I wasn't surprised. The activity helped soothe his anxiety. "She's gotta talk to Parker."

"Of course." Chloe nodded. "We'll loop her in."

We'd hired Parker Gagnon a while back to help us investigate and work through some of the strange occurrences that had taken place since my father's arrest. Thefts and vandalism had both been problems, and Lila and Owen had discovered accounting issues. Then there was the attack on Hugo.

Parker had worked for the state police for a time and had FBI contacts, but so far, we were still chasing down leads and trying to follow the money to the top.

"Do you think she'll take off again?" Finn asked. He'd shown up with his shoulder-length hair down but had pulled it up into a bun as we talked.

"Doubtful," Cole said, saving me from having to vouch for her. "She was adamant about not calling the police or going to the hospital. We had to hold her down while Willa popped her shoulder back in. Trust me. She's scared and hurt. I think it's best if we let her lie low while we coordinate with Parker."

Noah fidgeted beside me. We'd been in here too long for him. I was surprised he wasn't up and pacing or doing pushups to work off his pent-up energy; he was an outdoors kind of guy, always moving. "Can she stay with you?"

I nodded. She was already at my house, and it was secluded and private, so it made sense.

"No," Gus said. "It's not safe for you if she's there." He gave me that big brother glare he'd mastered before I could even remember. "Who knows what kind of trouble she'll bring with her."

I took a deep breath and collected my thoughts. Mila was my responsibility. It had only been twelve hours, but that fact had already sunken into my bones. "I'll deal with this," I said. "You've all sacrificed so much. And you've got families."

Finn cleared his throat. "Do you think she really has evidence to take them down?"

"I fucking hope so."

I thought about her smile, her freckles, and the mischievous glint in her steely gray eyes. She was trouble personified. But I couldn't help but feel like she might be the missing piece we'd spent years looking for.

"What if this is our opportunity?" I scanned the table, making eye contact with each of my brothers and Chloe. "To end all of this, once and for all?"

"What do you mean?"

I closed my eyes and searched for the right words. Public speaking was not my thing.

"We've been living under this cloud for so long," I eventually said. "Chloe, you've been followed by sketchy people. Cole and Willa stumbled on some kind of illegal deal, and then Cole was drugged and framed. And Noah—"

I looked over at my twin, and a wave of panic washed over me. It happened every time I thought about the fire. About what could have happened to the person I cared for most in this world. What could have happened to his daughter. I couldn't even fathom it.

I swallowed back the emotion and lifted my chin. "We're not safe. This isn't going away unless we do something about it. And she's our best chance."

Gus, the quietest of all of us, spoke up. "But we hired Parker."

"And she's amazing, but she's just one person. When she's officially sworn in as the new chief of police, she can do a lot more. But right now, we've got a resource with hard evidence."

"Have you seen this evidence?" This question was from Owen, ever the cynic.

I shook my head, then forced out a "no" when I realized he couldn't see me.

"And you trust her?" Lila added. "Believe her?"

I ruminated on those questions for a moment. Did I believe her? Yes. Undoubtedly. I couldn't imagine her dislocating her shoulder in order to pull something over on us. But more than that, the fear in her eyes was genuine. So was the jut of her jaw when she talked about what she'd done. And the love and care that oozed from her when she spoke of her brother.

"I do. I trust her."

"What does this mean practically?" Finn asked. "How do we proceed?"

"Guys," Gus said, crossing his arms. "It means she meets with Parker and tells her everything. Then we decide what's next. We're not going to do anything reckless."

"Agreed," Owen said from the phone. "We proceed cautiously. Give all the evidence to Parker. Try to rope in the FBI at the right time. I've got the lawyers on standby in case this goes sideways."

"I think we're gonna need more than lawyers," Finn grumbled. "Like a couple of shotguns."

Chloe rolled her eyes. "Okay, it's decided. She stays with

Jude and lays low while she heals. We'll get Parker looped in, find out what this girl knows, and go from there."

"And," Gus said, putting his arm around her. "No one does anything reckless or dangerous. We consult each other, and we do not take any unnecessary risks. We've had too many close calls already."

Murmured agreements went up around the table.

Meanwhile, my mind was spinning. What did Mila know? And could it help me put a stop to this? Because after this meeting, it was more obvious than ever how much this ongoing fiasco was weighing on my siblings. They had all sacrificed so much, and now they were happy. So it was up to me to wrap it all up so we could move on.

Chapter 4
Mila

I did not leave the house. Instead, I spent the day sleeping on Jude's couch, petting his dog, and flipping through his books. The shelves in the spare room were meticulously organized, and I found all sorts of gems, including an entire shelf of poetry. That one had been a pleasant surprise.

I'd raided the kitchen as well. Like the rest of the house, it was well-organized. But sadly, the only foods I found worth consuming were dried mango and lentil chips. Ripley followed me around, probably confused by my presence.

All day, try as I might, I couldn't stop memories of the last time I was in this house from bubbling up. Filled with grief and scrambling to make sense of what had happened to Hugo, I'd lost all sense of self-control.

I'd never been good at denying myself the things I wanted, and when I'd looked at Jude standing on that stage with his guitar, there was no doubt in my mind that, in that moment, what I wanted was him.

He was at once both powerful and gentle. Feral and tame.

We'd gone back to his house, this little place up on the side of the mountain, hidden by a dense canopy of trees, and we'd spent a magical night together.

There had been plenty of fucking, yes.

But that was only one facet of what made the encounter so incredible. We'd lain in his bed, naked, gazing out the picture window at the sea of stars above. Downeast, the stars didn't shine this bright. The city lights drowned them all out.

Eventually, we'd bundled up and taken his dog for a late-night walk, listening to the hoots of the barn owls and the songs of the insects.

He'd made chocolate chip pancakes for me, then he'd eaten me for dessert.

When I snuck out, just as the sun was rising, it took all the strength I had not to lean down and kiss him again or wrap my arms around him and thank him for giving me such a precious memory. For providing such pure fun, a connection unlike anything I'd ever experienced, a desire I'd never known was possible.

But I couldn't.

So I tiptoed out, hopped into my rental car, and took off.

I didn't have time to get swept up by the sensitive lumberjack. Not then. And not now.

I'd thought of him so many times over the past year. Every time, I'd smile, wondering if he enjoyed the sexy memories as much as I did.

But then I had to go and show up here like a wounded animal and ruin it all. Now I was lingering. A helpless, unwanted guest.

Great job, Mila.

Every muscle ached, and my skin itched. What was worse, though, was the boredom. I was restless, desperate to search for my phone. To listen to recordings, do research, and feel useful. I'd been going so fast for so long, and now, the compulsion to be productive was overwhelming.

My all-day nap had shown me that I was in worse shape than I'd realized. If I left the house and was discovered, I had no hope of getting away. The exhaustion, and then the wild hunger, had kept me here. Warm and safe. I hated being weak like this, but even I knew my limits.

I was seconds away from entertaining myself by counting the fibers in the carpet when the low rumble of an engine caught my attention.

Ripley happily trotted over to the door, instantly assuaging the panic that had flared at the sound. If she was at ease, then it had to be Jude. As the sound grew louder, I considered lying down and pretending to be asleep to avoid him but dismissed the idea quickly. That would be weird.

I was in his house, alone, looking at his stuff and eating his food. I felt guilty and awkward for being here, for allowing him to take care of me.

What was wrong with me? I'd never experienced this kind of self-loathing.

I was Mila Barrett. I'd hidden in a foxhole while bombs went off. I'd trekked across deserts and negotiated border crossings with no passport.

And I was panicking because a nice guy was walking into his own house?

Ridiculous.

I pushed the instinct to hide from him down and sat on

the couch, pretending to serenely read a book of Emily Dickinson poems. Balancing a hardcover book in my lap and turning the pages with one hand was a bit awkward, but at least I had something to look at. Otherwise, I'd probably appear as expectant as his dog, who was panting at the door.

When Jude stepped inside, he was loaded down with several large shopping bags. With a silent nod to me, he hung his coat and keys on the rack by the door, then toed off his work boots.

When his hands were free, he sank to his knees and scratched Ripley's ears. She returned the affection by licking his face.

"Hey, girl," he said in that deep, husky voice. "Did you do a good job today? Did you protect the house?"

Ripley's large tail thumped against the floor loudly. She was totally in love with him.

I tried my best to stare blankly at the poetry in front of me rather than at the hot guy showing affection to an animal.

The effort was in vain.

He stood, pushing his glasses up his nose, and focused on me. "Hi. How are you feeling?"

I gave him a tense smile. "Okay. I slept a lot. Helped myself to some food. Is that okay?"

"Of course. Sorry I was gone for so long. After the meetings, I picked a few things up for you. But if I shopped in town, people would talk, so I went to Bangor."

He held up the white plastic bags with the red Target logo.

"You went all the way to Bangor?"

"It's only forty minutes." He lifted a shoulder. "And I figured you could use some clothes and toiletries and stuff."

He set the bags down on the coffee table, the plastic rustling, and I peeked inside.

There were a couple of pairs of what looked like black leggings and several T-shirts. An oversized fleece jacket and thick socks and—

Snapping back, I cringed. "You bought underwear for me?"

His cheeks turned the most adorable shade of pink.

Dammit. Why did he have to be so endearing?

"I called Willa. She gave me a list and guessed your sizes. If any of it doesn't fit, I'll take it back." He held his hands up in surrender.

I couldn't help but laugh. "You did good," I said as I pulled out a set of PJs and a package of tank tops with built-in bras. Under it was a soft cotton bra, as well.

"She said to buy those because they would be easier to put on than a regular bra for now," he explained.

"Thank you."

The next bag was filled to the brim with toiletries. Moisturizer, a hairbrush, and a box of tampons.

"Willa gave me a list," he said. Again. He was careful to avoid eye contact as he explained this time.

I was impressed. I didn't know many men who willingly bought tampons, especially for a woman he barely knew.

As that thought hit me, so did another. One that knocked the wind out of me.

I was alone.

And I was helpless. Forced to rely on the kindness of strangers. Unable to care for myself and failing at my one mission.

I couldn't hold back the tears. Head bowed, clinging to the package of underwear, I gave into them.

One after another, they dripped onto the plastic still in my lap, plopping audibly. I was trying to sniff them back, determined to wipe them away, when Jude appeared at my side.

"I'm sorry," he rasped. "If I fucked up, I'm so sorry. I'll go back tomorrow."

"No." I shook my head and instantly regretted it when a sharp pain shot through my shoulder and down my arm. "No," I whispered. "I'm grateful, I promise. This is too kind. It's too much."

"Mila, no." He tentatively rested a hand on my back. "It's only a couple of things from Target. That's all."

"But I'm such a failure," I cried, cupping my face with my good hand. "Look at me. I can't even shake my head. I'm literally hiding out in your house, and I've got dried blood and rotting leaves in my hair. I've fucked up so badly."

"You haven't fucked up," he urged, scooting a fraction closer. "You're hurt. And while I don't know what you've been up to for the past year, I have a feeling that if you filled me in, I'd be impressed by your bravery and annoyed by your recklessness."

Sniffling, I staunchly avoided his eye. I didn't usually subscribe to defeatist tendencies. In fact, I'd been accused of being overconfident on many occasions. But at this moment, every aspect of my life was crumbling. I'd backed myself into a corner, and the hot guy giving me pitying looks was not helping me regain my composure.

"How can I help right now?" He sat back, crossing his arms over his broad chest, his forearm muscles bulging and a deep kindness in his eyes. There was no use fighting it. I needed his help.

Closing my eyes, I sighed. "For now, I just want a shower. I feel so gross."

He nodded. "I'll get towels. Redid the shower last year, installed a rainhead and the works. The water pressure is excellent."

I gave him a faint smile, my vision still blurred with tears. "Good water pressure is underrated."

"Couldn't agree more." He stood and offered his hand.

Too tired to fight the urge to handle everything myself, I took it and let him help me up.

"Thank you," I whispered as I found my balance.

He swiped the rough pad of his thumb across my cheek, wiping away a tear. "Anytime, Trouble."

I'd visited the bathroom a couple of times today. Like the rest of the house, it was clean. The walls of the shower were white subway tile, and the space was separated from the rest of the room by one of those fancy glass doors instead of a shower curtain.

He hung giant white towels on the rack and set my new clothes on the vanity, then turned, hands in his pockets. "Anything else you need?"

I swallowed past the lump in my throat. "Can you help me get the sling off?"

Slowly, he removed it, the screech of the Velcro deafening in the small room.

While he worked, I assessed the shower. It was beautiful. Had he tiled it himself? He mentioned a few times that he'd done a lot of the work on this house.

He eased the sling down carefully, being sure not to

jostle my arm. It had been hours since I'd taken the painkillers, but I wasn't feeling all that much pain yet.

Once he'd set the sling on the counter, he turned back to me. "I'll pull the T-shirt over your head and right arm first, and then we'll ease it down the left, okay?"

I nodded as my face flamed with embarrassment. As badly as I wanted to shoo him out, I'd been lying to myself when I thought I could do this on my own.

At least it was only a shirt.

It wasn't until he'd gotten it off and had dropped it to the floor that I recognized the flaw in my plan.

Eyes squeezed shut, I whispered, "Can you unhook my bra?" Without waiting for him to answer, I turned and faced the wall. Cradling my left arm over my bra-clad breasts, I fought back tears again.

This overwhelming need for modesty was unwelcome. He had, after all, already seen me naked.

"I can do the rest," I said when he'd undone the clasp, keeping my back to him.

"I'll wait outside. yell if you need me."

I grimaced. I'd be fine, and even if I wasn't, the last thing I'd do was ask for his help. When the door clicked shut behind me, I let my bra straps slide down my shoulders. The fabric was gray with sweat and dirt. There was no saving it after what I'd been through. So I picked it up with my toes and deposited it in the trash.

I pushed the sweats down and shimmied out of them, then stepped into the shower.

He wasn't wrong about the water pressure. The way the water pelted my back was incredible. I tilted my head up and let the water cascade down my face. Every inch of my being hurt, but the sensation of clean water running over me made going through the motions of bathing worth it.

With my bad arm clutched to my chest, I reached for the body wash, desperate to scrub away the grime and dirt. But as my fingers brushed the bottle, it slipped off the shelf and crashed to the floor. I bent over, grasping for it, but as I did, my injured arm bumped the wall. White-hot pain shot through me, and I was hit with a wave of dizziness. I threw my good hand out, steadying myself on the wall, and hung my head.

God, I couldn't even wash myself. This was so pathetic.

I thought a nice hot shower and a good night's sleep would be enough to allow me to keep going. But I was so far away from fixing this.

Without my permission, tears sprang to my eyes again. Because of pain, because of humiliation, and because of defeat.

Doing anything more than existing felt impossible.

The door creaked open, adding insult to injury. "Are you okay?"

I wanted to say yes. I wanted him to go. But I was mid-sob, so when I tried to speak, a hiccup escaped me, followed quickly by a wail.

The door shut, and when he spoke, his voice was closer. "Are you hurt?"

I forced my head up, noticing then that he was standing only a foot or two away from the steamed-up glass of the shower door.

"I'm fine," I said, still crying.

"Can I help you?"

Unable to form a response, I leaned against the wall and gave in to the sobs racking through my body.

When the door swung open, I was too defeated to even try to shield my nakedness.

Jude was all business, methodically removing his glasses and placing them on the vanity, then pulling off his T-shirt and shucking his jeans. He tossed his clothes into the hamper, and then he was standing on the bathmat in nothing but a pair of black boxer briefs.

My heart lodged itself into my already clogged throat. "What are you doing?"

He stepped inside the shower, careful not to bump into me. "I'm helping. But if you want me to go, I will."

I turned away, hiding myself from him. I wasn't sure what was more embarrassing: my nudity or my pathetic sobs.

"Don't go," I said. "I can't wash my hair, and I dropped the body wash. My stupid arm hurts too badly to even move."

"I can help. I'm going to touch you, okay? I'll start with shampooing your hair."

Still facing away from him, I nodded.

With a touch gentler than a man his size should be capable of, he scraped my hair back, ensuring all the strands were wet. Then he squirted shampoo into his cupped palm. Its honey lemon scent hit me before his fingers were massaging my scalp. This was my shampoo. I couldn't move to check the label, but I'd know that scent anywhere.

He moved in gentle circles, sending a cascade of bubbles down my neck. Eyes closed, I leaned into the sensation, hints of tension oozing from my body and swirling down the drain with the suds. I bit my lip to hold back a sigh. The last thing I needed was to add weird moans between my sobs.

He rinsed the shampoo out and picked up another bottle.

"Conditioner?"

"Yes."

He worked that in next, taking his time, then carefully rinsing. I shouldn't be surprised. From the moment I met him at the dojo, I'd seen the gentle-giant nature he possessed. I'd seen those fingers work the strings of his guitar. I'd felt them work me over as well. I knew what they were capable of.

"Can I bend down and get the body wash?" he asked gently.

"Yes, please."

"Would you like me to help with the dirt and iodine on your skin?"

No. I didn't want that. I didn't want him scrubbing every inch of me. I didn't want to turn around and give him a full-frontal view of my unkempt bikini line and sad, deflated breasts. I wanted a time machine to magically appear so I could jump into it and go back to a time before I stepped into this shower. Before I woke to the pounding on my door. Before the day my brother was assaulted.

But want had nothing to do with it. I needed his help. "Okay."

He leaned over and picked the bottle up, his arm brushing the curve of my ass.

Once he'd dangled the body wash over my shoulder and I'd snatched it from him, he stepped back. The shower door opened, and I was hit with a wave of cool air. Then he was back with a washcloth.

He knelt next to me, gently washing my legs, which were no doubt caked with dirt and grime. He cleaned around my cuts and bandages and worked his way up to my back. The lemon scent that had faded after he'd rinsed the conditioner from my hair returned even stronger this time.

"Do you want to turn around?" His deep voice echoed off the tile walls.

I wanted to say no, but while I'd stood here, mortified, I'd discovered how badly my ribcage and arm were bruised. There was no way I could get rid of all the grime on my own, and the mottled bruising ensured there was nothing sexual about this.

"It's okay. Nothing I haven't seen before." He let out a deep chuckle.

Unable to hold back a grin, I turned slowly. As much as I dreaded showing him how much I'd changed in the months since my brother had been hurt, I was more afraid of seeing him. All the muscles and chest hair with a few small tattoos. If memory served, Jude was a delicious specimen of a man who was very, very hard to resist.

I kept my chin tucked and focused on my breathing while he washed the iodine off the areas on my knees that Willa had treated.

Like a true gentleman, he remained focused on the task at hand, keeping his gaze where it should be, and treating my skin as if it were precious to him. When the washcloth swept over the purple bruise on my thigh, my knees buckled and the air whooshed out of my lungs.

He grasped my other thigh, looking up on instinct, and I put my good hand on his shoulder to steady myself.

"It's okay. I've got you," he said, his eyes shifting back to the floor.

He made his way up over my hip to my stomach and moved very gently over my ribs.

As he worked there, I focused on the suds pooling at the bottom of the shower and keeping steady. It had been difficult to breathe before, but now, even the shallowest of breaths was excruciating. My heart pounded in my ears as he made his way up, avoiding my breasts and moving to my good arm.

He stood and carefully grasped my hand, scrubbing the dirt from my nails. My muscles locked up at his proximity. Suddenly, all I could sense was his body and the steam rising around us. The pain in my shoulder dulled, but the rest of me throbbed. Every nerve ending lit up, sensing each fiber of that washcloth.

I closed my eyes as he stepped closer and rinsed off my collarbone.

"You okay?"

The words rumbled through me. His chest was so damn close to mine.

My body desperately wanted to close the gap between us, to wrap my good arm around his waist. No one had ever cared for me like this. No man had ever touched me as if I was delicate, precious.

While this encounter had started as a nightmare, I wasn't sure I wanted it to end.

Eventually, though, he reached around me, careful not to let his body touch mine, and turned off the water.

"Gimme one sec."

He hopped out and closed the door behind him, trapping the steam inside with me. With one of the fluffy white towels he'd hung up, he dried himself off. The glass door was foggy, but before he secured the terry cloth around his waist, I was pretty sure I saw a large bulge in the front of those boxer briefs.

I was so entranced by the idea that when he pulled the door open, I startled.

Though he'd definitely noticed, he didn't mention it as he wrapped the second towel around my shoulders and guided me out.

"Stand right there." He slid his glasses on and raked a hand through his hair, then stepped in close again.

Just as he'd washed me, he carefully dried me off. Once again, when he brushed the towel over the stubble on my legs, mortification swamped me.

Unbothered by any of it, he stepped back and tore into the package of cotton bikini briefs, then held out a blue pair.

I steadied myself on his shoulder as I stepped into them, my whole body heating, and not in a good way.

The stretchy cotton bra clasped in the front. I was sure I had Willa to thank for that detail. He took it off its little plastic hanger, then threaded my bad arm through it. After he'd guided it back to my chest, his touch featherlight, he walked around me, trailing his fingers across my back. Once my good arm had also been guided through and he was working the clasp between my breasts, his focus intent on my chest, my feelings toward Willa and her thoughtfulness soured a little.

I let out a little squeak as the clasp snapped, more from embarrassment and his proximity than anything else.

His head snapped up. "Did I hurt you?"

"No." I squeezed my eyes shut and tried to ignore the sensation of the pads of his fingers on my ribs.

"Do you want me to brush your hair?" Without waiting for a response, he guided me to sit on the toilet and draped a dry towel over my shoulders. Gingerly, he separated my hair into sections and worked a wide-tooth comb through it. He secured it with a hair tie, creating a stubby ponytail at my nape.

"Time to put the sling back on. You ready?"

With a nod, I stood. From this angle, I caught a glimpse of myself in the mirror. I was in nothing but my underwear, and his chest was bare. Eyes closed, I forced the image from my mind.

After helping me into my pajamas, he slid the sling on, adjusting it like Willa had shown us and fastening the Velcro.

"That feel right?"

"Yes," I said, sighing as I let my arm relax into its cradle.

The pain was returning quickly, making my legs weak and my head pound.

"Thank you," I said as we exited the bathroom and my common sense started to return. "I owe you so much after all of this."

He pulled up short and rounded on me, his eyes narrowing.

"You owe me nothing. You're my guest and my friend. I'll always help you."

The sharpness of his tone was so uncharacteristic for the

man I'd met a handful of times. It was enough to have me teasing, in hopes of lightening the mood.

"But you didn't invite me," I said. "I crashed your pizza party."

"I have a feeling that's what you do, Trouble." He rested a hand at the small of my back and guided me toward the living room. "This isn't the first time you've crashed into my life and shaken things up."

Chapter 5
Jude

I closed the door to my bedroom and rested my forehead against it.

This was bad.

She was hurting.

I'd gotten her settled on the couch, then hustled back in here, hoping like hell she hadn't noticed my raging hard-on.

I was trying to be a good person. She could barely move, after all. But my cock hadn't gotten the message. Throughout the entire shower, I'd harnessed all the self-control I had, worried that if I made one wrong move, she'd run away screaming and file a restraining order.

With every swipe of the washcloth, I'd wanted to scoop her up and carry her to the safety of my bed. Then make her come over and over, make her feel so good she'd no longer even notice her injuries.

It had been more than a year, but she'd made an impression. When I closed my eyes, I could feel her in my arms. I could remember the sounds she made when she came. How she gasped when I pushed inside her.

Since she returned, those memories had played on a loop in my head. Maybe I was an asshole. She was injured; she could have been killed. But the visions were a lovely distraction from the reality of guns and drugs and criminals crawling around our town.

There was no way I'd survive her stay if I didn't get myself under control.

I tore the towel from my waist, shucked my drenched boxer briefs, and pulled on a pair of sweats and a T-shirt.

When I had reined myself in again, I strode out to the living room, where she was still sitting on the couch, petting Ripley and speaking to her softly.

Damn, the woman had even charmed my dog.

"I got something else for you." I picked up the bag the surprise was stashed in and turned, keeping my back to her as I removed it.

When I spun around and presented it to her with a dramatic flourish, her eyes widened, and her face lit up with a bright smile.

"Scrabble?"

That expression made my stomach clench. "I took a guess. Thought you'd like it since you're a journalist and all."

She kicked her feet. "I'd clap if I could. I love Scrabble."

I sat on the other end of the couch and pulled the coffee table closer, then set the game up.

"When I was a kid, we used to have big family games. My dad always won; he was so damn smart." Though her tone was light as she began the admission, by the end, her face was shrouded in sadness. "Sorry." She shook her head, squeezing her eyes shut. "He passed away a few years ago, and sometimes I miss him so much."

"I'm sorry for your loss." It was the best I could come up with. My father was an asshole at best, and a career criminal at worst.

"He was awesome," she said. "Coached my basketball team. Took us camping and fishing every summer. Sat and did math homework with me every night."

Silently, I held out a box of tissue.

She plucked one out, then another, and clutched them in her lap. "I don't know why I'm telling you all of this."

"When did he pass?" I asked gently.

"Eight years ago. From an overdose."

My stomach bottomed out. I had not been expecting that.

"But really, we lost him ten years before that. It's a common story. He got injured, and when the painkillers ran out, he went looking for something more."

"I'm so sorry. I didn't realize."

She looked up at me, her cheeks tearstained. "I told you this was personal."

Her words hung in the air between us, her eyes swimming with a pain that had clearly lingered a long time.

My heart clenched as I studied her. This woman had been through so much, and I'd thought a game of Scrabble would boost her mood? Fuck, I was an idiot.

I pulled the game box back over and snagged the lid. "We can skip the game. No big deal."

She rested her good hand on my forearm. "No. I wanna play. Kicking your ass would really help me turn this day around."

There it was, the spitfire energy I'd been so attracted to that night. "Okay, then. But first, we need snacks."

"Got any Flamin' Hot Cheetos?"

"No. But I've got almond meal crackers, hummus, and some decent Vermont cheddar."

She dropped her chin, her expression unimpressed. "Good enough."

After I'd had a second lucky break, her competitive side finally made an appearance.

"Come on, Yale. You can do better than that," I teased.

She tapped her chin and glared at me. "You're smarter than you look, Jude."

I shrugged. "Not really. I got good letters. You're the one who got the Q."

"Query was pretty decent, if I say so myself." She laughed.

The sound lit me up inside. This was the most carefree she'd been since she showed up on my doorstep yesterday.

"Qaid was even better, in my opinion. I seriously didn't think it was a word."

She smirked. "I noticed. But if scrabble.com confirms it, then I'm good. And it was pure luck that I hit that sweet triple-word score. I'm going to catch you and then bury you."

Her eyes danced as I lined up my tiles, sending a thrill through me. I couldn't remember the last time I'd had so much fun. I tried to make one ridiculous word after another, but she rejected them all. That morphed into stringing letters together, creating nonsense to make her giggle.

"I know it was awkward, but thank you for the shower." She studied her letters, avoiding my eye. "I feel so much better."

"No problem," I lied through my teeth. It had been a major problem, actually. Being in such close proximity to

Mila's naked body like that had been pure torture. I think I may have permanent blue balls from that little interaction.

"I can't believe we use the same shampoo." She ran her good hand through her clean hair. "It's hard to find."

I nodded but kept my mouth shut. There was no way I'd tell her that I'd been so obsessed with the scent of honey lemon shampoo she'd left on my pillows after we hooked up that I'd driven to store after store, sniffing shampoo bottles like a fiend until I found it.

Pinning down the mystery shampoo was a strange coping mechanism after a one-night stand, I supposed. It was how I handled the utter disappointment that consumed me when she disappeared without a trace. I used it all the time, eager to relive the memories produced when I did.

Round after round, I pulled out all the stops to keep up with her prowess on the Scrabble board. We devoured an impressive amount of cheese and fought over words and spellings endlessly.

It was the most fun I'd had in months.

In the end, she beat me. I had a respectable showing, but I slyly downloaded a Scrabble game on my phone so I could practice before our next match.

After, while she brushed her teeth, I cleaned up and let Ripley out. When she returned, she arranged the pillows on the couch with her good arm, her expression still bright.

"Why don't you just sleep in the bed?"

That stole all the light from her eyes instantly. "I'm sleeping on the couch."

"You're injured."

"I'll live."

I shook my head. Damn stubborn woman. She'd let me

wash her naked body today, yet she drew the line at sleeping in my bed?

After all these years, I still wasn't good at reading people.

It was one of the reasons I enjoyed my solitude here. People were so confusing. Especially women. I always worried about saying the wrong thing or not saying enough.

For the life of me, I could not understand why she was passing up a very comfy bed, but it wasn't worth the argument. Like last night, I'd wait until she was out cold, then I'd pick her up and take her to the bed.

I brought her a glass of water and her medicine.

"This was fun." She popped the pills into her mouth, then washed them down easily. "Rematch tomorrow?"

"Yes." I dipped my chin. "I will redeem myself."

Her lips twitched. "I was rusty. I'll double this score."

"Sure you will, Trouble."

Once she was settled on the couch, I let Ripley inside and turned off the exterior lights.

"Being stuck here," I said slowly. "It's not so bad, is it?"

She scrunched up her nose. "No. It's nice. I adore Ripley, and you're growing on me."

I couldn't help the smile spreading across my face.

"But," she continued. "I'd give my left tit for some Doritos, or maybe a bag of Skittles."

I shook my head. This woman wanted to kill me. With a couple of steps closer, I crossed my arms and loomed over her.

"Shame," I said, biting my bottom lip. "The left one is my favorite."

Her eyes widened in shock, and her jaw dropped.

We'd yet to discuss our hookup. We'd danced around it

and ignored it, but she'd opened the door wide and let the topic in.

While she gaped up at me, a flush crept its way up her neck.

I held on to my cocky expression for another moment before laughter burst out of me.

At first, she reared back, bewildered. But she quickly joined in, laughing gently while holding her ribs.

"Don't... make... me laugh." She sucked in a shallow breath. "Ow. It hurts."

Cringing, I reined myself in, stuffing my hands into my pockets. "Sorry."

Once she'd gotten herself under control too, she looked up at me. "Were you messing with me, or did you mean what you said about lefty?"

I put away the Scrabble box, then padded to the hallway. Before I disappeared, I spun around. "Just messing with you," I admitted.

She sagged in relief, which only made me want to rile her up a little more.

"The right one is my real favorite." I spun around, grinning, when she gasped behind me. "Night, Trouble."

Chapter 6
Jude

The crisp air, the changing leaves, and the knowledge that we'd be back in the woods soon, ready for winter cutting, made fall my favorite time of year.

Since Chloe had promoted me, I'd been spending far too much time in an office, so I was beyond ready for the season. Weeks out at camp, no cell service, just me and the guys, cooking together and playing endless games of darts after long days in the forest. I brought my guitar and usually played while Ripley stole leftovers off the long wooden tables in the main bunkhouse.

I ran my hands through my hair, taking a deep breath, then took a slow sip of coffee. My neck was sore from sleeping on the couch, and I wanted nothing more than to hit the trails, but I had a lot to get done today.

As I lifted my steaming coffee cup to my mouth again, a "damn you, Jude" echoed down the hall.

I smirked into my mug. Ripley picked her head up off the

floor and stared at me. I gave her a shrug, then stood and slowly made my way to the master bedroom.

When I stepped through the open door, I grinned. "You rang, Trouble?"

Mila was sitting upright, my dark green blanket pulled up to her waist and her hair plastered to one side of her face. She looked pretty cute, save for the snarl she had aimed at me.

"I said I was sleeping on the couch."

I took a sip and nodded.

"And you moved me?"

I nodded again.

Her huff caused the hair framing her face to float. "Don't do that."

"I told you to take the bed. If you'd listened, I wouldn't have had to move you."

Eyes narrowed, she tried to cross her good arm over the one in the sling. She stopped abruptly, though, her face pinching in pain, and rested it at her side again. "How do you even do it? The painkillers aren't strong enough to keep me from waking up if I'm jostled."

I shrug. "I'm careful. And you're welcome, by the way. I hope you had a good night's sleep."

She scrunched up her nose, her eyes darting around like she was trying to formulate a denial. In the end, she slumped. "I can sleep on the couch if I want to."

"No guest of mine, especially one who is seriously injured, is sleeping on the couch when there is a perfectly good bed. I don't know who raised you, but Debbie Hebert would beat me with a wooden spoon if she knew I let a lady sleep on the couch. While you're here, you sleep in the bed and I take the couch."

Her eyes flared. "You are impossible. What kind of macho bullshit is that? Don't manhandle me."

"If you weren't so damn stubborn, I wouldn't have to."

She didn't have a retort ready, but her mouth worked like she was trying to come up with one. For the space of several breaths, we stared at one another, neither of us willing to back down.

"Parker is gonna be here in thirty minutes," I said when she didn't snap back. "Do you need help getting dressed?"

She glared at me. "No thank you. But I'd love a cup of coffee."

I gave her a salute and closed the door behind me. As I padded down the hall, I shook my head. Why did she have to fight everything? She should be taking it easy. Instead, she was duking it out with me at every turn.

I looked down at Ripley, who cocked her head in response, as if confused. I owed her a really long game of fetch for all the disruption to her routine.

With a sigh, I scratched her ears. "I don't know either, girl."

PARKER GAGNON WAS A WOMAN WORTHY OF BOTH respect and fear. We'd hired her to help us untangle some of the secrets and unknowns around my dad and the family business. When it sold, inconsistencies had been discovered, and pulling those threads had led to even more questions.

Since she began working on our situation, I'd spoken to her a few times, but since my job was to run the machines and keep the crews moving, I wasn't a lot of help when it came to the questions she had regarding the company's financial records.

Chloe loved her, which meant she was probably excellent at her job. And I had no reason to think otherwise.

But we'd been stuck for quite some time, and with each day that passed, frustration grew.

Now that Mila was here, I prayed she was the missing piece we needed to finally put all this mess behind us.

Parker was tall and sporty and wore her dark hair in a ponytail. She didn't mince words and was always taking notes.

Unsurprisingly, Mila did not share my fear of the woman. I couldn't imagine Mila being scared of anyone. Even while she was dressed in baggy sweats and still recovering from her injuries, she was sharp, intense, and confident.

Parker lobbed a few softballs, testing Mila's responses, probably ensuring she actually knew what she was talking about. But before long, she really dug in.

I poured coffee as they went back and forth, Parker asking questions, using a tone she'd clearly perfected in her law enforcement training and Mila keeping her answers clipped and full of sass.

Despite never wanting any part of it, this mess had somehow landed in my living room.

Most days I focused on the things I could control. I worked and took care of myself and my house. Played my guitar and hiked with my dog.

The fallout from my dad's crimes honestly felt too big. If I focused on it, I'd lose myself.

A couple of my brothers had been shocked, even upset, when our dad was arrested. And even more so when we learned the extent of his crimes, his responsibility for the death of Frank Gagnon.

Me? I was sad.

My brain couldn't accept it. Wouldn't accept it.

Even when all the evidence had been laid out, even after he'd confessed, I struggled to understand.

He'd never been a good father to any of us, even to Gus, who he'd molded to follow in his footsteps. But the man had a great life. He ran the company his grandfather had founded with his brother. He had six sons and the respect of the entire community.

It was hard to believe that wasn't enough for him.

My brothers all had their theories about why he'd done it. Gus thought it came down to greed, but Owen was convinced he was a sociopath. I wasn't sure where I fell. I couldn't put that much energy into trying to decipher his motivations. What I did know was that I wanted this over.

His arrest hadn't been the end. Not by a long shot. In fact, it was only the beginning of a long nightmare for my family. One that was getting more dangerous by the day.

Mila described the Ape Hanger, a biker bar she'd worked at, and some of the people she'd met—as well as the things she'd seen—to Parker, who furiously scribbled notes.

"So you showed up there like a vigilante Nancy Drew?" Parker asked.

"Yes," Mila replied.

The comment was likely intended as an insult, but Mila seemed to bask in it.

"One thing I've learned as a journalist is that the story is in the people. Always. So getting close to the people was essential. It's a shady place. No one asks questions. So I kept my head down and observed."

Parker made a noncommittal hum and scribbled in her notepad.

"Otter, he's the owner," Mila explained. "He's clean, but he turns a blind eye to his patrons who aren't. And most of them aren't. His son Razor gets himself mixed up from time to time but isn't a major player."

"And who are the major players?"

"They call themselves the syndicate. Some are bikers, some are loggers, and some are business types. They're the ones responsible for the stream of opioids coming in from Canada. Some of them have matching tattoos."

Parker's eyes widened. "Can you describe it?"

"Haven't seen them up close. A tree or something. Razor doesn't have one. Probably because he isn't fully in on the trafficking. I don't think they trust him not to fuck it up. But some of the guys who run back and forth to Quebec have them. Usually on the hand or forearm. When I went up there for Winter Carnival with Razor, we stayed for a few weeks and met some of the guys on that side of the border."

"You met with the Canadians?" Parker asked, scratching notes at a ridiculous speed.

"I think so. Eagle seemed to be the one doing business, but he was speaking French, so I couldn't decode any of what he was saying. Razor was more of a hanger-on."

Parker pinched the bridge of her nose and closed her

eyes. "Do you have any idea how much danger you were in palling around with an international drug trafficking organization like that?"

Mila glared at her. "I'm acutely aware, thank you. And I got a pretty good reminder the day before yesterday, when they shot at me and chased me through the woods on ATVs. But I've been in war zones before. I know how to take care of myself."

Parker frowned, her expression dubious. "Okay, then. So where is this evidence?"

"I have to go back for it," Mila said, her gaze drifting down to the table. "But I have so much. Recordings, notes, photos, paper files."

I was still trying to wrap my head around this. Mila—or Amy, as I knew her before—had infiltrated this criminal organization and was working to single-handedly take them down from the inside?

As impressive as her bravery was, I was mostly terrified for her.

Parker looked up from her notes. "You didn't take it with you?"

"Long story. But I can get it," Mila said.

"How do you know they didn't get to it first?"

Mila chuckled. "I don't. But I'd be impressed if they found everything. Razor and his crew are not exactly masterminds."

Parker pinched the bridge of her nose. "I appreciate the work you've done as a civilian—"

Mila huffed.

"But we need to get law enforcement involved."

"I thought you were law enforcement."

"I'm going through the background check process. Becoming chief of police in a small town comes with a shocking amount of red tape. But I have great contacts at the FBI."

"As I explained already, the FBI is compromised." Mila seemed annoyed.

"How do you know that?"

"They used to joke around about a fed on their payroll. They'd laugh about this investigation being the longest in Bureau history because their guy kept delaying things."

Parker's face paled.

The FBI had been sniffing around Hebert Timber for years. We'd had meetings, investigations, and numerous drop-ins. Yet they still hadn't come up with enough concrete evidence to bust this ring. The only arrest they'd made was an arsonist who torched our machine shop in full view of our security cameras.

With a long breath out, Parker sank down in her chair. "Do you know who it is? Or have a description?"

Mila hummed. "White guy, in his forties or fifties. I saw him once, and I recorded his voice on my phone. At the poker game."

Parker was back to jotting notes. "This could be worse than we thought." She peered up at us, pen still moving. "But we can keep it local for now if we need to."

"What about your last police chief?" Mila asked. "He came into the Ape Hanger all the time."

Parker's brows shot up, and I straightened in my seat.

The whole town knew Chief Souza was a bad guy. What he had done to Cole was probably only the tip of the power-abusing iceberg. But involved with drug trafficking?

"Yes. He always ordered a shot of whiskey and an Alla-gash White. I know he's on leave, but he's not locked up, and he still has influence around here, right?"

Parker winced. "Do you know for sure he's involved?"

"I've seen him walk out of the bar with duffel bags full of cash. Does that answer your question?"

"Any other Lovewell PD?"

"No one ever came in dressed in uniform, so I couldn't tell you. I only recognized Souza because I met with him after Hugo was attacked."

"Wait a second." Parker tapped her pen on the table, her lips turned down. "You met with him, and he never recognized you at the bar?"

Mila shrugged. "I cut and dyed my hair before I started this and dressed differently."

"Fuck." Parker shook her head. "That dumbass was terrible at his job."

Mila pushed her hair behind her ear with her good hand for what had to be the third or fourth time, which got me thinking it was a tic of hers. That was further evidenced when she stood abruptly, wincing at the movement.

"Respectfully," she said through gritted teeth. "I'm not going to stop. This situation." She pointed to the arm cradled in its sling. "Is unfortunate, but I'm too close now."

"I'm going to ask you to please stand down." The authority in Parker's tone was natural. Clearly, it came with the territory in law enforcement. "This is complex and, while I'm impressed with what you've put together, one injured woman is not going to take down an entire opioid cartel."

Mila's expression darkened as she pulled herself up straighter.

"You should lay low," Parker said. "Leave town."

Leave town? No way. Abruptly, I stood. A second later, sensing my mood, Ripley appeared at my side.

"No. She'll stay here," I growled.

The response was out of character for me. I was the calm, quiet Hebert brother, and I certainly didn't make demands like this. But I couldn't imagine Mila being safe anywhere else. And that was all I wanted, for her to be safe.

"I'm not running away from this," Mila argued, her good hand balled into a fist at her side.

"You should." Parker sighed and closed her eyes. "You should go far away and live your life."

Mila's eyes flashed with rage. "Whether or not you want to believe it, this isn't only about your family and your town. My brother's in a damn coma because of these assholes. My mother has been threatened by goons. So excuse me for caring."

She stepped up to the table and splayed one hand on it, leaning closer to Parker.

"I'm sorry this is coming at an inconvenient time for you professionally, but I will push forward, and I will find law enforcement to help me."

My blood ran cold. While I respected her passion, she was hardly in any condition to do this. And in the thirty-six hours she'd spent in my house, I'd learned that she had little to no regard for her personal safety.

"Parker," I pleaded.

She sighed. "Let me poke around with the FBI. Off the record. See if I can get a sense of where the investigation has stalled. Even if someone there is compromised, the bureau is likely still collecting evidence. There have got to be threads we can pull."

"I'll get you all my evidence." Mila straightened again, her demeanor calming.

"I can't use illegally obtained evidence."

"Yes, I'm familiar with the fruit of the poisonous tree doctrine, thanks," Mila snapped. So much for her mood settling. "But in the state of Maine, there are several exceptions, including independent sources. Of which I am."

Parker tilted her head, regarding Mila, then nodded. "You're good."

"No shit," she replied. "So let's make a plan."

Despite the fear still consuming me, I couldn't help but be proud of her for fighting for what she believed in.

Parker put up a hand. "Okay, okay. We will. But for now, you should lay low. When I'm officially on the job in a month or two—"

"We can't wait that long." Mila's pitch rose, her breathing coming in short pants like she was in pain. Her ribs were probably killing her. "Things change day to day. Who knows how long this information will be good for. You've got to move now."

With a shake of her head, Parker looked at me. "I thought being a small-town police chief would mean dealing with speeding tickets and lost pets."

"Sorry." I shrugged. "But we've waited years for a lead like this."

"I need to go pick my daughter up from daycare. Can I trust you to stay here?"

Mila grimaced. "For how long?"

"Give me two weeks. Stay in the house. Let your shoulder heal. Read, relax, spoil the dog. Do not get yourself killed or do anything that would clue them in to your whereabouts or give away that we're on to them."

"But my evidence—"

"Let me worry about that. Just hit pause for a damn minute and give me time to catch up."

Mila bit her lip and narrowed her eyes. From her expression, she wasn't thrilled about being told to stand down.

Parker arched a brow at me. "Jude, can I trust you to keep her contained?"

Honestly, it was unlikely. Though I didn't know Mila well, I could guarantee she wasn't the kind of woman who could be contained or controlled. But I'd do everything I could to protect my family and end this once and for all. If that meant babysitting her, even if she fought me over it, I'd do it.

"Yes. She'll stay here. I'll keep her safe. We're out of the way up here, and I've got access to our camps if we need to get off the grid."

Mila glared at me. It was the same expression she wore when she woke up and discovered she was in my bed. I was getting used to it pretty quickly.

Parker gave me a tight nod. "I'll be in touch."

I saw her out, and when I returned to the living room, Mila was pacing. Ripley was on her heels as she wore tracks in my area rug.

"I can't wait weeks," she said. "You're gonna have to help me."

A long breath escaped me. "Parker said to stand down."

She halted her movements and tilted her head, looking unimpressed. "Not the first time I've been told that."

I scoffed. "Shocking."

She stuck her tongue out, her body relaxing a fraction. "You sure you don't mind that I'm here?"

I stepped up to her, taking in the fading bruises on her face. "It's no problem." My hands itched to reach out and cup her jaw, but I fisted them at my sides, resisting the urge.

She grinned, clearly not as affected by our proximity as I was. "Because you're gonna help me take these fuckers down?"

I frowned. "No, because I'm gonna keep you safe."

With a step back, she rolled her eyes. "Who said we can't do both?"

Chapter 7
Mila

I woke up in Jude's bed again. Propped up on a throne of pillows like a princess with my favorite blanket tucked around me.

Damn him.

Damn his lumberjack strength and gentle hands. I blamed the painkillers for sending me into a state of unconsciousness so deep I'd slept through being manhandled.

What good was being manhandled if I didn't even remember it?

It had been a very long time since I'd had a good manhandling. And this man had been the one to do it.

I shook my head. There was no time for sexy flashbacks today. I swung my legs over the side of the mattress and headed to the bathroom to brush my teeth. From there, I'd brainstorm how to continue my mission despite the inconvenient setbacks.

While I'd love to hang around this cute house, playing Scrabble, snuggling with the world's sweetest dog, and staring at Jude's shoulders, I couldn't afford to lose time.

Especially if Razor and his crew were out there searching for me.

Getting dressed was almost impossible with the sling. But I'd be damned if I asked Jude for help again. The thought of the pity I was certain I'd see in his eyes as he touched me made me want to run screaming into the woods.

The last time I'd been here, he'd looked at me with pure lust. After we'd torn each other's clothes off, he'd taken a step back, his eyes wide behind his thick-framed glasses, flexing his fists while he drank in the sight of my naked body spread out on his bed. I'd felt like a fucking goddess then, and again when he made every inch of me scream with pleasure.

Now? I was a skinny invalid fugitive he had to carry to bed every night. That truth was somehow more painful than any of my injuries.

Once I'd rinsed the toothpaste from my mouth, I assessed myself in the bathroom mirror. The bruises on my face had started to fade, turning a mottled yellow.

How did I end up here?

I splashed water on my face with my right hand, racking my brain for some kind of solution. I'd been so careful, with systems and procedures in place, and I'd gotten so close to the finish line. Yet I'd blown it. All that work, all that sacrifice, had been flushed down the drain. I could practically taste the justice I'd found for Hugo. And now I'd gone and fucked it all up.

I squeezed my eyes closed, fighting back the tears. I would not show Jude any more weakness. No matter how badly things hurt, I wouldn't be that girl.

I'd managed to put on a tank top and sweats when a light knock sounded on the bathroom door.

"You need some help?"

I let out a sigh. No, I didn't want any fucking help. But with one look at the sling that I'd shimmied off and dropped to the floor, I knew there was no way I'd get it back on myself.

I opened the door, finding a rumpled lumberjack who looked equal parts concerned and scrumptious.

Ripley pushed her head in too.

With a sigh, I nodded to the sling I'd left on the floor.

Wordlessly, he shuffled in and scooped it up. He kept his focus on his work as he eased my arm into it and slid the strap over my shoulder. When it was in place, he plucked my hairbrush from the counter and sidestepped me. While he worked, brushing my hair gently, we locked eyes in the mirror. He towered over me, his height and bulk surrounding me like a protective cocoon.

I averted my gaze, overcome with a self-consciousness that seemed to be seeping in more and more these days. I was pale and skinny and bruised. As terrible as I looked, it had nothing on how I felt. Even so, in such close proximity to him, my pulse fluttered.

God, what I'd give for the circumstances to be different. To not be so damn helpless. To stand on my own two feet, secure in my identity again, and offer myself up to this man.

He still hadn't spoken when he leaned around me to grab the hair elastic I'd set on the counter, his arm brushing my hip.

Tingles spread through me from that point of contact, but his expression didn't change and his movements remained easy. Carefully, he gathered my hair into a little ponytail at my nape, like he had before.

"I've got to head to work soon," he said, avoiding eye contact. "But I got you something."

He walked out, leaving me flushed and confused. Needing a moment, I pushed the door closed and leaned into it, letting my head gently thunk against the dark wood. What was it about Jude that made normal, run-of-the-mill things like what he'd just done seem so significant?

It was a ponytail. But my nervous system had turned it into so much more. In my mind, it had become a moment of intimacy. But I was alone in that feeling, clearly. And even if I weren't, I didn't have time for the emotions that sprang up when he was close. Not when the clock was ticking.

Eventually the smell of coffee dragged me out.

I found him standing in the kitchen, sipping from a mug, looking like a woodsy snack in a dark blue flannel shirt. It was open over a T-shirt that did nothing to hide his sculpted chest.

God, I was down bad. Maybe it was the pain meds. Was it possible that antibiotics could cause lustful delusions? That would be a great investigative piece. I could pitch it to the times.

My mind was wandering around potential reporting angles when my attention snagged on a small box on the countertop.

"Here," he said, sliding it closer.

I looked down at the white package, frowning. "A phone?"

He nodded. "It's one of those prepaid ones. It's charged, and I put my number in. Parker's too. And Willa's. She says she wants you to keep her updated."

My stomach twisted. "You bought me a burner phone?"

He nodded, continuing to sip his coffee with an ease I wasn't sure I'd ever experienced.

"This may be the nicest thing anyone has ever done for me," I gushed, lifting the lid and shaking the box lightly until the bottom slid out and landed on the counter. "And you charged it?"

He nodded. "That way you can reach me. As we get closer to winter, I'll be away more."

My heart panged at the thought. Jude belonged here, being all inscrutable and helpful. At the same time, I needed him out of the house so I could search for my phone and finish this once and for all.

He was so kind and helpful. I couldn't put him in danger. He was already doing so much by letting me stay here. So maybe it was best that he would be gone so much.

And the sooner I found what I needed, the sooner I could walk away and ensure he was safe.

My instinct was to dawdle this morning. To hang out with him, then spend the day resting and eating and avoiding hard truths. In a matter of days, I was already succumbing to the cozy charm of this house.

I couldn't let it continue. I had work to do, and I refused to overstay my welcome.

With a smile, I rounded the counter and threw my good arm around him.

"Thank you, thank you, thank you." I pulled him in for a hug. "Connection to the outside world!"

It took a moment to realize his body was rigid and that he hadn't spoken. Shit. With a big step back, I chastised myself for making things weird.

"I owe you big-time," I said.

Those dark blue eyes were fathomless as he assessed me. But the message he was sending was loud and clear when he backed away and busied himself with putting his coffee mug in the dishwasher.

"We can unpack that later, Trouble. But I'm late for work."

Chapter 8
Mila

LUMBERSNACK:

Test

TROUBLE:

New phone, who dis?

LUMBERSNACK:

I take it everything is in working order?

TROUBLE:

Oh yes. I'm reading up on celebrity gossip and playing word games.

LUMBERSNACK:

As long as you're resting…

TROUBLE:

Resting is boring. I just watched a YouTube video about how to build a birdhouse. Do you have a circular saw?

LUMBERSNACK:

No power tools. You only have one good arm.

Daphne Elliot

Chapter 9
Mila

I squeezed my eyes closed, teeth gritted against the pain. Willa had come over to check my healing and was now measuring the range of motion in my shoulder.

She'd busted in here not long after Jude had left for work, looking all sweet and concerned. It was all an act. She was an evil, evil woman who was putting me through actual torture.

It was luck that I was here when she pulled up. I'd lingered to drink another cup of delicious coffee while putting together a plan for the day. If I'd pushed myself out the door immediately like I'd intended, there was no way she wouldn't have called Jude.

I'd found a mountain bike in the garage while inspecting the property yesterday and figured I'd ride to the state park to retrace my steps, praying I'd find my phone. I'd found a pair of gloves that fit me, as well as a headlamp and extra batteries in the oddly organized junk drawer in Jude's kitchen.

So far, I'd decided that every morning, after Jude left, I'd search for a few hours. And I wouldn't stop until I found the damn thing.

Maybe I didn't know how I'd ride a mountain bike with one arm, but that was a small detail. I wouldn't let it stop me.

But the good doctor had shown up and fucked up all my plans.

I winced as she pushed my arm higher. Her hands were deceptively strong, pushing and kneading while she felt around my tendons.

"I've kept the sling on," I said through gritted teeth.

"Good." She lowered my arm gently. "It's time to start moving it. Getting the blood flowing is important."

With a step back, she dug around in her large bag. When she straightened, she held up a small tube.

"I'll roll BioFreeze into some of the accessory muscles and massage it in. That'll get the blood around the injury moving and help with the swelling."

As she began, the menthol smell hit my nostrils and made my eyes water.

"So," she said, digging into my neck with those skilled hands. "Do you mind telling me how on earth you ended up working undercover at a biker bar and trying to take down a drug trafficking operation on your own?"

I closed my eyes, relishing the pain that came with the way she worked my muscles. "When you say it like that, it sounds insane."

"Nah, when I say it like that, it sounds brave but reckless." She pushed her fingertips into my bicep.

I closed my eyes, willing, unsuccessfully, my twitching muscles to relax. Despite the debilitating pain, I'd remained in denial about just how badly I'd been hurt. This, though, was proving I had a long way to go until I was healed.

"My brother," I said, wincing as she moved to a new spot. "When he was attacked, something inside me broke. I became fixated on bringing his attacker to justice. In the process of trying to identify that person, I discovered the breadth of what was going on. I have the skills to track down information, gather data, and build a case, so why wouldn't I put them to use? It's what I've done since I was a second grader investigating missing Halloween candy."

She chuckled. "So you're one of those. I performed surgery on dolls at that age."

A chuckle escaped me.

"The more I dug, the more I uncovered about the criminal organization working around here. This is so much bigger than Hugo." My throat tightened. I'd been in so deep for so long, and the weight of it was all beginning to hit me.

"So I let myself become Amy," I continued. "No one had succeeded in stopping it, so I took it upon myself to infiltrate the ring and find the evidence and gain the access required to shut them down."

Hugo was still my primary concern, but this was so much more now. It was part of me.

Willa continued to poke, prod, and massage in silence.

I was quiet too. There was nothing more to say, no way to make it make sense for someone like her.

Once she'd massaged every inch of me from my neck to my forearm, she put away the cream and helped me back into the sling. "Maybe you can't do it all on your own," she said softly.

My muscles locked up tight. "Did you just stare into my soul and articulate my greatest fear? Jesus, Doc."

A warm smile spread across her face. "My mom is a psychologist. I get your thought process. For a long time, I thought I had to do everything myself, that if I wasn't over-achieving, I was failing."

"Amen, sister. I'm the oldest daughter. My whole life, it's felt as though the weight of responsibility has been placed directly on my shoulders. I was supposed to protect my little brother, but I failed him."

She squeezed my hand. "You didn't fail. Something terrible happened, and you have no control over that."

Familiar guilt rose up within me. The feeling that I was so close to a breakthrough but still far enough away to worry that I'd never get there.

"How about I make tea?" Willa asked. "I brought treats too."

I joined her in the kitchen where she filled the kettle and bustled around, pulling mugs from a cabinet and tea bags from a canister. "Jude's a coffee guy, but I've been slowly building up a stash of tea here. And..." She reached into a cloth grocery bag. "I brought peanut butter cookies. My husband makes them. They're life changing."

"Thank God." I barked out a laugh that had me wincing and clutching my ribs. "Everything in this house is made from spelt."

With a snicker, she peeled the lid off the plastic container. "Try one."

Without hesitation, I snatched the biggest I could find and took an enormous bite. When the flavor burst on my tongue, a loud moan escaped me. Sweet, salty, chewy, and rich. Damn, that was good.

"I know." Her eyes danced as the kettle whistled. "Sinful. It's my mother-in-law's recipe, but Cole has perfected it." She poured the scalding water into our mugs and nodded at the stools along one side of the island. "Sometimes a really good cookie can help heal a person."

With a huff of a laugh, I eased onto a stool. "Is that your medical opinion?"

"Absolutely. Our bodies are complex." She set both mugs down and picked up her own cookie. "The mind-body connection is so strong we still don't fully understand it. You've been through some traumatic stuff, and while your body will heal quickly, it'll likely take more time to recover emotionally. That's why a really great fucking cookie can help."

She lifted her cookie up to me, and I tapped mine against it in a toast.

"You're kind of amazing," I said.

She blushed, fidgeting with her steaming mug. "No. I'm a work in progress, same as everyone else. And you're gonna be okay."

Head lowered, I gave it a shake. "Probably not. I'm in a wild mess of my own creation, and right now, I can't see a way out."

She pressed her lips together, considering me for a moment. "You're smart and capable. But I think patience and support are the key here. What did Parker say?"

I slumped against the counter. "To sit tight and heal and let the adults handle it."

Willa burst out laughing. "So the odds of you listening are...?"

I rolled my eyes. "Zero. Like I'm going to sit around here, doing nothing."

She hummed. "I figured. But..." Her eyes twinkled with mischief. "Jude's not bad company."

With a noncommittal grunt, I sipped my tea.

"You know." She reached for another cookie. "You never did tell me how you met him."

I took a bigger sip to avoid having to answer, this time burning my tongue.

"I ask because I'm protective of him," she said, her inquisitive stare making me squirm. "I'm an only child, but I grew up with the Heberts, and Jude is my brother now. He's the quiet one, but he feels deeply."

It would have been easier to tell her to fuck off and mind her own business if I didn't like her so much. But Willa had gone out of her way to help me, providing medical care and emotional support. Not to mention the excellent cookies. So giving her at least a little of the truth felt like the right thing to do.

"Okay," I sighed, closing my eyes. "I first met him at karate. I signed up for a women's self-defense class. Figured I could use the training. He was assisting the instructor."

She nodded behind her mug.

"I went pretty regularly for a couple of months, and each time, he was so kind and helpful."

"Women's self-defense?" She straightened. "I wanna take that class."

"When this is over, we'll do it together. I need a refresher. And you'll feel like such a powerful badass after."

She leaned in, resting an elbow on the granite, her green eyes growing wide. "Okay, so you fell in love with my brother-in-law while karate-chopping him. Adorable."

My heart lurched, and I reared back enough to make my shoulder throb. "I did not fall in love." I cringed. "I just thought he was good-looking and nice. We chatted, but I chatted with everyone there. I was making myself known as Amy, the bartender who was new in town."

She raised her eyebrows. "But?"

Cringing, I considered whether to give her the full story.

I was leaning toward no when she tapped her nails on the counter. "I'm waiting."

Shit. I blew out a breath and wrapped both hands around my mug. "Fine. Last year, some women I'd met at the bar mentioned that there was great live music in Lovewell. They said the band playing that weekend was amazing and went on and on about how hot the lead singer was."

"Jasper?"

"Yes."

She shrugged, unimpressed. I could understand the reaction. Why bother ogling a decently good-looking musician when she was married to a seven-foot-tall hockey God?

"Anyway, I was still getting my bearings here. It hadn't been long since my brother had been attacked, and I was anxious about what I'd gotten myself into. So I went. Had a beer and a basket of fries."

She hummed. "They do have excellent waffle fries."

"Then the band came on stage," I continued, spinning my mug on the countertop.

"And you made eye contact and fell in love." Willa squealed, popping up straighter.

"No." I huffed. "I saw him and immediately recognized him. And... I can't explain it. He was different from the man I'd met at the dojo. The man I knew had been shy and reserved and serious. But playing guitar?"

A dreamy sensation floated through me, making me feel as if I'd been lifted off the stool.

"He came alive right in front of me."

I barely blinked during the entire set. I was too enamored by the passion radiating from him, too caught up in the mix of pain and passion in every movement of his fingers.

"And I couldn't take my eyes off him."

"So this is basically a rock star romance," she said, her tone light. "If you need recs, I have several. The knitting club is deep into smut right now. Jodie, who was my elementary school PE teacher, is all about knotting." With a shudder, she shook her head.

I huffed a laugh, hoping she'd run with that change in topic, but no, she zeroed in on me again, her expression expectant.

So I continued. "Even from halfway across the bar, there was this tether connecting us, urging me closer to him. And when the set ended. He put his guitar on the stand and walked through the crowd, his eyes never leaving mine."

"Oh my God." She kicked her feet and fanned her face with one hand. "So hot."

"He strode right up to me, all muscly, with those sexy glasses, and took the beer bottle out of my hand. Without looking away, he took a swig, then handed it back."

"Jude?" Willa froze, her hand pressed to her chest. "Jude Hebert did this? The mild-mannered dog dad who has a 'system' for folding his towels? That man took a sexy swig from a stranger's beer bottle?"

I nodded, willing the heat the memory brought with it to subside.

I considered stopping there. The rest of that night was illicit. The most provocative experience of my life. But Willa, with her infectious smile and amazing healing hands, was kind of a friend now.

So I said, "It was so fucking hot. All I could think was *I need to get this man naked.*"

She rubbed her hands over her face. "I can't even wrap my mind around this. Obviously I don't blame you." She shook her head, her blond curls bouncing. "But I didn't know he had it in him. I'm impressed. Sometimes the brothers joke about him. How he's the most eligible bachelor in Lovewell. How girls are always throwing themselves at him."

My stomach clenched at that tidbit of information.

She didn't seem to notice. "One time, I mentioned that I worried about him being lonely up here with only the company of his dog." She took another sip of her tea. "Cole laughed and swore that Jude has plenty of company. He's quiet about it. Now I know how he does it." She shook her head and laughed.

I shifted on my stool as unease rolled over me. I didn't want to think about him going home with lots of other women after they'd gotten all hot and bothered watching him play the guitar.

"But," I said, forcing the conversation on before I could spiral, "I didn't come here because of that. Yes, we had a great time." Cheeks heating, I fixed my focus on the pattern of the granite. "But I came here mainly because he's a Hebert and I needed help. I was in the woods—"

"How did you find this place?" she interrupted, clearly seeing through at least some of my bullshit. "It's not exactly easy."

"I don't know. I hid out in the state park, and when they were gone, I started walking in this direction."

Her eyes went wide. "Wet, freezing, with a dislocated shoulder, and in shock?"

"Yeah, I guess so." In the moment, it felt as though this was the only place I could go. I couldn't go home and put my mom and Hugo in danger, and the police were probably compromised. It was highly unlikely anyone would draw a connection between Jude and me, so I had no other options.

She got up and spun in a circle, waving her arms and shaking her hips. "You're getting married," she sang, dancing around the kitchen.

"*Stahp,*" I whined. God, I sounded like a preteen girl. I needed to rein it in before I embarrassed myself further.

Willa tossed her head back and cackled.

"It's okay. When I woke up in Vegas and discovered I'd drunkenly married Cole and then had to move in with him, I had many giddy moments. Those Hebert boys can reduce the most self-assured, confident women into giggling mush. It's genetic."

She wasn't wrong, but I didn't want to confirm the squealy, giddy sensations that Jude inspired in me, so I kept my mouth shut tight. It was more mature to keep those thoughts and feelings bottled up and deny their existence to the outside world. *Right?*

She came to a stop and let out a sigh. "Just promise me something."

"Sure."

"Stay safe. Don't go running into another dangerous situation."

I sat up straighter. "I'm not planning on it."

Brows raised, she crossed her arms. "But?"

"But danger kind of finds me," I said weakly.

She shook her head and sighed. "That's what I was worried about." Easing back onto her stool, she said, "How about this? Do not put my brother-in-law in danger." She swiveled so she was facing me head-on. "He's one of the best people I've ever known. I don't want him to get hurt."

"Neither do I."

One brow cocked, she scrutinized me, wary.

"I know I'm shady as hell," I explained. "And I'm so grateful to you and Jude. To your whole family, really. I won't do anything to hurt any of you."

Seemingly satisfied, she turned back to her tea.

"Once the dust settles, I'll be out of here. I'll collect my evidence and go to the police. I've given too much to this to quit now, and I don't want anyone else getting hurt."

She nodded slowly. "What you're doing is ridiculously dangerous, but I admire the hell out of you." She smirked. "Chief Souza drugged my husband and then tried to frame him. There's no way that's not connected."

"If you're implying that wasn't the first illegal activity that sad excuse for law enforcement was involved in, then you would be correct."

"Excellent. Make sure you take him down too, okay? Get

him a nice long sentence. Because no one fucks with my husband."

"I will." I dipped my chin. "He attended many poker games with the traffickers. He's dirty as hell."

She smiled broadly and stood. "Okay, I'll get out of your hair. Ice, rest, and do the exercises I showed you. No need to sleep with the sling, but keep it on when you're awake. And *please* try to stay out of trouble."

Once she was gone, I paced around the house, my mind spinning and adrenaline coursing through me. The longer I stayed here, the more danger I put Jude in. The more danger I put his whole family in.

There was no more time to waste.

I snagged a large dark hoodie from Jude's closet and pulled a gray beanie over my head, then loaded up on supplies. I couldn't risk another injury, especially after learning that I was healing well, so riding the bike was out. I'd have to go on foot.

I had about six hours until Jude would return. If I jogged through the trails, I could make it to where I'd hidden in an hour or so. I'd search that area first, and if I didn't find the phone before I had to return, I'd work from there.

I found a small backpack that I could loop around one shoulder. Once I'd filled a water bottle, I tossed a few snacks into the bag, along with my headlamp and another sweatshirt in case this one got wet from digging around.

I was tying the laces on my muddy sneakers when Ripley padded up to me, her nails clicking on the hardwood floor.

She stood in front of me, wearing a disappointed look on her face. Like she knew I was going against Jude's orders.

"You can't tell." I stroked her ears. "He won't under-stand, and I don't want him getting hurt."

She lowered her head, as if acquiescing. But when I walked out the door, she followed. Okay, then. I guess I had a friend. Once I hit the edge of the forest, I took off at a jog, wincing as each step made my shoulder ache.

Ripley matched my pace, clearly not letting me out of her sight.

I was anxious and in pain, but at least I wasn't lonely.

Chapter 10
Jude

The diner was the hub of our small town. On any given day, half the population dropped in, sometimes for breakfast and other times for a to-go coffee and gossip.

It was also *the* place to see and be seen. And to get updates on what was happening around town.

It may come as a surprise, but I didn't avoid the place. The eggs Benedict was too good for that. Though I limited my visits, unlike Finn and Cole, who practically lived here. Which was why I'd swung by this morning. So I could pick their brains.

Cole, who worked at city hall, coordinating and planning town festivals and events while getting his master's degree, was one of the most connected people in Lovewell.

Finn ran a wildly popular flight tourism company, and since he was the friendliest and most approachable of the six of us brothers, he had a tactical advantage.

I had barely seen them in the week since Mila had

arrived, so when they'd texted, suggesting breakfast, I jumped at the chance.

Every day she was here, I woke up a little more panicked, concerned about how much longer I could keep her hidden.

What worried me more, though, was the concern that she wouldn't allow herself to remain hidden much longer. I could feel it—her restlessness, her itch to do something, to make headway.

"Morning, assholes." Gus, the oldest of the six of us, approached our booth, looking as grumpy and sleep-deprived as ever.

"I texted him," Finn said, studying the menu like he'd never seen it before.

"We need to strategize," Gus said, signaling for Cole to slide over to make room for him.

The four of us must have looked ridiculous, crammed into the red vinyl booth, hunched over our coffee mugs.

"Tell me what you've heard," I said, bringing my mug of black coffee to my lips. The coffee I made at home was better, but Mila was there, and it was getting harder and harder to look at her sleepy smile and brush her hair and not give in to my impulses and kiss the life out of her.

So this morning I'd programmed the coffee pot, left her a note, and escaped the house before she woke up. I was desperate to pull myself together. My protective instincts were growing exponentially by the day. The longer she stayed, the more I wanted to pick her up, carry her to my bed, and fix all of her problems.

She didn't want a hero. She'd made that clear. What use could I be, anyway? The issues she was dealing with were pretty damn monumental, and they were only getting worse.

"Folks have been sniffing around," Cole reported. "One guy, Maurice Murphy, apparently went to the technical school in Heartsborough with Erica's son. According to what she told me at knitting club, he's a bit of a shithead."

I winced. That was quite a name.

"He's a biker. Thirties. Shaved head," he explained.

"I've seen him," Finn said. "At the gym here and there with some of the other biker guys. Some of them are decent dudes. They spot me from time to time. But there are several who are pretty shady and twitchy."

"Names?"

Finn shook his head. "They all have biker names. One of them is Viper, but I don't know about the others."

"Anyone asking about Amy?"

Cole nodded. "According to my source, there's been a lot of talk about her at the Ape Hanger. They're saying she stole something."

I shook my head. "As far as I know, she didn't steal anything. But then again, getting information out of her has been a challenge, to say the least."

Cole shrugged, sipping his coffee.

"We've had two visits from the FBI," Gus said. "One at the office and one at our house."

"Chloe must have loved that," Finn quipped.

Gus grimaced. "She did not appreciate it, especially because we'd just gotten Simone down for a nap." He shook his head. His infant daughter was a notoriously difficult sleeper.

"What did they want?"

Gus ran his hands through his chin-length dark hair. "Asking more questions. Same old bullshit. The guy they arrested for the arson at the machine shop still isn't talking, so I'm not sure they've got much at the moment."

I wasn't sure how to feel about that.

"Two visits in a week?" Cole asked, raising an eyebrow.

Gus grunted. "I know. They go months without responding to emails. We think they know more than they're saying and are trying to sniff out what we know."

Fear gripped me. "Did you tell them about Mila?"

He shook his head. "Fuck no."

I let out the breath I was holding. "Good."

"Chloe and I both agreed it felt off, so we decided to play dumb."

I closed my eyes, filled with gratitude.

"What did Parker say?" Finn asked, his voice low. Parker was his sister-in-law—married to Finn's wife's brother—and even he was a bit scared of her.

"To wait. Not to do anything crazy until she's named police chief. Then she can open an official investigation and root out the assholes involved," I explained.

Cole sipped his coffee. "That's reasonable."

"Yes." I unrolled my silverware and fiddled with the paper ring. "But not practical. We don't have time to waste, especially if these goons are hunting around for Mila."

Finn lifted his chin and scanned the diner. "It's only been a few days. Give it time. They'll get bored and move on. They probably assume she went back to where she came from."

As much as I wanted to believe him, I wasn't convinced. While Mila had described most of the guys on the ground as idiots and lackeys, this organization had evaded detection for a long time. They couldn't all be stupid. If Owen and Lila's research was accurate, this was a complex organization with a lot of financial and political power.

They wouldn't let her get away with what she'd done.

My father had gone down for a lot of the crimes these fuckers had committed. Yes, he was guilty as hell of plenty of them, but he'd kept his mouth shut, clearly concerned about the repercussions if he named names.

Day by day, Mila grew more restless. She was holding so much information in, keeping it to herself. I wanted to trust her, and a big part of me did. But the shadows in her eyes warned me that there was more to the story. She was hiding something.

"She's not going to sit around waiting," I said. "She's already itching to get back out there."

"So let her." Cole lifted a meaty shoulder. "We barely know her, and while I certainly don't want anything bad to happen to her, she seems like the type of chick who can handle herself."

A wave of anger washed over me at his words. "I know her," I snapped, "And she's under my roof and my protection. I'll do everything in my power to help her."

Her presence was driving me out of my mind. Throwing me off and scrambling my brain.

I bounced between losing myself in sexy memories and being overtaken by a blinding urge to protect her.

Every night, when I scooped her up and carried her to my bed, my heart thumped heavily against my chest, as if trying to get closer to her. The thoughts and feelings plaguing me since she showed up weren't healthy. I couldn't afford to get too attached. But at least I could breathe easy, knowing she was safe at my house.

"Hello, handsome," Bernice, the owner, said as she filled my coffee cup. "Been a while since we've seen you. Your usual?"

I shook my head. I'd been out of sorts for days. This called for something indulgent. And maybe Mila was rubbing off on me with her constant discussion of junk food.

"Eggs Benedict, please." I handed her my plastic menu.

My brothers murmured that they'd take the same, and once their coffees had been refilled, Bernice was gone.

While Finn filled us in on the latest hijinks of his toddler son, Thor, and debated sleep strategies with Gus, I observed the various groups of folks in the diner. It was a cross section of our little community. A community I loved and wanted to protect.

But how? I wasn't brilliant like Owen, and I didn't have military training like Finn. People a lot smarter than me had been working to stop this for years with no success.

I was no one. Yet Mila had landed on my doorstep, putting me smack dab in the middle of all of this.

"Just be careful," Cole warned. "You have a history with this girl."

Finn's eyebrows almost met his hairline as he angled forward. "What?"

I glared at Cole. It wasn't a secret, per se, but I preferred to keep my love life quiet. And I had, but Cole had been at my house when the FBI had visited recently, inquiring about Mila's whereabouts.

"I knew her. Sort of," I admitted, staring down into my coffee mug.

Gus scratched at his beard. "Was she one of your groupies?"

Cole snorted.

"First of all," I seethed, hitting them both with glares. "I do not have groupies. That's a derogatory, sexist term, and I do not treat women like objects."

Finn and Cole froze, their eyes going wide. Gus shook his head and drank his coffee. He knew me better than anyone, and he knew how much I hated the assumptions people made about my private life.

It rankled me, the way they treat me like I was some kind of lothario rock star instead of a normal guy who liked to blow off steam by playing my guitar, having a few beers, and occasionally hooking up with women.

"And regardless of that, Mila is no groupie. She's brilliant and fierce. If circumstances had been different, I would have spent a hell of a lot more than one night with her."

"Shit, man." Finn ran a hand through his long hair. "I didn't mean it like that."

I grunted out a response. I'd been taking shit from my brothers for years for any number of things. Not going to college, defending my dad when the accusations were first hurled his way, playing music for fun rather than trying to make a living off it. My dating habits too. I took it all in stride. Kept my head down and did my thing. But this was getting out of hand.

"I'm sorry," Cole said. "As the family fuckup, I should know better than to judge."

That had my hackles rising. "You're not the family fuckup."

"Course not," Gus jumped in. "You do more than any of us to help out."

Cole lowered his head and gave it a shake. "Maybe not anymore. But I used to be, and I'm working through the effects it had on me." He elbowed Finn and forced his gaze to mine again. "We're doing this all wrong. We're trying to protect you."

"Yeah," Finn agreed. "It seems like this girl has gotten under your skin."

"She's a woman," I corrected. They meant well, but the words still chafed.

He nodded. "It's just... How do I explain this?" He rested his elbows on the table. "You're a Hebert, and we all know that we tend to catch feelings."

"Big feelings," Cole added.

He would know, what with his accidental marriage to Willa.

"At the end of the day," Finn went on, "we're all just golden retrievers in flannel shirts. You may be the broody musician of the bunch, but you're built like the rest of us in that respect."

Gus laughed again. "You sound like Chloe. She'll love that."

"I can handle myself." I unclenched my fists, annoyed but no longer angry. "Mila's only staying at my house. It's not a big deal."

"Don't let yourself get dragged into danger. Please," Cole said. "Let Parker and the feds handle it. She may be staying with you, but that doesn't mean this is your fight."

"It sure is my fight." I leaned in, lowering my voice so we wouldn't be overheard by gossipy townies. "You've both been targeted. Noah escaped a potentially deadly house fire. I've got nieces and a nephew to worry about. This is my family and our business. It's the only life I've ever known."

I straightened and cocked my head one way, then the other, trying and failing to relieve the tension that had built in my neck and shoulders during this conversation.

"You're dead wrong. This is my fight."

Chapter 11
Jude

LUMBERSNACK:

It will come back tomorrow expecting more.

TROUBLE:

That's the plan.

LUMBERSNACK:

You cannot befriend dangerous wildlife. You could get hurt.

TROUBLE:

Stop being so overprotective, Lumberjack.

LUMBERSNACK:

If you fed a baby, it means its mom is nearby and could kill you.

TROUBLE:

Oh, I saw the mom. But it may have been the dad. It had huge antlers. That was a little scary. But we went back into the house. You're really overthinking this. I'm fine.

Chapter 12
Jude

I pulled into the driveway, rolling my neck again. It still wasn't helping. Chloe had insisted I spend the day in the office, learning about the new software she'd implemented. Its purpose was to track shipments and load values. Apparently, it would be installed in the trucks this winter. The online training program had sucked up several hours of my afternoon, along with what was left of my sanity.

Now I was home, working up the nerve to go inside, where Mila would undoubtedly be doing something to drive me over the edge permanently.

Like dancing in her underwear, or playing one of my guitars, or reading poetry aloud to Ripley. Every day was a delightful new surprise wrapped up in an excruciating test of my self-control.

For years, I'd come home to a clean, quiet, peaceful house after a hard day's work. That was before a hurricane of a woman swept in with her constant chatter and restless energy.

I never knew what I'd walk in and find.

Her clothes were all over my house. Bras hanging from doorknobs, hair ties next to the sink, and the smell of lemons everywhere I went.

It was distracting.

My home, my sanctuary, had been overtaken.

In this moment, the lack of my quiet, safe space annoyed me, but honestly, more often than not, I looked forward to seeing Mila and talking to her about how she'd spent her day.

As I climbed out of my truck, the morning's conversation with my brothers played in the back of my head. It was true —I barely knew her. But the connection between us was unlike anything I'd ever experienced. But I didn't know how to even begin to explain that to them.

Though she'd lied, it was undeniable: I trusted her. Though some of her methods may have been questionable, she was a good person who was trying to do the right thing. And against my better judgment, I found myself getting pulled in, wanting to help.

The sun was low in the sky and the air was cool as I walked into the house and flipped on the lights. The place hadn't been this dark in a while. Not since Mila had shown up. And it hadn't been this quiet either.

Assuming she was sleeping, I toed off my boots, hung up my stuff, and headed to the kitchen for a glass of water. My head was pounding, so I popped a couple of aspirin and chugged the whole glass.

Aside from dirty dishes in the sink, there was no sign of the woman who'd infiltrated my life.

I whistled softly for Ripley, and when she didn't come, I assumed she'd been shut in my bedroom with a sleeping Mila.

As silently as I could, I opened the bedroom door. Rather than being met with my dog and a hurricane of a woman in my bed, the room was empty.

"Mila?" I spun around, my heart thudding against my sternum.

Where was she? Was she hurt? Had they found her?

I raced around the house, opening every door, scouring each room and closet.

Vision tunneling and hands shaking, I darted to the back door. It was locked, and there was no sign of a break-in. I hadn't noticed an issue with the front door, but I checked again to confirm. Nothing. The place looked as it had when I left this morning.

"Mila," I called as I jogged out onto the driveway, boots untied, and scanned the yard.

I turned in a circle, surveying the tree line, at a loss.

My heart pounded in my ears, worsening my headache, as I formulated a plan. She had no car, and Ripley was with her, so it was unlikely she'd gone by road. I jogged to the back of the house, where a path led into the woods. Could she have taken Ripley for a walk and gotten lost?

The possibility of her being lost in the woods, in the cold, hit me like an arrow to the heart. Fuck.

I picked up the pace, headed down the back of the hill toward the trail system. Quickly, I was ensconced in the thick canopy of forest.

It wasn't dark, but it would be soon. I needed to find her before then.

When I hit the fork in the path, I only hesitated for a moment before choosing the direction that led toward the state park.

A wave of nausea hit me as I ran as fast as I could down the trail, jumping over roots and scanning the ground and surrounding trees for any sign of her.

The slightest jingling sound—barely audible over my pounding heart and labored breathing—eventually caught my attention. Coming to an abrupt stop, I turned one way, then the other, letting my ears adjust to the sounds of the forest.

I whistled loudly, and seconds later, Ripley appeared, trotting toward me, tail wagging.

"Good girl." I crouched and scratched behind her ears. "Where is she?"

With a yip, she took off down one of the side paths. I darted after her, pulling my phone out of my pocket, ready to call for help if needed.

In a matter of seconds, she came into view. She was walking along the overgrown path, wearing one of my old sweatshirts, her expression serene.

"Mila." I pulled up short. "Where have you been?"

She walked toward me slowly, her dark brows knitting together. "I went for a walk."

"This far from the house? Are you crazy? It's not safe," I spat.

Adrenaline coursed through my body. Over and over, I silently told myself that she was fine. That she was safe. Everything was okay.

But that wasn't true.

I was not okay.

"In daylight, in the woods. And I brought the dog. Not a big deal." She walked past me without slowing.

"Yes, it's a fucking big deal." I spun on my heel and

stomped after her. "You're being hunted by violent criminals."

She threw a weary expression over her shoulder. "Don't exaggerate."

Eye twitching, I caught up to her and grasped her good arm, pulling her to a stop. "Exaggerate? You're the one who got shot at."

She rolled her eyes. Actually rolled them at me.

Annoyance flared hot in my veins, making my head pound harder. Why was she not getting this?

"That was a week ago. These kinds of idiots have short attention spans."

I pinched the bridge of my nose and followed after her as she picked up the pace.

"Bikers have been poking around town," I said to her back. "Asking questions about you. The FBI is here too. Trust me, there's a lot of heat right now. You have got to be careful."

It made my stomach roll, how unafraid she was.

Without slowing, I took off my glasses and cleaned them with my T-shirt.

Mila spun around and glowered at me. Ripley stood between us, looking back and forth, confused.

"Why were you out there?" I asked again, trying to keep my tone even.

"Because I'm stuck in the house." She threw her good arm up. "It's a nice house, and I'm grateful that you've let me stay here, but I'm going stir-crazy."

The movement caught my eye, highlighting the small backpack she'd slung across her chest as to not disturb her sling. Eyes narrowed, I slowly surveyed her, noticing the headlamp that hung around her neck like a necklace.

Something was off here.

"There are plenty of trails close to the house. Why did you come this far? Why would you venture onto public land where you could be seen?"

She shifted, her attention flitting away, a clear sign that she was hiding something.

All the suspicion my brothers had brought up rose in my chest.

Was she playing me? What was really going on here?

"I need the truth, Mila," I said softly. "I don't appreciate being lied to."

She said nothing. Her eyes were on me again. Staring me down. She had one hell of a poker face, but I wouldn't put my family in danger for her if she couldn't tell me the truth.

"What are you doing out here? Tell me. I won't ask again."

Her eyes fluttered closed and her body deflated. "I'm out here searching for my phone."

I frowned. "What?"

"When I fled, I stuck my phone in my bra, along with my ID and cash." She sucked in a harsh breath and let it out again. "I used it to record the secret meeting that took place at a poker game. The big bosses were there, and they were planning something significant."

I took a step closer, wanting to reach out and touch her, soothe the anxiety radiating from her.

"I took it with me when I ran, but I lost it along the way." Head lowered, she wrapped her good arm around herself. "It's all I've got, Jude. It was supposed to be the smoking gun. With it, I could have finished this once and for all. But I fucked up." Her shoulders rose and fell as she breathed, face still averted. Eventually, she straightened and looked at me. "While you're at work, I come out here and look for it."

"But your search area—"

"Is massive. I jog, and Ripley comes with me." She gestured to the backpack. "I bring food and water and then jog back and shower before you come home from work."

"You're not supposed to jog. You're supposed to be healing."

"I take it as easy as I can, but this is too important."

Arms folded, I kicked at the ground, reining in my anger. All this time, I'd assumed she was safe and sound, but in reality, she had been running around the woods with one arm and my dog?

"Why?" I threw my arms out and let them fall to my sides. "Why did you lie to me? If you'd told me about the phone, I could have been helping."

She turned and continued her way down the trail. I followed, still trying to wrap my mind around this development as the sky above grew darker.

Was this the rock-solid evidence she'd told Parker about? Had it all gone missing?

"Mila," I said, rushing to catch up again.

She wheeled around, her eyes filled with tears. "I've got nothing. Is that what you want to hear? That I gave up a year of my life for nothing? That I thought I was an investigative journalist, but it turns out I'm nothing but an idiot who lucked out and got close, only to fuck it all up?"

She stomped away, wiping at her eyes.

Heart lurching, I jogged to catch up. "You're not an idiot."

"I sure as shit feel like one. Can we go home? Please?"

With a nod, I fell back and let her lead the way back through the state park. The whole way, her shoulders remained slumped, tempting me to console her.

Instead, I kept my hands to myself and my mouth shut.

I should be angry about the lies. I should be frustrated that she'd put herself in danger.

But all I felt was admiration. This woman was fierce and fearless.

The closer we got to the house, the firmer my resolve to help her became.

While she showered, I built a fire and got started on dinner. I'd never been good with words, and as I heated up soup and sliced bread, I struggled with how to explain my thoughts in a way she'd understand. How to tell her that whatever she needed, I was in. That she could trust me. That I would see this through with her.

After silently slurping soup in front of the warm fire for several minutes, she wiped her mouth with a napkin and said, "I owe you an apology. You could have kicked me out or called the cops. Instead, you opened your home to me, and you've taken care of me." She swallowed thickly. "And I really adore your dog."

Ripley lifted her head from where she was curled up in front of the fire.

"So please know how grateful I am for all of that when I say that I'm losing my shit, Jude." She stirred her soup, her gaze averted. "I should have told you the truth. I know that. But I can't rest. Not while those men are out there." When she finally lifted her head, her face was gaunt, her eyes ringed with dark circles. "I've got to stop them."

"Your plan was riskier than necessary. Sneaking out of my house and running around the woods alone wasn't wise," I snapped. "Like it or not, your body needs the rest."

She stood abruptly, brows pulled low and her good hand on her hip. "You're being an overprotective caveman."

I had to stifle a smile. Her attitude was adorable.

"I wish. Do you have any idea how much easier my life would be if I could club you over the head and drag you home? Chasing you around, trying to keep you safe, is exhausting."

"I can't live any other way." She huffed. "This is how I'm wired. Ever since I was a kid. And it's exhausting for me too most days. Trust me." Her body deflated a little. "I don't want this. I don't want to single-handedly try to take down an international opiate trafficking ring."

I stood, set my bowl down, and padded toward her. "So don't do it alone."

Her eyes widened as I got close and flared when I ran my knuckles along the edge of her jaw, then cupped her face.

"Let me do it with you," I whispered.

"Who are you?" she asked, and I swore she leaned into my touch a little bit. "My knight in shining armor?"

I leaned closer, unable to fight the pull of her atmosphere. "I'm just the guy who wants to protect you."

"Why do you care?"

My breathing picked up, and hers did too. With each inhale, our chests came dangerously close to touching.

Desperate for her to understand how I felt, despite how terrible I was at putting the emotions into words, I said, "I care about you." I brushed my thumb over the light bruise that lingered on her cheek. "I respect you. And I want to help. But you can't lie to me. You have to let me in, and you can't be wandering off and putting yourself at risk."

She bit her bottom lip, her teeth sinking into the plump flesh there in a way that had electricity coursing up my spine. What was it about this woman that made me lose all control?

"I want to protect you."

She placed her hand on my chest and held it there, her breath hitching. Then, her expression going hard, she pushed. "Too bad. Because I'm trying to protect you."

Frustration and a little fury swirled in my gut as I stepped in again, closing the distance she had created between us. "Then it looks like we'll have to protect each other."

She tipped her head back, glowering. "You are so damn stubborn."

"And you are so damn beautiful."

The moment I said the words, my body went rigid. Shit. Those words were not meant to come out.

Gasping, she clutched a fistful of my shirt.

"Fuck, I want to kiss you right now," I gritted out. "But I won't. I respect you too much to cross that line when you're healing."

Chopping wood would help. Or maybe I'd punch a wall. The fire that was rising up inside me had nowhere to go. A cold shower might help while I reined myself in. I wasn't the kind of guy who shouted or argued, but Mila had a way of pushing me out of my comfort zone.

She let go of my shirt and took a careful step back.

"Calm down, caveman. I'm not exactly kissable right now. I'm bruised and in a sling, and I'm wearing your sweats."

My instincts urged me to reach out and pull her close. Wrap my arms around her and beg her to let me in, to let me help her, to insist she never lie to me again.

Instead, I choked them back and took a step back, smirking. "You underestimate yourself, Trouble. You are very kissable."

Chapter 13
Mila

"What is that?"

Jude, who'd just walked into the house wearing a huge grin, carried a cardboard box toward the kitchen island. After our argument last night, I'd agreed to stay near the house today. I had, but now I was itching to get back out there and find the phone.

Though I wanted to argue when he'd made me promise not to leave—I was not in the habit of obeying orders—I was wiped out after yesterday. So I settled in with one of the books Willa had lent me.

The story distracted me for a bit, but a few hours later, I was pulled back to the real world when Ripley got up and padded toward the front door. I straightened on the couch, listening for sounds outside the house, but heard none. A minute later, Jude's truck pulled in, his tires crunching on gravel, and my heart leaped. My body wanted to jump up and greet him like an excited dog, but I forced myself to sit back, despite how thrilled I was that he was back so early.

The excitement was centered around getting out there

and finding my phone. It had nothing to do with being excited to see him. Nope, not at all.

In journalism school, the instructors had driven objectivity into us. The ability to see all sides, to distance oneself, and to reject potential bias before it had a chance to form were some of the most important traits a journalist could possess. I was used to creating distance, to examining situations carefully.

But maintaining objectivity and appropriate emotional distance while trapped in a house with a sweet lumberjack twenty-four seven was virtually impossible.

Especially a sweet lumberjack wearing thick glasses and holding a large bakery box.

"Got you something." He broke into a smile that would have made my knees weak if I were standing. "These scones are famous."

At the word *scones*, I was on my feet, grabbing at the green box.

"The blueberry is a big deal. But I'm partial to the maple bacon."

The pastries smelled like heaven. The anticipation of carbs and sugar hitting my bloodstream sent a zing of excitement through me.

Or maybe it was Jude's proximity. Or the dimple barely visible beneath his beard.

He skirted around me and set the box down. Only then did I notice the cardboard tube he had tucked under one arm.

"I got you something else." He cleared off one side of the island, then slid a piece of rolled-up paper from the cardboard tube.

"We have a large format printer at the office," he explained, smoothing it out.

I snagged a scone and took a too-big bite as I circled the granite countertop. "Is this—"

"A topographical map. From the trailer park to here. This way we can plot out the route you took and use GPS coordinates, then make a search plan so we don't miss anything."

I scanned the map, then locked eyes with him. "This is brilliant."

He grinned again. Damn. I didn't think I'd ever get tired of that expression. He was so serious and stoic, his thick beard and glasses only adding to the façade. But when he smiled, his expression turned boyish and a bit naughty.

"I told you I could help. We've got to be smart about this. We'll construct our search perimeter and then strategically comb the area."

I smoothed my hand over the thick paper as hope swelled in my chest. I'd been running around like an idiot, searching with no plan and no sense of where I'd been. This was so much better.

"Thank you." This entire thing was beyond logical, and yet here he was with his giant map and his plan, ready to help me.

He shrugged. "I told you—we're in this together. But what if the phone is damaged?"

"I had a fancy case. Waterproof and shatterproof. Obviously that's no guarantee, but it's something."

He nodded. God, I hoped this wouldn't be a complete failure. It would be bad enough if I messed it all up on my own. I wasn't sure I could live with myself if I dragged him into it with me and it was a bust.

"Let's work through the path you took." He held out a pencil. "Then we can prioritize the areas we're more likely to find it, like where you had to crawl."

I walked around the table, finishing my scone, and oriented myself. I took the pencil from him, and for several seconds, I studied the details of the map, taking in landmarks. Then, tentatively, I leaned over the island and plotted where I'd started, where I'd ridden the motorcycle, and where I'd entered the state forest.

It was difficult to tell, even with a detailed map, where I'd veered off the trail.

"We can drive over there tomorrow and use the app on my phone to record the coordinates of some of the spots you remember."

"I do. I remember some of the rock formations and the trees. I can find my hiding spot again." Eyes trained on the map, I circled the island, trying to recreate the feel of running through the forest.

"I think it was roughly around here." I used my index finger to circle a small area. "But if I see it, I can be more precise. I haven't been able to hike out that far yet."

He covered my hand with his large, warm one.

It took willpower, but I did my best to ignore the small tinge of heat that shot through me.

"We'll drive out tomorrow and retrace your steps." He squeezed my fingers gently. "We'll find it together."

Affection surged through me. For so long, he'd lived in my memory as a sexy one-night stand. The cute musician I'd lusted over.

But over the last week, I'd seen so many sides of him, and my affection had grown exponentially. He was smart, curious, and caring. And the more time I spent with him, the more at ease I felt.

In my experience, words were cheap. Most people could say the right thing and even offer to help, but few would dive in the way he had. And it was rare to find a person who could match my intensity and not be scared off.

This moment was a simple one, but it felt as though he was showing me who he truly was. Someone who wasn't afraid to get his hands dirty. A man who was not intimidated by me. A man who could handle me. All of me.

My cheeks heated under his scrutiny. Why had I come here? Yes, I needed the help, but why had my first instinct been to seek out this man I'd spent a single night with? And why did the help have to come with a side of orgasmic memories and sexy banter?

"Thank you." I kept my focus on the map, feeling more hopeful than I had in the past week. "I really need the help."

"Partners," he said, holding out his hand.

I squeezed my eyes shut, digging deep for bravery.

"Yes." I forced myself to zero in on him and slide my palm against his. There was no denying the rush of electricity I felt this time. The longer I stayed here, the less control I had. One of these days, our hair-brushing routine alone might be enough to cause an orgasm.

"But we need some ground rules," I said, my tone harsher than I meant for it to be.

He squeezed my hand tighter and pulled me closer. "I happen to like rules, Trouble. Tell me what you need so we can get to work."

At the flirtatious flash in his eyes, I jerked away. Boundaries. Yes. They were a necessity if I had any hope of surviving him.

I took another step back for good measure. When it came to scruffy lumberjacks, distance was always helpful.

"No more flirting," I said, my pitch a little too high. "And you can't mention the, uh..." I paused, sure I wouldn't have to finish the sentence.

But his only response was to widen his eyes in question. Dammit.

"You know." I cleared my throat, my cheeks burning. "That we had sex."

"So you want to ignore it?" He crossed his arms, which made his stupid biceps bulge and my core twinge.

"Yes!" I shouted.

He was way too calm and looked way too good. I couldn't handle the teasing. "Wipe it from your memory. You want to work together, then we have to pretend there's no sexy history between us."

"Can't do it." He shook his head, chuckling.

"Jude," I hissed. "Be serious."

"I am serious. I told you I was all in. I told you that you could trust me. So what if we had sex multiple times and on multiple surfaces?"

I covered my face and groaned.

"And yes, it was fucking great," he went on, uncaring that I was slowly dying of mortification. "But I'm a gentleman, Trouble. If it embarrasses you or bothers you, I won't mention it. But I'm not gonna let you take those sexy memories away from me."

I peered at him from between my fingers. This entire conversation had gone off the rails.

"I won't do anything or say anything to make you uncomfortable. I promise."

"I know that." I dropped my hand. "You've been so good to me. Truly. I didn't mean to imply otherwise."

He smirked. "This is important. And we need to trust each other."

"Strangely, I do trust you," I admitted. "Maybe it's your awesome dog, or maybe because you're a single guy who keeps hand soap in the bathroom. But you need to understand what you're getting into with me."

Hand held out, he took a step closer.

Despite my better judgment, I took it and gave it a firm shake, pushing away thoughts of how warm and strong his calloused palm felt.

"You have my word," he said. "I will do whatever I can to help you, and I won't let our sexual history get in the way."

"Friends," I declared, my stomach fluttering obnoxiously in his proximity.

It was the broadness of him, the way he took up space, that pulled me toward him. Or maybe it was his warmth and strength. As much as I'd like to step into his arms and let him comfort me, I needed to keep this friends boundary firmly in place.

"Can I get my friend more coffee?"

With a nod, I released him.

We got back to work, and while I used Google Earth to pull up images on his computer in order to better orient myself, he measured and calculated distances. After an hour or so, we had a decent search area mapped out and a plan for how we would get started.

We'd leave early tomorrow morning, when we'd have a lower chance of being seen, and drive as close as we could to the most likely spots. There, we'd comb carefully through the area, searching for the phone. It would take time, but the plan was far more strategic than running into the woods and stopping to look in places that seemed familiar.

The device was the definition of a needle in a haystack, but I was more hopeful than I'd been since I arrived.

He'd kept the flirtation to a minimum. Not that it helped much, since everything about Jude oozed sex appeal. I'd love to brush it off to hormones and broad shoulders, but it was more. He was smart, strategic, and invested.

The way he studied the map and asked questions was hotter than I could have imagined. I'd been working alone for so long that I'd forgotten how helpful it could be to have another person pushing me, questioning me, forcing me to be my best.

He stood up to stretch, making his T-shirt rise a few inches above his belt, revealing a sliver of taut, pale skin covered in a dusting of hair that took concerted effort to ignore.

"I need to get back to work, but tomorrow"—he pinned me with a look and tapped the map—"we're doing this." Before he could go on, his phone rang.

He dug it out of his pocket and quickly swiped the screen to answer. "Hey. Gus," he said as he brought the device to his ear. "I'll be back in a —"

His words cut off, and his face fell. In the next heartbeat, the blue of his irises was the color of a tumultuous storm.

"When? How many?"

He paced the room, silent, as Gus continued speaking. With every lap he made, his shoulders drew up farther and my stomach knotted more painfully.

At one point he closed his eyes and tipped his head back, as if asking for help from the heavens.

"Fuck," he said again. "Yeah, I'll stay here. No, she's fine."

He eyed me, and when the pity in his expression registered, my heart sank.

"Chloe did what?" He huffed. "Of course she did. Do you have a photo?"

He turned on his heel and headed the other direction again.

"Send it over. I don't have the criminal file, but the pictures are in there, right?"

For a moment, he paused, and when there was a murmured response on the other end, he started up again.

"Okay, great."

When he finally ended the call, he studied me from the other side of the island. The concern in his eyes made my breath catch.

"What's going on?" I asked, anxiety rolling through me.

"I'm gonna stay here with you for the rest of the day." He pulled his glasses off and cleaned them with the hem of his shirt, moving in a methodical circular motion. "We had some visitors over at the office."

Dread joined the anxiety, the two sensations dueling to take over inside my body. "Visitors?"

"A group of bikers drove around the campus, looking in

some of the outbuildings and the newly repaired machine shop."

I clutched my good hand to my chest. "Oh shit."

"A couple of them walked around the property, taking photos and trying to get into locked buildings. Chloe went out there and threatened to have them arrested for trespassing. They left without much fuss, but she's shaken up."

"Did she recognize any of them?"

He pressed his lips together as he slid his glasses into place again. "Gus is getting the security footage. He'll send it over. Maybe you can ID some of them. Chloe mentioned seeing that tattoo on more than one of them."

I frowned. "The tattoo I mentioned to Parker?"

Chin dipped, he hummed. "Last year, a couple of guys followed her. Harassed her a little. They had this distinctive tattoo. He's gonna send me a picture. The guy they arrested for arson had ink on his arm. What do you want to bet it's the same design?"

He bent at the waist, petting Ripley, who'd been hovering close since the moment Gus called, sensing Jude's distress.

Nausea clawed up my throat. Were they looking for me? Or trying to start trouble?

"It's likely." I sighed. "But damn. Do the jackasses really think they can ride around and intimidate people?"

He laughed. "Guess so. Not that intimidating Chloe is an easy feat."

"Sorry." I squeezed my eyes shut, staving off a wave of tears. Chloe and Gus had a baby. These people had lives and families, all of which were being disrupted because of me.

"I need that phone, Jude." A tear crested my lashes. "I need to find it and figure out what they're planning."

"They're out and about today, which means it's too dangerous for us to hunt for it. But first thing tomorrow, we'll load up, and we won't stop until we find it. These assholes are threatening my family, and we're gonna take them down."

The determination in his eyes stole the breath from my lungs. I'd only seen those flames once before, and it was when he'd had his head between my thighs. Turned out this mild-mannered lumberjack had some fire after all.

Chapter 14
Mila

LUMBERSNACK:

I heard you singing in the shower this morning.

TROUBLE:

OMG. I am so embarrassed.

LUMBERSNACK:

Don't be. I'm glad you're feeling better.

TROUBLE:

I'd feel a lot better if I could have a Pop-Tart.

Maybe Swedish Fish too?

LUMBERSNACK:

There's chia pudding in the fridge and banana chips in the pantry.

TROUBLE:

I'm offended that you think I even know what chia pudding is.

LUMBERSNACK:

Offended?

TROUBLE:
Good day, sir.

Chapter 15
Jude

"I'm having second thoughts about this." I scanned the empty forest, searching for anything unnatural. This had seemed like a good plan yesterday, but after the bikers showed up at the office, I'd changed my mind. I wanted to lock Mila up in my house and never let her out.

"It's seven a.m. We're the only people awake, never mind hiking in the freezing cold woods," she quipped, tromping up the path from the parking lot.

"But those guys—"

"Are sleeping off last night's bender." She cut me off. "This is our best chance."

She pulled the gray beanie lower, tucking her hair inside. Between that and the sunglasses, she was almost unrecognizable. The Racine field jacket I'd pulled out of the closet for her made her look like another hiker, roaming the woods with me and my dog.

But I couldn't shake the fear, the feeling that we were in danger.

Though her injuries were healing, she still had a way to

go. Willa insisted she still wear her sling, and she'd only just finished the antibiotics.

Being out here must be terrifying for her.

The uncertainty and danger ate at me. This had to end. It had changed the lives of every one of my brothers. We'd never be the people we were before Dad went to prison. And Mila? How could she ever go back to the life she'd lived before her brother was attacked?

I consulted the map on my phone as we walked the path, headed to a more densely wooded area. We'd put a lot of time into planning our search grid and recreating the route she'd taken. From the parking lot, we'd have to hike a couple of miles before we hit our search perimeter. We sipped coffee from the thermos I'd brought and walked quietly as Ripley jumped over exposed roots and sniffed almost every tree.

"The forest reminds me of Hugo," Mila said, tilting her head to look up at the gray sky. "He's the outdoorsy one. A habitat biologist. Total idealist. Believes that business and nature can coexist, that we can protect plants and animals if we do it right."

I hummed in agreement.

She let out a humorless chuckle. "All that hope and belief in doing what's right, and he ended up almost beaten to death outside your office."

"I'm so sorry," I said, chest aching. That was a hard day for us. I couldn't imagine the pain she felt when she'd gotten the news. "Lila, my brother's fiancée, found him while she was on a run. Called 911 and gave him CPR."

She dipped her chin and tugged the collar of her jacket

up higher. "I've read all the police reports. Someday I'd like to thank her in person."

As we walked, our breaths puffed out in white clouds in front of us. It was shaping up to be a typical Maine fall day. Though it was freezing now, by midafternoon, the sun would be out, warming the air to a bearable temperature, and for a glorious few hours, we'd take off our coats. As the sun started its descent, the jackets would reappear, and by nightfall, it would be freezing again.

"He was the quiet, gentle one. He was born premature, and even then, when I was five years old, I remember looking at him in the plastic bassinet at the hospital, thinking he was so tiny and helpless, vowing that I'd always protect him.

"He's a grown man, but he'll always be my little brother. The two of us stuck together. We were both nerdy kids. He was the outdoorsy one who loved science, while I was reading *Sherlock Holmes*."

It was baffling, the mixture of joy and pain on her face as she talked about her brother.

"He loved his job," she continued, forging ahead. "He loved protecting the forest and its creatures. So every time I come out here, I feel that peace. Always have. Only now, it's tinged with rage. Because the person who loves this"—she held out her good arm, gesturing to the forest—"the most, who taught me to stand still and appreciate nature, is currently in a hospital room hooked up to machines."

My heart ached for her. "What's the prognosis?"

She kicked a rock, sending it skittering into the brush. "Not great. Comas are weird. Most are very short, and some are very long. But he still has brain activity. Some days a lot of it. So it is possible he'll recover. Now it's a waiting game."

I ducked my head and scratched at my neck, once again at a loss for the right thing to say. "I'm sorry."

"He'll come back. I know he will. I can't fathom the alternative. His body responds to stimuli. We've had specialists from Boston come in several times. Initially it was swelling and a brain bleed, but then he had a stroke during surgery, which put additional stress on his brain."

"Sounds like he's getting excellent care."

She shrugged. "Decent. I'd prefer he be in Boston. Mass General has a neurology ICU and the best doctors in the world, but given his odds, they did not accept him when I pushed for it. My mom doesn't want him moved there anyway. She can't afford to pack up and relocate to Boston to be with him every day. So it's fine."

"That's terrible."

"Eh, it's medicine." She lifted one shoulder. "They want the cases they can cure and write papers about in journals. But I don't care what the odds are. They don't apply to Hugo. He's better than the rest of us. Kind and funny and filled with so much joy. He will wake up and he will get his life back."

Her voice was filled with sadness, but the love she had for her brother radiated from her.

"You should have seen him as a kid, writing careful notes about the species of beetles in our backyard. So excited to talk our ears off about bird migration patterns or the role of moss in erosion control."

That comment brought with it thoughts of my own brothers. The six of us had complicated relationships, but every one was built on love and camaraderie. For years, I'd had to worry each time Noah deployed to a fire. And there were times during Finn's stint as a Navy pilot when he flew missions that demanded a level of security that kept him from contacting any of us.

"That was one of the reasons," she said softly.

So wrapped up in my own thoughts, I missed what she'd said. "Sorry." I shook the cobwebs from my mind. "Reasons for what?"

"I saw the newspapers about the fire at your brother's place, and I'd heard talk about the issues Souza had with Cole. I thought…" She sighed, her focus fixed on the path ahead. "I thought you'd understand the agony and the fear, and I hoped that you might want to help."

I did want to help. I was already mentally calculating how I could help her brother get better medical care, catch the bad guys, and solve every problem she'd ever had or ever could have.

The tug in my chest was firm enough to cause physical pain. Eventually, I'd have to examine the how and the why behind the impossible-to-ignore desire to be everything she could ever need, but right now, we were on a mission.

"This is it." She pointed ahead. "This is where I got off the path and headed into the forest." Coming to a stop, she turned slowly, surveying the area around us. "I hurdled over those." She pointed toward several fallen trees. "And down that hill is where I grabbed the tree and dislocated my shoulder."

Her face was impassive, stoic, her muscles locked up tight.

I put my hand on her shoulder, hoping to ground her as she relived what must have been a terrifying experience.

"You're really brave," I said softly.

Her lips tipped up almost imperceptibly as she peered over at me.

I knew the hike would be grueling for her in her injured state, but I hadn't anticipated how emotional this would be.

I wanted to gather her in my arms and promise to fix it all. I wanted to swear I'd find a way to take them down.

There was nothing I wouldn't do for Mila.

For now, though, I had to stay focused. I couldn't drift away along a current of memories of her touch, her sleepy smiles, or the way she'd whimpered when I'd pushed inside her for the first time.

Nope. That was totally out of bounds. I'd assured her that we could work together. And I was nothing if not a man of my word.

"We should get on with it. I haven't made it this far yet."

With a nod, I got my phone out and recorded our GPS coordinates, then added them to the map I'd created.

Then, as I tucked the device into my pocket again, I dipped my head. "Show me where you hid."

She pointed, and I got to work clearing a path with my boot, kicking leaves and twigs out of the way.

Ripley sniffed around, taking in all the details.

I was on alert, worried we'd be caught unaware. But Ripley had a keen sense of hearing. She'd bark if anyone approached.

"Over that way," Mila urged, kicking her way down the path, scanning the ground for the phone.

I rolled one rotting log away from another, scouring the cold, wet ground.

Fuck, she'd lain on the ground for God knew how long, injured and hiding. I couldn't imagine.

Together we followed her path as best as we could, scanning and searching, digging when necessary.

Despite the circumstances, it was peaceful work. I'd always loved the quiet of the forest.

After a few hours, though, her feet had begun dragging and her posture was stooped. She had to be exhausted.

We recorded the coordinates of a few more spots, and then she guided me back along the path she'd taken to the trail on the far side of the forest toward my house.

Once we'd done a thorough search of the hiding spot, I pulled out a Thermos of hot coffee and a couple of bags of snacks.

We sat on a large, flat rock, sipping coffee while my mind spun around in circles, alternating between hope and panic.

Mila surprised me, bracing her good hand behind her and tilting her face toward the sun. Eyes closed and mouth tipped in a smile, she said, "There isn't much better than this. I've always loved the smell and the sounds of the forest and the warmth of the sunshine on a chilly fall day."

She trailed off, taking in our surroundings not with the intent of searching for the phone, but in wonder, really drinking in the scene.

"The last time I was here, I was terrified. But sitting here with you, I feel safe."

My heart stuttered at her words. My instinct was to puff up with pride. Of course I could keep her safe. But I reined it in. In reality, that safety was only an illusion. She was in danger. We both knew it.

But her attitude was contagious. This place was beautiful. The foliage and the crisp air fueled me and encouraged me to keep going.

She reached into the pocket of the giant jacket I'd lent her and held out a treat to Ripley, who sat patiently, her tail beating the dirt path with excitement.

"I love this dog." She leaned forward and scratched her ears. "You are the best girl, Ripley. The best."

With a quiet groan that betrayed just how much this excursion had taken out of her, she sat up.

"Where did you get her?"

I opened my mouth, but before I could respond, a familiar sound interrupted me.

"Do you hear that?" I pivoted, scanning the trees. "There," I said, pointing at a massive curved oak up ahead. "That's an American redstart."

She squinted, one hand blocking the sun from her eyes. "The little black bird?"

I hummed. "See his long tail and the orange streaks?"
She nodded.

"They're a protected species up here. Listen."

We sat perfectly still, and eventually, the bird opened its flat bill and let out a series of melodic squeaks and chirps.

"That's different."

"Yes, their warble is longer than that of most birds. We've done a lot up here to protect habitats, and I did a lot of research, so I nerd out when I see one."

She picked at the trail mix and grinned. "You're a bird-watcher? Never would have guessed that."

"I'm a student of the forest." I leaned back on my hands. "Spent my life out here, getting to know the trees and the animals. And birds are fascinating creatures."

"You're full of surprises." She rubbed Ripley's head, her

expression softening. "Now where did you find this beautiful creature and how sad will you be when I steal her?"

Ripley watched Mila, her eyes full of love and devotion. The sight sent a surge of panic through me. She really could steal my beloved dog. Ripley would probably go willingly, and I didn't think I'd have the heart to stop her.

"She found me." I poured trail mix into my hand and tossed it into my mouth. "Up at the Northwest Camp, near the Montreal border. It's been about five years now, I think. We went up one early spring, while the ground was still frozen, to do a survey and collect some data. We were sleeping in an old camp hut with no heat. It was nearly impossible to sleep with the number of mice scurrying around in the walls and ceiling. I was lying in bed, wide awake, when I heard a crying sound. I shoved my feet into my boots and pulled on my coat, then went out to investigate."

Mila's eyes widened. "Was she hurt?"

I nodded. "I found her in the deep woods. She'd dug herself a little den under a boulder. She had a broken leg. Her fur was matted and she was scraped up pretty badly." I scratched her chin, assessing her now. My beloved Ripley. How far we'd both come since that day. She was the most loving, protective creature on earth. She went everywhere with me, and at night, she slept in her special bed, on the floor right next to mine.

"We were hundreds of miles from civilization. I couldn't tell you where she came from, but she was small and scared and I..." I dropped my head between my knees. The thought of how malnourished she was back then always hit me hard.

"You're a protector," Mila finished with a light elbow to my ribs. "No denying it."

"Something like that." I straightened, keeping my forearms on my knees. "So I brought her home and took her to the vet. After that, we were inseparable. I had no idea she'd grow into the size of a small horse, but I'm not complaining."

The gentle beast gazed up at me with those soulful dark eyes, showing me again that she understood so much more than I realized.

The vet had suggested she was part wolf hound. It made sense, with the dark gray fur with the occasional black spot. She had a white circle around one eye, which wasn't a wolf hound trait, but she was perfectly Ripley.

"She adores you," Mila said, pulling another treat from her pocket. "I've never had a pet. Always wanted one, even though I wasn't sure I was a dog person."

"Even as a kid?"

She nodded. "My parents worked a lot. I swore that when I was grown, I'd get a cat. I love cats."

Ripley wrinkled her snout as if disgusted by the suggestion.

"But then I traveled all the time, chasing stories and packing up with a day's notice. So it never felt practical."

"You're a dog person," I assured her. "And you can hang out with Ripley any time you want. She's pretty ambivalent about people, but she likes you."

A smile spread across Mila's face. "It's mutual." She stood, brushing crumbs off her lap. "We should get back to work."

I packed up the Thermos while she continued to scan with her flashlight, kicking leaves and dirt to clear a path.

"And I wasn't kidding about stealing her," she teased.

A couple of hours later, we'd covered a significant portion of our route, but we'd had no success, and the cold was setting in.

We'd been at it since sunrise, and after our snack break, I'd felt recharged, but now I was quickly losing steam.

Mila's calm from earlier had morphed into agitation. All morning, I'd reassured her that if we stuck to the grid, it would turn up. But the longer we searched, the harder it was to remain positive.

With her back to me, she hunched over, sniffling.

Gut lurching, I hopped over a fallen tree and darted for her.

"Are you hurt?" I took her good hand between mine to warm it and ducked, catching her sorrowful eyes.

She shook her head, her eyes filling with tears.

"We will find it," I said with a conviction I didn't feel.

"What if we don't?" she whispered as the tears crested her lashes and tracked down her cheeks. "What if it got smashed or broken and it's all gone?" Before I could respond, she pulled her hand away and fisted it at her side. "This is hopeless. I'm a complete failure."

The words had me snapping up straight. I was used to confident Mila, sassy Mila, and injured Mila. But sobbing Mila was distressing. She hadn't made an appearance since that first full day after she was attacked.

The pain and defeat in her tone tore at me, ripping me apart.

Without thinking, I pulled her into my chest and wrapped my arms around her, careful of her shoulder. I rested my chin on her head and held her as she cried into my chest.

This was all I could offer her. Warmth and comfort.

I'd fucked up. I'd promised her we'd find the phone, and I hadn't delivered.

I held her close, aching to make this all go away.

"Let's take a break. We can come back tomorrow."

"No." She sniffled. "Every minute that we don't have the evidence is another minute these fuckers are hurting people."

I eased back and surveyed her face, cataloging the fierce determination in her eyes.

In that moment, my world shifted.

As I held her shaking body while she spoke with such steel in her voice, I knew I was gone.

Life would never be the same.

And while that should have terrified me, the realization brought nothing with it but peace.

Chapter 16
Mila

As though he knew I needed junk food to steel myself after the disappointment I'd suffered today, Jude drove a solid thirty minutes to the nearest McDonald's.

We sat in his truck in a parking lot off 95 while I willed the carbs, salt, and grease to quell the panic inside me.

He'd been so kind in the forest. Searching tirelessly, keeping me fed and hydrated, and attempting to lift my spirits. As frightened as I was, I'd actually enjoyed the time with him a little.

"Admit it." I threw a fry at him.

It bounced off his shoulder and landed on the dash, where he plucked it up and popped it into his mouth.

"It's delicious."

He held his double cheeseburger up, studying it like it was a rare jewel.

"Good thing you let me order for you." I chomped on a scalding-hot fry. "I can't believe you tried to get a salad." I shuddered.

"Seemed like a good idea."

"McDonald's doesn't have salads. They used to, but no normal person ordered them. Why would they when they could have this instead?" I lifted up a McNugget like a trophy.

"Clearly." He gestured at the two bags filled with fries, chicken nuggets, and every type of dipping sauce.

Once he'd admitted that he hadn't had McDonald's since he was a kid, I'd insisted that we sample all the delights. So we may have over-ordered a bit.

I glared at him as I picked up my Coke. "Don't complain. I got the Filet-O-Fish for a healthy option."

He rolled his eyes and took a massive bite out of his burger.

Shit. That should *not* have been hot, but suddenly, my core was tightening.

He closed his eyes and chewed, his strong jaw working.

"I can admit it. After a day spent in the cold, damp woods, this has made me pretty happy."

He broke off a piece of his burger and held it out to Ripley, who was lounging in the back seat.

He took another bite and grinned at me, one cheek puffed out.

My stomach flipped, and not because I'd shoved an eleventh McNugget drenched in sugary barbeque sauce down my throat.

I should not be having fun. I was on the run from criminals, I'd lost valuable evidence, and I was exhausted and in pain.

But I was at peace here, sitting beside him, listening to country music, and devouring fast food.

He took another enormous bite, the move leaving a glob of ketchup on one side of his mouth.

"You have ketchup on your face." Without thinking, I leaned over the console and used my thumb to wipe at the condiment. When the soft yet scratchy sensation of his beard registered, I yanked my hand back. Shit. This was exactly the kind of physical contact we needed to avoid.

"Sorry," I said, grimacing.

He snatched my wrist and, gaze heated, brought my thumb to his lips and gently licked it clean.

My heart practically leaped out of my chest.

His tongue. Oh God, did the memories of his tongue haunt me.

I must have briefly hallucinated, because before I could truly register the sensation, he dropped my hand and went back to devouring his burger, completely unaffected.

I blinked a few times, willing my heart rate to slow. Suddenly, the car felt too small, and I had the overwhelming urge to run straight into the woods and never look back.

But good sense prevailed, I'd already done that, and it hadn't exactly helped matters.

When he turned the music up, probably to drown out the awkwardness, I let myself relax. Emotions were running high. I had to keep my focus on the search. On my brother. Not the sexy lumberjack beside me.

"Do you want to head home?" He crumpled up the Filet-O-Fish wrapper and tossed it into the bag. He'd polished that off, along with the double cheeseburger and a large order of fries. It was impressive.

I hummed. "I need some time to think through my movements again so I can pinpoint other locations where I could have lost it."

He rolled the top of the bag down and nodded. "Makes sense. If I take the scenic route back to Lovewell, maybe the view will stir memories. As painful as it is, try to go through every move you made that day. Where you went, how you felt, sensory details. It can help."

I'd relived the events a dozen times already, but since we turned up empty-handed today, it wouldn't hurt to go through them again. Though I was at risk of falling into a food coma on the drive after spending the day in the mountains and consuming so many carbs.

I reclined the seat a bit and closed my eyes, letting the memories wash over me. I started from the moment I woke up. The sense of triumph that came with the realization that I'd gotten the evidence. Then came the mounting panic when Razor pounded on my door.

I was going through the movements I made as I escaped my trailer when a comforting warm pressure rested on my shoulder.

With an eye cracked open, I peered at Ripley, who'd placed her snout on my shoulder and closed her eyes. She understood I needed her in that moment.

I smiled. What a good dog. When this was over, I'd adopt all the dogs.

Eyes closed again, I envisioned slipping my phone into my bra and climbing out the bathroom window. The panic that hit me as the SUV pulled up returned, causing Ripley to snuggle closer to my neck. Then came the hair trigger decision to take off on Razor's bike.

Struggling to balance and steer, getting to the stop sign

and then flooring it. Wobbling, desperate to get away from the scary dudes who would have done God only knew what if they caught me.

The air was chilly that morning, the dew soaking into my sneakers as I ran.

Bathroom window, looking out at the road, noticing the motorcycle keys were still in the ignition.

"Wait." I kept my eyes closed, pushing away thoughts of the physical space to make room for sensations.

The wind stinging my eyes. The fear that I'd lay his bike on its side and kill myself since I wasn't wearing a helmet or any kind of protective gear.

"I stopped the bike a few times, to get control and to get my bearings. I'd ridden before, but not a lot, and without a visor, it was difficult to see."

He hummed, the sound vibrating through me. "Keep talking, Trouble."

"They were chasing me. Just the SUV at that point. The bike was almost out of gas, but I didn't have time to stop. I headed up Route 2, and after the old service station, I picked up Route 16, thinking I could lose them."

Jude turned the music down. "What happened next?"

The engine sputtered. I knew then I had to ditch the bike and hide. I pulled onto the shoulder and jumped off.

"That's where I bruised my knee. I jumped off the bike and then caught my foot. It was a steep drop-off. I fell, and that's when I made a beeline for the woods, looking for cover."

"That's where you cut through to get to the state forest."

I nodded, still reliving the moments, taking in the details I may have missed the first time.

"I almost fell a few times. I was leaned over the bike, struggling, wobbling. I thought the phone had fallen out in the woods, but what if it happened just off the road?"

I sat up, itching to search again.

"Can we go back? To the trailer park? It may spark more memories."

He winced. "If it fell out on the road, it's probably destroyed."

I shook my head. "No. It can't be." That was an outcome I couldn't accept. I'd find that damn phone if it killed me.

"Take me to the trailer park," I urged.

"I'm not sure that's a good idea." He blew out a long breath, his focus fixed on the winding road. "What if you're recognized? I won't put you in danger."

"At this point, not finding the phone is more dangerous." I leveled him with a glare. "I'll put my hat back on, and I'll stay out of sight."

When he flipped the turn signal on, I was hit with a rush of hope and affection for him. He was pushing aside his caveman instincts and trusting me. I wasn't sure when I'd last felt so respected.

"But you're not going into that trailer," he warned.

"They probably trashed it." I lifted a shoulder. "If I think there's anything worth salvaging, I'll send you."

He shook his head and continued on. As we rode in silence, I sent up prayers to any deity who might be listening that the phone was out there and the evidence was still accessible. That all this work and anguish hadn't been for nothing.

Thirty minutes later, we turned into Pine Tree Acres. I pulled my hat over my head and slumped down in the seat, watching carefully out the window for people I recognized or anything out of the ordinary.

As we drove farther into the park, I was hit with a wave of embarrassment. The place was a dump. I should have come alone.

Pine Tree Acres was gross by rural Maine trailer park standards. And that was saying something. But it was cheap and close to the main hub in Heartsborough. It had been a good cover, living here on my own, keeping quiet about my past.

I shifted, grimacing as we passed a car with four flat, rotting tires. "I'm sorry for bringing you here. This may have been a mistake."

The homes near the entrance were nicer. The residents there lived in double-wides with potted plants out front and outdoor furniture. My single-wide was *much* farther back.

"Where was your place?" Jude's expression remained impassive, free of judgment.

I pointed to the back road, where most places were deserted and crumbling. One nicer trailer was clearly a meth lab, but the people who worked there were quiet and clean. So I kept my distance.

The owner of the park, Betty—a chain smoking seventy-something with teased hair and a Harley—had been more than happy to accept cash when my rent payment was due. She didn't ask questions and I didn't offer any information.

At the time, it made sense.

But now, as I cataloged the details through Jude's eyes, this all felt wrong. What the hell had I gotten myself into?

My heart rate picked up, and my breathing went shallow. "I had a home," I babbled, my face heating. "Or I used to. Before I ended my lease. A townhome in the East End of Portland. I used to walk along the harbor and go to trivia night with my colleagues on Tuesdays."

Jude was silent as he navigated through the park. The farther we got, the shabbier the homes looked. With each passing second, the shame that had hit me grew.

"My mom and I went to the outdoor summer concerts in Payson Park. She'd get whoopie pies from Becky's Diner for my birthday every year," I rushed out. "But." I snapped my mouth shut and eyed him.

He glanced my way, his brow furrowed in concern.

"But I fell apart after Hugo was attacked. The same kind of fear I'd felt when I was overseas in a war zone took over, and when the adrenaline joined in, it was as if I had to be alert and ready to go at all times."

He looked over at me with nothing but compassion. God, I wished I could go in for another hug right now. The way he'd held me in the woods was more comforting than any hug had the right to be. Like he was there to keep me on my feet when I no longer had the strength to remain upright. Against my better judgment, I trusted him.

"I think I got addicted."

"Addicted to what?"

"Living in survival mode." I let out a shaky breath. "Waking up ready to fight. I've been cooped up at your place for over a week, and my nervous system has been twitchy for days already. It feels like I can't function unless I'm digging and investigating and moving forward."

He gently placed his hand over mine and gave it a light squeeze.

"It's PTSD," he said. "You've been through so much."

It was unnerving how he could practically see into my soul and read my innermost thoughts so easily. I wasn't the heart-on-my-sleeve kind of girl. No, I was battle hardened. Elusive. Mysterious. I'd been living as Amy for over a year, for God's sake.

Yet after only a few days with this guy, he was diagnosing my trauma.

Discomfort rolled over me. This was too intimate. Too much. All the hugs in the world wouldn't help my brother.

I squeezed my eyes closed, steeling myself. Reminding myself of my mission. Jude was helping me find the phone. Nothing else.

I forced myself to give him a sassy grin. "Didn't know I was hanging out with an armchair psychiatrist," I needled. "I think it'd be best if you stuck to lumberjacking."

His eyes flashed, but rather than get angry about my jab, he grinned. "My job is not lumberjacking."

Shifting his way, I arched a brow. "So it's just your hobby?"

"No," he replied. "My hobby is beating your Ivy League ass in Scrabble. Now lead the way so we can find this phone."

Chapter 17
Jude

"This way." Mila pointed up the road.

I eased off the gas and pulled onto the shoulder. We were slowly retracing her steps from the trailer park, searching for the exact spot where she'd fallen off the motorcycle. The sun was sinking lower in the sky. Soon, we'd lose the daylight.

We'd been at this since sunrise, and my head was pounding.

But I wouldn't give up. I was in this now, and there was no going back.

We drove up Route 16, stopping periodically and combing each area. Taking breaks so she could focus on details of that day and so Ripley could stretch her legs.

My gut had twisted painfully at the sight of Mila's destroyed trailer. Even if it hadn't been trashed, I couldn't imagine her living in the dilapidated single-wide for so long.

She hid behind a tough façade, but the fissures and cracks were there if one looked close enough. The pain, the uncertainty, and the fear.

She'd been living in fear for so long, and I wished I could fix it for her. Show her there were other ways to live. Free her from this burden and these threats.

"Can we walk this way a bit?" She pulled the hat down over her hair again. "See how the shoulder slopes and then drops off? This may be the spot."

We jumped out, and I retrieved two flashlights from the set of tools I kept in my truck for emergencies.

"Be careful," I cautioned as we walked along the shoulder.

The grassy area was steep, with several large tree roots protruding from the dirt. Running here would be dangerous.

We took our time, scanning the ground, using our flashlights to search every inch of dirt, grass, and rocks.

"Jude," Mila said, her tone pitching high. "I think this was the spot. See that fallen tree?"

I nodded. At the bottom of the embankment was a large oak that served as a gate to the dense forest behind it.

"Pretty sure I jumped over that when I went into the woods."

"Let me help you down."

I held her good hand, and we shuffled down the steep drop toward the forest floor.

"Let's scan in grid formation from here to the tree. Then we can shift and do the next section."

She nodded, her gaze already sweeping the area in front of her.

The ground was damp and covered in fallen leaves, sticks, and debris, so it would be slow. But it was the best lead we'd had in hours.

I focused on my section of this area, shuffling my feet to

kick up anything that may be covered, all the while saying every prayer I knew that we'd find the damn phone.

Just as I was starting to lose faith, Mila screamed.

Heart pounding, I took off running, picking my feet up to avoid tripping on tree roots. Ripley darted past me, as concerned that she was hurt, I was sure.

Mila kneeled on the cold ground, her back to me. As I rounded her, she was trembling, clutching what looked like a muddy phone in her hand.

"Is that...?"

Face tilted up, she nodded, her teary eyes glistening in the light of the rising moon.

I helped her to her feet, taking the phone from her hands. It was muddy and scuffed up and dead, of course, but there was hope.

"We found it," she whispered, her voice shaking.

"You found it," I said.

"But you." She sniffled. "You got me here. You helped me remember. Fuck, I'm so relieved."

Grasping her hand, I led her back up to the car, both nervous and excited. She had started to softly cry, and I wanted to scoop her up into my arms and make everything better. But we had work to do. We had to get this phone to work.

By the time we pulled up in front of the house, I was shaking with adrenaline. Could this be it? Was it possible that the phone would power on? The moment the truck was in park, Mila threw her door open and hopped out. Ripley followed, dashing for the house. I was hot on their heels.

Inside, I kicked off my muddy boots and shrugged out of

my jacket. "I'll find a charger," I shouted, heading to the kitchen.

"And I'll wipe off the mud," she replied.

I wasn't even sure the front door was closed, but in less than sixty seconds, the device was plugged in and resting on the kitchen island.

We stood shoulder to shoulder, both zeroed in on the dark screen. The scratches all looked superficial, though there was a chance it had been damaged by water.

Regardless, we had it, and we had to try.

Mila was still trembling beside me. "What if it's really dead?" she whispered.

"Then we take out the SIM card," I said. I had no clue what the fuck a SIM card did, but it sounded right, and she immediately perked up in response.

She bounced on her toes. "Yes. Good call. I hooked up with this NSA guy when I was overseas a couple of years ago. Now I remember. We can get the data out of it even if it's damaged. Okay. Okay." She sucked in shallow breaths, still vibrating with a mix of anticipation and fear.

My eyelid twitched at the mention of a former hookup. Especially after we'd spent the last twelve hours sharing stories and opening up to one another, all while skirting danger.

We were still staring at the blank screen, silent again, when the little green battery icon lit up.

"It's alive!" Mila shouted.

I let out the breath I'd been holding, and euphoria surged through my veins. We'd done it.

She jumped up and down carefully, her good arm wrapped around the injured one, as happy tears rolled down her cheeks. With a hiccupping breath, she turned to me and threw her arm around my neck. "Thank you," she mumbled into my T-shirt. "I wouldn't have found it without you."

I wrapped my arms around her and held her close. God, what I'd give to pick her up and spin her around. I was that fucking elated. But with her injuries, this was the best I could do.

Today had been a marathon. We'd really gotten to know one another. We'd been vulnerable in ways I didn't think either of us had allowed ourselves to be in a long time. Though we'd spent hours in the cold, this moment made the aching feet and freezing fingers worth it.

With any luck, this would be all we needed to guarantee her safety. That knowledge felt as good as having her in my arms.

I slowly released her, worried I'd hurt her.

But she was still smiling, beaming up at me. With a happy squeal, she popped up onto her toes and slammed her lips to mine.

The feel of her soft lips sent me hurtling back to our night together. Her scent flooded my senses, urging my hands to roam all over her body.

This felt right.

So I kissed her back, meeting her firm pressure, showing her how good this felt.

I wrapped my arms around her, craving the feel of her skin as I deepened the kiss.

She let out a whimper and grasped a fistful of my shirt, pulling even closer, and I was fucking gone.

It was the sexiest sound I'd ever heard.

A fire ignited inside me, burning only for her. For this

moment, this kiss. This was so much more than attraction. So much deeper than lust.

It was possibility.

The instant that word registered, logic kicked in. There was no possibility. Only danger and heartbreak.

I pulled back and steadied her, putting space between us.

This was wrong. She was hurt. She was reliant on me in so many ways. My job was to protect her.

I took off my glasses and cleaned them, averting my gaze. Even when I put them back on, I couldn't look at her. It took every ounce of self-control I had not to carry her straight to my bed, and if I saw even a flicker of need in her expression, I was worried I'd give in.

"What. The. Fuck. Jude?" she hissed, stepping into my line of sight.

Fuck. It was impossible to avoid looking at her now. Her eyes were lit with a fire that burned with a combination of need and fury.

The anger there did nothing to extinguish the desire building inside me.

She stood in the dim light of the kitchen, her hip cocked, focus fixed completely on me.

I loved her confidence, her bluster. But beneath it, there was exhaustion. She couldn't hide the dark circles under her eyes. This woman had been through hell. She needed a safe place to heal. I wouldn't take that from her.

"We wouldn't stop at just a kiss," I said, hoping that explanation wouldn't result in her kicking me in the balls. Thankfully, the kitchen knives were on the other side of the counter.

"And that's a bad thing?" She bit her bottom lip, still glaring at me. The expression was the equivalent of waving a red flag at a bull. Fuck, I wanted her. But this wasn't right.

"Yes." Though it pained me, I forced the word out.

Her face fell, but the hurt quickly morphed into an angry scowl.

"We didn't stop last time. And if memory serves, it was pretty great."

Great didn't even begin to cover it. It had been the best night of my damn life. But there was too much at stake now to go back. And although Mila brought out every one of my animalistic caveman urges, my honor won out.

"I won't take advantage of you," I said through gritted teeth.

She huffed, sending the little hairs at her temples flying, and stalked toward me. "I'm no damsel in distress."

I clutched the countertop behind me to keep from reaching for her.

"Fuck, I'm an idiot," she said.

My gut sank. "No, I'm the idiot, Trouble. It's not you. Trust me, it's not you. My job is to protect you. Keep you safe. I can't cross the line."

When her eyes narrowed to slits, I wished I could take the words back. "Your *job*?" She huffed. "I can protect myself. And it's not taking advantage if I'm ready and willing."

I couldn't move or speak. My self-control hung by a thread. All I wanted was to protect her, but by shutting her down, I was hurting her instead.

I didn't operate at this speed. I needed time to process and understand. In every aspect of life, with every decision, I took my time, did things right the first time. I did not shoot from the hip and I never took big risks.

Lust, longing, and whatever the strange ache in my chest was? Those things didn't matter.

Eyes squeezed closed, I sucked in a harsh breath, then another. Anger flooded my veins. Anger at my dad and the assholes who'd hurt her brother. Along with every mother-fucker who'd ever threatened the happiness of either of our families.

Because in another world, another life, I would have picked her up and carried her straight to my bed.

In another world, we could be something. I'd felt it that first night together.

But it could never be. I had to make my peace with that.

I'd long ago accepted the fact that I'd be alone forever. And it was so fucking unfair, the way the universe had delivered the one woman I'd ever imagined a future with right to my doorstep while the world around us was burning. While everyone we knew was in danger.

With one more glare, she unplugged the phone. "It's a shame," she said, somehow eye fucking me while shooting daggers. "I still dream about your cock. Biggest I've ever had. Guess I'll charge this in the living room and go to bed. Please leave me alone."

With that, she sauntered away.

Zeroed in on her round hips, I clutched the countertop more firmly.

Fuck me.

I needed a shower. Immediately.

Chapter 18
Mila

LUMBERSNACK:

How many packages did you order?

TROUBLE:

You said to get what I needed.

LUMBERSNACK:

This is a lot of stuff.

TROUBLE:

The rest is coming tomorrow.

LUMBERSNACK:

Did you order a pink sparkle collar for
Ripley?

TROUBLE:

Yes. Poor girl. The boring black collar
makes her so sad. She needs to feel good
about herself.

LUMBERSNACK:

She's a dog. They don't perform gender.

TROUBLE:

She deserves to sparkle, Jude.

Chapter 19
Mila

"What are you doing?"

"Research," I said, a pencil between my teeth as I opened another browser window.

"That's the wall?"

The wall in question had been covered with very nicely framed vinyl covers, but I'd taken them down and gently stacked them in the closet.

In their place were a few dozen Post-it notes.

I didn't glance up. The post-kiss awkwardness was killing me. So I did what I did best. I avoided and evaded.

Jude had given me free rein of his laptop, and we'd dug in.

I'd uploaded all the recordings from the phone to the cloud and was going through them one at a time, creating notes and transcripts, connecting the dots as best as I could.

In this state, it was imperative that I keep busy.

Finding that phone had been a sign from the universe. It was time to get serious.

"I've got your deliveries." He disappeared, and when he returned, he was carrying a stack of Amazon boxes.

"Ooh. Yay," I said, focused on the screen again. "Can you set up the printer for me?"

"Printer?"

"Yup. And the cork boards should go on that wall." I thumbed over my shoulder.

"Shouldn't you be resting? Not"—he waved, gesturing to the chaotic state of the room—"whatever this is."

Halting my search, I lifted my head and narrowed my gaze on him. "We're building a command center. We need a place to ideate."

"Ideate?"

"Yes. Work through it all. You said I could order stuff and ship it to your office."

"I was thinking clothes and things like that..." He trailed off.

"I don't care about clothes." I huffed. So maybe I was still in my feels about our kiss. "I care about justice."

He gave me a tight smile. "Okay, let me get the rest."

As he stalked out, I tore into the first box. Pushpins, red string, printer paper, ink. Great.

"What's with the string?" he asked as he set the massive printer box down.

I cocked a brow. "You can't make a proper evidence board without red string."

He lowered to his knees and opened the printer box. "So you're making a murder wall. Like crazy people on TV shows."

"I object to the use of the term crazy. Being organized is not a sign of illness, Jude. You, of all people, should know that." I gestured to the wall of bookcases with meticulously displayed books, graphic novels, and vinyl records.

"Touche," he muttered.

We unpacked, and while he broke down the boxes and hauled them to the garage, I set up our new equipment. I could feel a buzzing sensation under my skin. Purpose. Exactly what I needed.

While Jude broke down the cardboard for recycling, I gazed out the window at the firepit and expansive yard that led down to the edge of the dense forest. If this was my house, I'd probably plant a flower garden and add some of those flat pavers to make a pretty path.

Huh. It was the first time I'd thought about something like that. I wasn't exactly the domestic type.

"Jude!" I squealed in delight as I saw my friend emerge from the woods. Ripley came running over and pushed her nose against the glass.

"What is it—shit," he hissed.

We watched as the moose walked around the yard, bending down every few yards or so to graze.

"Isn't it adorable? I've been calling him Sir Antlerstein, but then I realized I don't know whether it's a boy or a girl."

He continued to stare as it meandered around the grassy area. "This is bad," he said, shaking his head. "That's an adolescent. They're even more unpredictable."

I brushed him off, continuing to marvel at the majestic creature.

"Oh, fuck," Jude hissed, taking a step back and lacing his fingers on top of his head. "That's Clive."

The big one came trotting out of the woods, looking

annoyed at the younger one. Or maybe that was just his moose face? Either way it was so cool.

"You managed to lure Clive into my yard." He yanked his glasses off and cleaned them on his T-shirt.

"Who's Clive?"

He frowned at me. "He is a menace. A massive bull that is way too comfortable coming to town and wreaking havoc. He made a huge mess at the Fourth of July festival a few years back and recently crashed a wedding."

Laughter bubbled out of me. "That's hilarious."

"It's not. It's dangerous. See the big scar on his flank?" He pointed out the window.

I followed his line of sight, taking in a thick whitish scar that cut across the moose's thick brown fur.

"No one knows how he got it, but it's always been there. It's how we identify him. Not that it's hard. The other moose are smart enough to stay deep in the woods."

"So he's the dad? That's cute." I watched as Clive nudged the younger one with his antlers, and then they both took off running toward the forest.

"Nature is awesome," I said with a smile.

Jude rolled his eyes. "Please do not feed that baby again. We can't have Clive hanging out around here. He could cause damage or a car accident."

Crestfallen, I nodded. I didn't want anyone to get hurt, but I was bored out of my skull most days, and moose sightings were pretty damn exciting.

"You need rest." He scanned the office supplies and the unassembled ergonomic desk chair lying on the floor.

"Yes." I huffed. "But my brain doesn't really do rest.

While my body sits around, my thoughts switch to overdrive. I gotta get all the ideas out."

I was energized in a way I hadn't been in years. My journalistic instincts had come back online. For so long I'd been living in survival mode, I'd lost my objectivity, as well as my ability to contextualize and work through problems.

Maybe it was the peace of this house or the presence of a person who was willing to do the work with me.

"You know things, I know things, Parker knows things. We've got to combine it all and organize it in a way that makes sense," I explained. "And Owen has been so helpful."

He frowned. "You've talked to Owen?"

"Yes. Willa gave me his number. He's great. Super efficient."

With a sigh, Jude shook his head. "If you need help, just ask."

"It's fine. Willa said he had the financial records, and apparently Lila is an absolute genius with numbers, so it made sense to go to them for that." I shimmied where I sat. "Honestly, I may be sexually attracted to the Excel spreadsheet she made. The pivot tables are immaculate."

Jude burst out laughing. This wasn't a chuckle. It was a full-blown belly laugh. He took off his glasses, shoulders shaking, and used his shirt to clean them, even though he'd done it only a moment ago. He was a sexy laugher, especially when his ab muscles peeked out from beneath the hem he had pulled up, contracting and releasing. His eyes crinkled in a way that suggested both maturity and intensity.

And here I was, sitting on the floor beside him, arm in a sling, waxing poetic about spreadsheets.

I couldn't help but give in to laughter too.

It was absurd. All of this. Him. Me. The situation I'd gotten myself into.

Ripley padded into the room, as if to check on us. The silly humans who were on the floor, surrounded by cardboard boxes, losing their minds.

"Sorry," he said, wiping a tear from his eye. "I'm sleep-deprived, and the way you said that—"

"I know I'm ridiculous." I chuckled, holding my ribs to ease the pain.

"And just, all this." He gestured around the room.

"I need something to do," I argued. "And regardless of what Parker says, I have to be ready. Things are happening, and when the shit hits the fan, I can't be caught off guard. Plus, I can only sit around reading dragon smut for so long."

His breath hitched and his eyes widened behind the lenses of his glasses. "Dragon smut?"

I lifted a shoulder. "Technically it's romantasy. The smut only involves humans, but they ride dragons."

He scratched his beard, head tilted to one side. "I don't want to be pedantic, but dragon smut would probably involve the dragons in the smut."

A rush of humorous affection for this man washed over me. "Fair. And honestly, the dragons are the best characters in the book." I threw a packing peanut at him.

"I'll read it. I love dragons."

"You are such a nerd."

He shrugged. "I love reading, especially epic fantasy. And then we can talk about it."

Cheeks heating, I looked down at my lap. That was so goddamn sweet. Why did he have to be like this, all considerate and thoughtful, after turning me down?

Why couldn't he have been a good lay with a shitty personality? That was how the universe was organized. There were basic truths about men. Many were dumb, and many were terrible in bed. Some were both. And the ones who were neither were usually narcissists, players, or sociopaths.

Jude Hebert was breaking all the rules, and it was making a difficult situation impossible.

He got up, thankfully sparing me from having to stare at his stupidly handsome face any longer. This room was too small, and I needed the distance so I could focus.

"I've been going through the recordings." I cleared my throat. "Most of it is hours upon hours of stupidity, but I've come across a few interesting things."

I eased myself up to my feet and shuffled to my wall of Post-its. Though my movements were still slow, the pain was lessening every day. "I've heard some chatter about Friday the thirteenth. During the poker game, they were talking logistics. They were using some kind of code. But it's come up multiple times, and then there was a reference to Jason. But not as a person. Like Jason was an object. I was so confused."

I wound a piece of string around a thumbtack, then looped it around another on the corkboard.

"But then I realized that Jason is the bad guy in the *Friday the Thirteenth*."

He hummed. "How does that relate?"

"If you look at a calendar—wait. Do lumberjacks keep track of dates on logs?" Lips pursed, I tapped my chin.

He let out a snort. It was alarmingly cute.

"October thirteenth is a Friday," I continued. "And I

think Jason could be a big shipment coming in that day. There seems to be a lot of activity and planning, so something must be happening."

I pointed to the maps of the Quebec border where I'd crossed with Razor. The forest around it was privately owned, which meant trafficking without being detected was possible.

"I've got to figure out where and how. Then it's lights out."

He nodded slowly. "Okay, I'm following."

"Which is why I needed those financial records. And I'm gonna need more. Parker has done a ton of legwork. Your family too. But I've got a different perspective. I know I can connect the dots."

I trailed my fingers over the Post-its and closed my eyes. I was so fucking close. I could feel it. And while I probably seemed like I'd lost my mind, he was at least listening, so maybe I wasn't totally gone yet.

"And let's say, for the sake of argument, you do figure it out," he hedged. "Then what?"

"Then we go to the police. Or the FBI or Parker. Whoever."

He dipped his chin. "As long as you promise you won't put yourself in danger."

With a hand pressed to my heart, I bowed my head. "Promise. Will you help me?" I gave him my best puppy dog eyes. It would be so much easier if he could be my man on the inside, collecting all the business records.

"You're insane," he said with a smirk.

Yes. I knew he'd be on board.

I flipped my hair, only slightly regretting the sassy move when pain shot down my arm. "Insanely brilliant?"

"Something like that," he grumbled.

"You need to trust me."

He crossed his arms, and I got momentarily distracted by the veins in his forearms, wishing I could run my tongue along them.

"I want to trust you," he muttered. "But you're trouble in human form."

"Eh." I waved away his concerns and wound the thread around another pushpin.

"Seriously, Mila." He sighed. "You were literally being shot at less than two weeks ago."

I took a step closer, looking up into his stormy blue eyes.

His concern, while annoying, was adorable.

Grinning, I patted his bearded cheek. "Jude, if I let being shot at stop me, then I'd never get out of bed. We've got work to do. Buck up."

Chapter 20
Jude

Since finding the phone, Mila had transformed. She was energetic and focused, spending hours in the spare room, talking to herself and slapping Post-its all over the walls.

Noah wanted to meet at the Caffeinated Moose this morning, and though I was loath to leave Mila, she'd kicked me out with a to-go order for scones and a latte. Then she'd gone straight back to work. Even Ripley barely acknowledged me when I said goodbye, too intent on watching the every move of her new favorite person.

Day by day, she was healing. And recovering her phone and the evidence it contained had been a huge leap toward ending this nightmare once and for all.

But, and I'd never admit this to anyone, the discovery made me sad. It was bittersweet, I supposed, because I enjoyed helping her. A tiny glimpse of her and a whiff of her delicious scent were enough to brighten my days. But now that she had what she needed, it was only a matter of time before she could go back to her life. And when that happened, I'd be me again. Except this time, I'd have the memories of her smile, her laugh, the sighs she let out when I brushed her hair.

The coffee shop was buzzing when I walked in. This place was one of several new businesses that were transforming the feel of our downtown, bringing it back to life.

When I stepped inside, I quickly found Noah settled in a back booth with two coffees in front of him.

He slid a black coffee across the table as I reached out to my niece, who was making grabby hands at me.

"She keeps growing."

She pawed at my beard, giggling.

"Toddlers do that," Noah replied. "She just learned how to walk, and already, she's full-on running. I thought I was terrified before." He shook his head.

"Things are working out okay in the new place?"

He nodded. "It's beautiful. I'm beginning to see why you like the mountain life."

Noah's apartment building in town had burned down this summer, so he and Victoria were renting a cabin from Henri Gagnon on the other side of Lake Millinocket for the time being.

"Ude," Tess said, breaking into a big smile. Her curly blond hair was in pigtails and her face was covered in crumbs from the giant cookie she'd probably suckered her dad into buying. She talked constantly and signed even more. I'd picked up on a few baby signs here and there, but she and Noah had a pretty vast vocabulary.

He'd been granted custody of her when her biological

parents passed away, and for months, they'd only had each other. Their bond was so strong, and now that Vic was in the picture, they'd developed the same kind of devotion for her.

"I love you, Tessie girl," I said, giving her a nuzzle.

She replied with a wet kiss to my cheek. I'd have to pressure wash my beard to get the chocolate chips out, but it was worth it.

As Noah chatted about Tess and the job he'd interviewed for, a unique sense of completeness hit me. He'd been gone for almost twenty years, and now that he was back, it was as if the limb I'd learned to function without had suddenly reappeared.

We were twins, always connected, even when he was in California. But with so much distance between us, I'd been incomplete. I'd made peace with that. I never thought he'd settle here in Lovewell. But Tess changed everything. And meeting Victoria sealed the deal.

Thoughts of them led to Mila. She'd almost lost her brother—and until he woke, she had, for all intents and purposes, I supposed—and she hadn't been granted the kind of support my hometown had always given me. The kind of support I'd been taking for granted my entire life.

I had so much. A great job, a home, and a big, messy family. But I'd isolated myself, keeping my life small for so long that I'd lost sight of how fortunate I was.

I bounced Tess on my knee and shot my brother a grin.

In return, he pinned me with a glare that was out of character for him. He was the wild twin; I was the serious one. That meant something was up.

"Are you being safe?" he asked quietly.

I nodded.

"I have something for you. Here."

He slid his hand across the table, palm down, all the while chatting with Tess, as if he was working not to arouse suspicion from the patrons around us.

He darted a look at me, then glanced at his hand. So, casually, I covered his hand with mine.

With an almost imperceptible nod, he drew his hand back and picked up his coffee.

I dragged my palm across the table. Only when the object was in my lap did I give it a cursory glance.

It was a small silver thumb drive.

Frowning, I looked up at him.

"Don't ask," he murmured. "Take it. Use it. Share it with Mila."

My heart thumped painfully in my chest. "But."

He shook his head. "I don't know what's on it. But we want you to have it. Hopefully it helps."

I nodded and slipped it into my pocket.

"How?"

I'd tried so hard to keep Noah and Tess out of the mess our family had been embroiled in. He'd wanted nothing to do with our father or the family business for years. And after the fire, I couldn't bear the thought of them being in danger.

"You didn't get that from me. Or Vic."

I nodded.

"Just finish this." He reached for Tess, who went willingly, burying her face in his neck. "We've got so much to look forward to. It needs to end."

His words hit me square in the chest. When the two of

them were packed up and gone, I still hadn't found the words to respond.

After they'd headed to the park, I sat, sipping my coffee and trying to orient my brain. We had more information and access than ever before. I was flattered that he had such faith in me. But I wasn't that guy. I wasn't the brave, strong hero type. As ready as I was for this to end, I didn't know what I could do to make that happen.

Abandoning my plans to run errands in town, I headed straight home to show Mila the thumb drive. When I stepped into the house, I expected to find her slumped over my old laptop, researching.

Instead, she was standing in the living room, wearing a pair of my baggy sweatpants and a sports bra.

One of the black sports bras I'd bought for her at Target. Willa had guessed that she'd need a small, but based on the distractingly tight fit and how her breasts spilled out of the top, I should have bought a medium.

But if I'd done that, then I wouldn't get to enjoy this spectacular view.

"You okay?"

She whipped around, a blush creeping up her chest and neck.

"Yes," she squeaked. "Just doing the exercises Willa showed me. I thought you were gonna be gone for a while."

"Sorry." I wasn't sure why I was apologizing for walking into my own home, but this encounter was hellishly awkward.

I lowered my gaze. "I'll get out of your way."

"Actually," she said, garnering my attention again. "I need help." With her lip caught between her teeth, she gestured at a tube of BioFreeze on the table. "I'm supposed to massage this into the shoulder and the tendons in my neck, but it's hard to reach all the right places myself."

I took a step forward, my mouth going dry at the suggestion.

"S-sure," I forced the word out. "Gimme one second. I should wash my hands."

In the bathroom, I turned the faucet on, giving myself a moment to think. I'd reined in my control as best as I could. After our kiss, I'd done my best to put space between us. And now I had to touch her?

I splashed cold water on my face.

Get it together, dumbass.

There were a lot of people counting on me. Especially Mila. I had to keep my feelings in check.

My dick would have to behave. There was no other option.

When I returned to the living room, she was squeezing a stress ball with her left hand while petting Ripley with her right. Mila was beautiful. I'd noticed that the first time I met her. But the determination in her expression, the determination she maintained in the face of adversity, only made her that much hotter.

"Tell me what you need me to do."

She looked up at me from where she sat on the couch, those dark eyes blinking rapidly, and patted the cushion beside her. "Work it into the muscles and tendons around the injury." She shifted, giving me her back. "The idea is to get the blood flowing so it heals faster."

I squeezed a nickel-sized glob into one hand and gently stroked along the column of her neck, following the line of her shoulder. My skin tingled as I used my fingertips to rub circles against the muscles of her back, the gel working its magic.

"Is this okay?"

She nodded. "You can push a little harder, especially in my lat."

Having my large, calloused hands so close to her injuries unnerved me. The last thing I wanted was to hurt her. She was so delicate and beautiful, her skin so soft.

I'd touched her before. Past Jude, that lucky bastard, hadn't realized what an incredible privilege it was. The more I learned about her, the more impressed I was. I'd seen her laugh and cry. I'd borne witness to the sounds she made when she ate french fries.

She'd wanted me. After our kiss, she had been very clear about that. Even so, I'd been a gentleman. The good guy. I'd done the right thing. No matter how much I regretted it, I wouldn't cross that line.

My heart pounded as I focused on applying pressure in the right spots.

"Yes," she whispered softly, angling her head to give me more access.

God, what I wouldn't do to kiss that neck.

Fuck, I'd bite it too, if I could. Every inch of her was so delicious.

Focus, idiot.

I dug my thumbs into the muscles in her neck.

In response, she let out a contented sigh.

My body locked up.

Control. Control, I chanted in my head. If she thought this was good, she had no idea what else I could do with my hands, my mouth, my dick. God, the thought had my jeans getting tight.

Every time she sighed, her chest heaved, and from my vantage point, I had the perfect view of the tops of her breasts as they spilled out of the too-tight sports bra. As I worked, I was assaulted with memories of how they felt, the light weight of them in my hands, and how fucking good her skin tasted when I licked and sucked and teased her nipples into peaks. Being this close was pure torture.

I squeezed my eyes shut, then tilted my head back. When I opened them again, I stared up at the ceiling, forcing myself to remember the cracks that I'd had to repair and all the days of painting I'd endured. This house was my solace, the project that had given my life meaning and purpose during some dark times.

For so long, I'd thought I was doing well. I enjoyed my job and was proud of my home. I spent time with my brothers and played with the band any time I wanted. The gigs allowed plenty of opportunities to socialize and hook up when it suited me.

In the two weeks she'd been here, Mila had changed this house, and she was changing me. I felt more alive than I had in years. Even my dog was happier.

"That feels so good," she said. "It hurts a little, but I think I like it."

I squeezed my eyes shut again and held my breath. *Dammit, Mila.* Did she have any idea how thin the thread I was hanging on to was?

"Great," I said, my voice almost cracking.

I scooted back, releasing my hold on her. I needed to get out of here. Go for a run. Jump in the freezing-cold lake.

Something. Anything to stop the hormones raging inside me and tame my attraction to this woman.

"Thank you." She turned and gave me a shy smile.

"Yeah." I stood abruptly, turning so she couldn't see the bulge in my jeans, then strode to the kitchen.

"I've, um, I've got chores to do. Gotta go."

Chapter 21
Mila

Fuck a duck on a goddamn truck. Jesus.

Had I seriously asked the man to give me a massage?

My instincts were screaming for me to run. To throw my shoes on and hide in the forest. Paint my face with mud so I'd blend in with the trees and die a slow death from exposure. I'd be alone, and it'd likely be painful, but at least I'd be spared this embarrassment.

The look on his face when I turned? He'd looked angry.

And he didn't even have it in him to be a dick.

As always, he'd been kind. Practical.

And he'd looked like a goddamn snack.

I paced the living room. Ripley followed me for a bit, but before long, she lost interest. This house was too small. Even this state was too small.

This humiliation would follow me forever. There was no way he hadn't noticed how heavily I'd been breathing, how hard my nipples were.

Fuck. I'd thought the hair-brushing was hot. But his

hands on my skin? Kneading away the tension? It was on another level.

I could take a shower, try to calm myself that way. But that would defeat the purpose of having him apply the BioFreeze. I could take Ripley for a walk, but if I did, Jude would insist on coming along.

So I hid in the spare room, throwing myself back into studying the recording and photos, searching for more clues. Desperate to push away the mortification that hit me when he shot up and darted away.

Apparently, I hadn't learned my lesson after the kiss the other night. If only I'd gotten the memo that he wasn't into me. Maybe then I would have stopped shamelessly flirting and saved myself the embarrassment.

But it was impossible.

He was so damn attractive. He was the definition of a man, yet everything about him, right down to the careful way he brushed my hair, was so sweet.

Jude was pure juxtaposition. Soft-spoken and quiet, yet mighty. And it wasn't only his powerful build.

It was in the way he carried himself. The quiet, contemplative confidence.

The careful way he considered everything, always observing and calculating. That was why he was so good at Scrabble, because he took the time to ponder every possibility.

I, on the other hand, became obsessive and formed tunnel vision, which sometimes led to chasing my own tail.

Back to work, Mila. Mooning over my hot roommate was getting me nowhere fast.

With a sigh, I sat at the desk and rolled my neck. It was

nice, the ability to take breaks from the sling. My entire left side was weak and useless, but at least I had two hands again.

My typing speed had plummeted, but it was better than hunting and pecking with one finger. Combing through these financial records was painful, but the devil was always in the Excel-spreadsheet details.

Just as I dug in, a loud noise caught my attention. I snapped up straight and spun, scanning the space around me, looking for an item that may have fallen. I was still searching when I heard it again.

Another loud thwack.

I stood and peered out the window. The forest looked as calm as usual, so I headed through the house in search of answers.

In the living room, Ripley was lounging in front of the wood stove, soaking up the warmth. Now that it was almost October, it was getting chilly up here.

Another loud thump sounded, this one even closer, so I headed to the kitchen and peered out the back window.

What I saw nearly knocked me on my ass.

Jude was outside next to the garage, chopping wood.

His chest was heaving and his hair hung in his face. And the focus in his eyes? Shit. It was unnerving and incredible.

I involuntarily squeezed my thighs together. What the hell was this? Was I dreaming?

He stood another log on its end and sized it up, walking around it and cataloging the grooves. Turning, he rolled his shoulders, the move forcing my attention to the rippling muscles in his back.

And... were those suspenders?

No. No way.

Jesus, take the wheel. Never in my life would I have considered suspenders sexy. But holy shit, the combination of tight white T-shirt, jeans, and suspenders was rewiring my brain.

He picked up a small metal wedge and stuck it into one of the grooves of the wood. Then he stood back and picked up his axe.

When, with one swing, he spit the massive log in half, my jaw hit the floor.

And my panties disintegrated.

I leaned in to get a better look.

The white T-shirt was smudged with dirt and clung to his pecs. If memory served me correctly, his body was ridiculous. I'd assumed he was one of those gym and protein shake guys.

Now that I thought about it, I'd been here for weeks, and he hadn't once mentioned hitting the weight room.

No, what he possessed was real, hard-earned strength.

And it was mesmerizing.

He rolled a log at least two feet wide onto his wooden platform and lined up his axe. In one fluid, graceful, precise motion, he swung.

This time, the wood didn't split all the way through. So he put one boot on it and pulled the axe out, then dropped it to the ground.

He walked around, inspecting the log.

I held my breath in anticipation of what he'd do next.

I never could have predicted that he'd pick the damn thing up, wedge his fingers into the crack left by his axe, and pull.

But fuck, that's exactly what he did. Every muscle in his

body strained with the effort, his biceps rippling as he pulled as hard as he could.

With a roar, he tore the fucking log in half.

I whipped around and slumped against the wall. What the hell had I witnessed?

Did mild-mannered, graphic novel–loving Jude Hebert rip apart a tree trunk with his bare hands? Like the Hulk in glasses and suspenders?

Sweat dotted my hairline, and my pulse raced as my legs wobbled, threatening to give out.

Goddamn him and his morals and his whole protector bullshit.

Yeah, I was hurt and on the run from homicidal drug traffickers, but I had needs, dammit. For God's sake, I was a red-blooded woman trapped in a small cottage with the hottest lumbersnack in history.

But he'd made it clear that he wouldn't cross the line.

So if I couldn't hit that, I'd at least enjoy the show.

With a deep inhale, I turned back toward the window, eager to get another look.

But when I zeroed in on him, my heart leaped right out of my chest. He stood, feet shoulder-width apart, arms crossed. Biceps bulging against the flimsy white cotton and the dark suspenders calling attention to the sheer breadth of his shoulders.

And he was looking right at me.

Shit.

I hadn't thought I could embarrass myself any further than I already had. I was wrong. But as white-hot shame washed over me, another feeling emerged along with it.

Anger.

Why was he taunting me? He was the one who'd turned me down.

And now he was out here, putting on a lumberjack show. The audacity.

He was waving a red flag in front of a horny, repressed bull.

So instead of hiding from him, I stepped into my shoes, pulled on one of his big coats, and marched my ass outside.

"What do you think you're doing?" I barked.

He looked at me, all sweaty and manly, and grinned. "Chopping wood."

"Why?"

"Because winter is coming. We'll need it to heat the house."

"Really?" I scoffed, propping my good hand on my hip. "You need it today?"

He nodded, blue eyes twinkling.

"What about that giant woodshed right there?" I pointed to the small structure next to the garage. "It's filled all the way to the door. You think we're gonna burn all that tonight and freeze to death?"

His cocky smirk faltered.

"It's bad enough you walk around looking so sexy and being so kind all the time." A low growl escaped me. "But now, when my defenses are down, you wander out here, wearing *fucking suspenders*, and start destroying trees?"

Silence.

I pinched my nose. "It's truly unfair."

Behind his glasses, his eyes were wide with bewilderment.

"You know, I expected better of you." I shook my head.

"I'm not sure I follow."

"You know I'm lusting after you, Jude." I dropped my arm to my side and huffed. "Could you let me live in peace for a little longer? I get it, you're not into me anymore. But come on. Cover up, for fuck's sake. You need to hide all this" —I waved a hand up and down, gesturing to his body— "manly goodness."

He crossed his arms, which only made his sweaty biceps strain more, and quirked a brow. "Manly goodness?"

"Yes," I whined. "A girl only has so much self-control."

With that, I spun, set on storming back into the house dramatically.

But his chuckle stopped me in my tracks.

"You're really something, Trouble."

With a roll of my eyes, I whipped around again.

"And if we're fighting right now, then I have a complaint to air as well. You're not making it easy on me either."

"Me?" I slapped a hand to my chest.

"I walked into the house, finding you jumping around in a bra in my living room. A bra that's too small, mind you."

Annoyance flared in my veins. "You bought it for me."

"Oh I know," he scoffed. "And the sight of your tits spilling out will haunt my dreams forever."

I opened my mouth to retort, but when the words registered, I snapped it closed again. His comment was... moderately satisfying.

He dropped his axe to the ground and stomped over. "You have been driving me insane since the minute you walked through that door. But I'm a good guy." He hitched a thumb and pressed it to his chest. "I can control myself."

I bit my lip hard, quelling the wave of need threatening

to engulf me. Fuck, he was mad, and it was hot. "What if I don't want you to control yourself?"

With a growl, he took a step toward me. "See? This is what you do. You use your feminine wiles." He squeezed his eyes shut. "And every day, it's harder to fight."

My pulse skyrocketed. This conversation was going in a very different direction from what I had anticipated. It was satisfying, really, to know that he was suffering as badly as I was.

"I have to ask," he said, his voice barely above a whisper. "Why did you come home with me that night at the bar?"

That was easy. "Because you're good-looking," I replied. "And kind. And when I saw you up on that stage, those big hands on that guitar, I was hypnotized, mesmerized by the thought of what they could do to my body."

His eyes flashed, igniting like blue flames, and then we were toe to toe, so close I could feel the heat radiating from him.

"Did my hands live up to your expectations?"

I could write a series of erotic novels about those hands. But I didn't want to show all my cards. So I lifted my chin and kept my expression even. "Yes. They exceeded them."

He grinned down at me. The satisfaction there made me want to kiss that stupid expression right off his smug face.

"I answered your question, so now I've got one for you. Why did you take me home?"

He crossed his arms again.

Fuck, the suspenders only made this hotter.

"Because I'm used to playing in front of a crowd. I'm used to the scrutiny. And I'm used to being hit on. Women are always interested in the quiet guy who plays the guitar."

I gave him a dramatic eye roll. Yes, I could only imagine the hordes of women who threw themselves at him every time he picked up a damn guitar.

"But when I saw you, when our eyes locked. Shit—" He ran a hand through his hair. "I thought 'she's the most beautiful woman I've ever seen.'"

A gasp escaped me, my knees buckling. That was *not* what I was expecting.

"And when we wrapped, I had to talk to you, to be near you."

"I felt the same way," I replied softly, my head spinning. What was it about this man that made every single cell in my body wild with lust?

"And then—"

Cheeks heating, I dropped my gaze to my feet and interrupted him. "Oh, I know what happened next. Trust me, I can't stop thinking about it."

"Really?" He scratched the back of his neck, head bowed, and peered at me, a lock of hair falling into his face. "You think about that night?"

"All the fucking time," I yelled, stomping a foot. "God, men are so dumb. It's like you don't get it at all."

Before I knew what was happening, he'd looped an arm around my waist and tipped my chin up.

"Trouble, be quiet."

I gaped at him, incensed. "You don't just tell a woman to be quiet, Jude."

"You do when you want to kiss her," he replied, lowering his mouth to mine.

Chapter 22
Jude

I couldn't stop myself. I wished I could. I wished I was strong and noble.

But I wasn't.

I was weak.

And Mila was the cause.

I cupped her cheek, caressing her smooth skin with my thumb, relishing the way her eyes widened.

And then my lips were on hers.

Her body melted into mine, her tongue sweeping into my mouth eagerly.

With a groan, I pulled her flush against my body.

Yes.

This is what had been missing for so long.

She threaded her fingers through my hair and tugged gently, making me even wilder for her. It seemed impossible, but she tasted and felt better than I remembered.

I was somehow both ravenous and sated.

This was it.

She was soft but demanding, passionate but not rushed.

Every sensation was thrilling yet comforting.

Exactly what I'd dreamed of.

This woman. This moment.

I could no longer resist.

With a hand beneath her T-shirt, I stroked the silky skin of her back, desperate to touch every inch of her.

She tugged at my hair with more force, and in return, I nipped at her bottom lip.

"Fuck, Jude." She groaned. "I've been dreaming about your mouth."

That guttural sound, combined with those words, obliterated any doubts I had.

I pulled away, cupping her face. "Trouble." I panted. "I—"

"Don't," she pleaded. "I don't want the excuses. Don't think. Kiss me."

"I don't want to stop." I ducked, kissing my way across her jaw. "I know we shouldn't. But I don't have the willpower to stop. Tell me to stop, Trouble."

"No." With her good hand, she palmed my erection, making my vision blur. "Don't you dare fucking stop."

"I need you," I groaned. "Just once. I know it's a bad idea. But this feels so good."

"Don't beg. It's beneath you. Just take me to bed, Jude."

Carefully, I lifted her, helping her cradle her arm, then strode for the house. And like every night since she showed up, I carried her to my bedroom.

This time, though, I'd join her. And there would be no sleeping.

I strode through the house, kicking doors closed behind me, and deposited her on my bed.

As I backed away, she reached for me and pulled me down for a searing kiss, her nails digging into my back.

I snaked an arm around her and grabbed a handful of her ass. When I squeezed, she let out a squeak.

I froze, loosening my hold, and pulled back. "I'm not hurting you, am I?"

She shook her head. "No. And stop worrying. I'm not breakable."

"But you're hurt."

"And I'll tell you if I'm in pain. Now get naked."

A laugh rumbled out of me. Even injured, Mila was not wasting any time.

"I mean it, Hebert. Strip!" She pushed at my chest. "I want a good look at you, Lumbersnack. Come on, don't be shy."

Biting back a smirk, I whipped my T-shirt off.

She whistled, spurring me on, but before I could do more, her hands were on me, running down my chest. She traced the lines of my tattoos along my ribs. "I will touch a hundred flowers and not pick one."

"Edna St. Vincent Millay," I explained. "She's from Maine."

"So the books of poetry aren't just for show, huh?" She angled in and pressed a kiss to the ink. "I like that you tattoo poetry on your skin," she said. "The quote on your back, it's Rilke, right?"

I nodded. "It's probably strange, but some words are so meaningful that I want them to be a permanent part of me."

She kissed my sternum, then a few inches lower. Her lips blazed a trail down my stomach until she reached the button of my jeans. "It's hot." She peered up at me from beneath heavy lids.

Though she wasn't wearing her sling, she kept her arm closer to her body for protection. "Can you help with my top? I know it's not sexy, but—"

"The hell it's not."

I circled her, then brought my lips to her ear, gently biting the lobe while gathering the hem of her shirt. As I lifted it, I kissed down her neck. Then I carefully helped her pull her good arm out, then the injured one, leaving her only in her front zip bra.

"Pants too." I pushed her sweats down a little more roughly, then I dropped to my knees and guided her hand to my shoulder so she could steady herself as she stepped out of them.

She stood before me, in her panties and bra, looking down on me with so much desire and affection it made my chest tighten.

I angled in and placed a kiss on her stomach.

"We don't have to do anything you don't want to," I said.

She grasped my chin and tipped my face up. "I want to do everything."

"As you wish, Trouble." I stood, then guided her back to the bed and eased her legs apart.

I kissed and nibbled my way up one thigh, relishing the softness of her skin, then edged around her undies, teasing her, making her shudder, then pulling back.

Unable to control myself, I grazed my nose along the crease of her thigh and then the line of her panties, breathing in deep, feral at the scent of her arousal.

Pushing the thin fabric to the side, I licked my way to her

center, and when I found her clit and she cried out, pride consumed me.

"Stay still, Trouble," I chided, smiling up from between her thighs. "I'm working here."

I tore her panties down her legs and tossed them to the floor. Then I teased her entrance with my fingers. Fuck I'd missed her. She was wet and sweet and already moaning. Stroking and caressing, I worked her into a frenzy before slipping my fingers inside her.

As I stroked her inner wall, she screamed, and when I sucked on her clit, her body bowed off the bed. Cock straining, I picked up my pace, eager for every moan, every shudder.

When she screamed again, her muscles coiled tight, I growled, "Come for me." Then I latched back on to her clit and doubled down. She tensed further, and then she was coming, her body convulsing as she pulled my hair and cried out.

Undeterred, I kept my rhythm steady until she was begging me to stop. As I sat back, she collapsed into an exhausted heap on the bed. Looming over her like this, I admired my work. Mila was laid out, naked and exhausted. The sight made me feel a hundred feet tall.

I was still reveling when she opened her eyes and gave me a wolfish grin. "That. Was. Spectacular."

Cock pressing painfully against my zipper, I stood, but before I could unbutton my pants, she was up, doing it for me.

She pushed them down in a hurry, leaving my cock standing at full attention, peeking out from the top of my boxers.

With a groan, she bent at the waist and licked the tip.

Stars danced in my vision and my knees buckled.

"No." I stumbled back, set on finding the box of condoms in the nightstand. "I want to be inside you."

She pouted, her lip stuck out.

Fuck. That mouth. As desperately as I wanted it wrapped around my cock, the need to be inside her was too great.

"Are you okay with this?" I asked as I yanked a foil packet from the box and tossed it onto the mattress. "I'll be gentle."

She sat on the edge of the bed and lay back, spreading her legs wide. "Please don't be gentle," she said. "You have no idea how much I need this."

I bent over her, braced on my forearms, and helped myself to a kiss.

When she cupped my face, I was hit with an over-whelming surge of affection for this complex, infuriating woman.

God, I had waited for what felt like a lifetime for this moment. I wanted to own her, claim her, and make her mine.

But she was injured. And I didn't trust myself not to hurt her.

I was brimming with pent-up frustration and desire.

"Change of plan, Trouble." I took one pink nipple into my mouth. "I want you on top."

With a wicked smile, she sat up, and once I was positioned on my back, she straddled me, pinning me to the mattress. "Gladly. But I'm taking my time."

She pressed a hand to my chest and drank me in with a predatory gleam in her eye.

"Where should I start?" She tapped her chin, then popped up on her knees and moved back, all the while biting that damn bottom lip and staring down at my throbbing erection. Carefully, she braced herself on one arm and kissed down my stomach, avoiding my cock.

"Tease," I gritted out.

She hummed. "Be patient." With more grace than should have been possible in a moment like this, she wrapped her hand around the base and slid her lips over my crown.

Jaw clenched and head thrown back, I groaned. I was in a state of pure agony.

Finally, she put me out of my misery, licking a bead of precum off the tip as she gave me a firm squeeze.

My back arched off the bed and stars danced in my vision. If I wasn't careful, I'd embarrass myself. So I racked my brain for the most unsexy thoughts I could come up with. *Spruce beetles, ultra-processed food, gray April slush on the side of the roads.*

Okay, that was better. I sighed. But just as relief worked its way through my body, her mouth was on me again, taking me deeper. Fuck. I had no hope of surviving this.

"Trouble," I hissed through gritted teeth, pawing at the comforter beside me. "Condom."

She snagged it, dragging her tits across my chest, then took her sweet time tearing the foil and rolling the latex down my length.

With a palm on my chest, she shifted up so her thighs caged me in, pinning my dick between us.

Then, with one hand, she slid my glasses from my face.

I caught her wrist. "No way. I need to see you."

She acquiesced without a fight, waiting while I adjusted them. Then, when I could see her clearly, she lifted up on her knees and positioned my cock at her entrance. Slowly, she lowered herself. As she took me in, inch by inch, her eyes widened and her breathing picked up.

Hit with a surge of pride, I bracketed her hips, steadying her. "That's it. Take it slow."

When she bottomed out, she gasped in a way that made her tits shake and my vision blur. This moment was perfection. Hot, tight perfection, with one hell of a view.

I sat up and devoured her mouth. Desperate to touch every part of her, I splayed my hands over her ribcage gently, then let them roam.

Slowly at first, and maybe even a little tentatively, she rode me. Her eyes went glassy as she found her rhythm, twisting her hips and grinding against me with every stroke.

She anchored her hand on my chest, and I took the opportunity to refamiliarize myself with her glorious ass, gripping her so hard I was sure I'd leave bruises.

It was thrilling, the idea of leaving marks on her. While she rode me like this, my better judgment had taken a back seat to the urges I usually kept in check.

"That's it." I took one nipple into my mouth and sucked hard. "Take all of it."

I grasped her hips, thrusting up to meet her. She cried out as our pace became frantic, tightening around me in a way that made my vision darken. Fuck. If she didn't come soon, I'd make an ass of myself. A vague memory came to me, reminding me that during our one night together, she'd needed extra stimulation, so I licked my thumb and brushed her clit.

The way her breathing hitched and her movements faltered told me I was on the right track. So I applied gentle pressure, circling the bud as she threw her head back and rode me harder.

"It's so good," she cried. "So big."

I bit my lip hard, barely holding on to control, watching her body for signals.

When her inner muscles fluttered around me, I gritted out, "You are such a good girl. You're gonna come so hard on my cock."

She squeezed her eyes tight and nodded, grinding her hips harder. I thickened inside her, dangerously close to losing the sliver of self-control I still possessed.

"Jude," she screamed, her body locking up. "Yes. Yes. Just like that."

I rolled my hips, keeping my pace steady and my thumb on her clit as she came, awash with wave after wave of pleasure.

Her voice was a rasp as she begged me not to stop.

Eager to give her what she needed, I obeyed. But in a matter of seconds, I could no longer hold back. She was still pulsing around my cock as I unleashed inside her.

Eventually she collapsed on my chest, sweaty and sated and panting.

I wrapped my arms around her, savoring every second of being joined together. For a moment, it was just the two of us, silent but for the pounding of our hearts and our jagged breaths.

Eventually, I eased her to the mattress beside me and went to the bathroom to dispose of the condom. When I came back, she was stretched out on her back, her naked body on display.

My cock twitched. Jesus, we'd just finished, but one look at her, and I knew I'd need a lot more to get Mila out of my system.

I lay next to her and closed my eyes. I had nothing to say. My world had been rocked. Now all I wanted was to be near her. She rested her head on my shoulder and ran her fingers through my chest hair.

I was nodding off when she whispered my name.

"Yes, Trouble?"

"It's even bigger than I remember."

A shit-eating grin overtook me as I drifted to sleep.

Chapter 23
Jude

Mila was propped up against the throne of pillows I'd constructed, her hair wild and her face flushed.

I'd never seen anything so beautiful.

"You really know how to blow a girl's mind, Lumbersnack."

I couldn't hide my massive grin if I tried. This woman had one hell of a mouth. I lay beside her, one arm behind my head, and stared at the ceiling fan, giving myself a moment to just be. My life had gone off the rails recently, but this was a very welcome development.

Now, the question was, when could we do it again? And could this become an indefinite arrangement?

I opened my mouth to suggest that very thing, but she spoke first.

"I want to level set," she said slowly. "This was a danger bang."

My stomach sank. "Sorry, what?"

"I've been in this situation before. Adrenaline is high,

and we're stuck together, running from bad guys. It's a cocktail for wild sex. Trust me, people in war zones fuck like bunnies."

I sat up, straightening my glasses. Talk about adrenaline. I was hit with a new rush of it.

"How many?" I blurted out. Bile rose up my throat. Calling what we had just done *banging* really stung my ego. "You know, uh"—fuck, I didn't want to use the term, but I didn't want to scare her off either—"danger bangs? Is this a regular thing for you?"

She sat up too, her breasts bouncing in a way that made my brain go blank.

"Don't you dare slut shame me." She poked me in the chest, her lip curling. "Like you should talk, Mr. Musician with soulful eyes and poetic tattoos."

Fuck. What the hell was wrong with me? I wasn't a possessive caveman. I didn't judge people and I certainly hadn't meant to imply that she'd done something wrong. But the mention of other men had made me see red.

"You," she continued poking my bare chest, "are sluttier than a pair of gray sweatpants, so you do not get to judge me."

I held my hands up. "I wasn't judging. I promise. I only got a little possessive." Grasping at straws, desperate to placate her, I kissed her neck. "Forgive me, Trouble. I'm drunk on you. The smell of you, the taste of your skin. Don't blame me for things I say while under the influence."

My hands had a mind of their own, already cupping her breasts.

She let out a sigh, head dropped back against the headboard. "You really know how to apologize to a girl."

With a grin, I cuffed her neck and captured her mouth. "You can't blame a guy for wanting more than one night."

She shifted beside me, giving me more access to her body. "I don't make long-term promises, Jude. Life is too volatile. Especially now."

With a noncommittal hum, I captured one of her perfect nipples in my mouth, sucking and lathing and nipping.

She was right, this probably was a danger bang. And yes, our entire world could come crashing down tomorrow. But that only made me want her more. A real connection. Something to hang on to when times were tough.

"The only promise I'm offering is to make you come as many times as I can." I kissed her sternum, then gave the other nipple attention.

She cried out and gripped my cock, which was hard and desperate for her.

"I like that idea."

IT WAS AFTER MIDNIGHT WHEN I LET RIPLEY OUT FOR the last time and emptied the dishwasher. Mila was out cold, but I couldn't sleep. My body was vibrating, itching to move.

I could only watch her sleep for so long. I'd already felt like a creeper. Any longer, and I didn't think I could live with myself.

Plus, I had to do something with my hands so I could process what we'd done.

I'd been impulsive. I'd followed my gut and not my brain.

Fuck. I couldn't even blame it on my gut. No, I'd followed my dick. And it had led to spectacular results. Even so, I was second-guessing myself. One night with Mila would never be enough.

I knew that from experience. I'd had one night more than a year ago and hadn't stopped thinking about her since.

How the hell had I ever thought I could get her out of my system?

Especially now that I knew her, now that I'd held her?

Her words chafed. What we were doing felt like a hell of a lot more than a hookup. It felt real and scary and beautiful.

But the moment those thoughts had formed in my mind, she'd brought me right back down to earth.

Though she'd fallen asleep in my bed, I had to assume I should sleep on the couch. So I gulped down a glass of water and looked out at the moonlight, grateful she hadn't bothered trying to move to the couch.

We had an established routine. She'd fall asleep out here, insisting that was where she preferred to sleep. Then, when she was out cold, I'd pick her up and carry her to my bed, arranging the pillows to support her shoulder.

My old routine consisted of work, running with Ripley, spending quiet evenings at home reading, and playing guitar.

This new life I'd fallen into was wild.

All day, I found myself itching to go home to her.

It had become second nature to pick up small things—food, necessities, books—for her from town.

And my typical evening routine had gone out the window. Thankfully Ripley wasn't afraid to alert me when she had a need, because I was distracted.

It was bizarre. I thrived on routine. I loved the simplicity of knowing what I'd be doing and when I'd be doing it.

But Mila had changed all that. She wasn't a hurricane or

a tornado. No, she was her own weather system: volatile, constantly changing, and requiring constant monitoring for surprise danger.

And I was beginning to think that was what my life had been missing. Why, though I fought against the thought, it had felt flat, empty.

I let Ripley inside, still lost in my thoughts. As I set my glass in the dishwasher, Mila let out a blood-curdling scream.

Heart in my throat, I darted to the bedroom. I pushed open the door, and as Ripley slipped past me, I found Mila still in bed, eyes closed, crying and thrashing.

Ripley spun in a circle, whining.

I kneeled beside the bed and cupped Mila's face. "Wake up. You're having a nightmare."

She continued to whimper, saying "please, please" over and over again.

Gently, I shook her good shoulder and called her name again.

Finally, her eyes popped open. She sat up straight, immediately crying out and grabbing her injured arm. "What happened?" she gasped.

"I think you were having a nightmare."

She nodded. "I feel like I'm going to be sick."

I rubbed circles on her back, noting the damp fabric. The dream had to have been intense. She was covered in sweat. "I'll get you a glass of water. Try to breathe."

When I returned, I sat on the edge of the mattress. My hands shook as I held the cup out to her. The thought that she was in danger, no matter how fleeting it had been, had completely fried my nervous system.

"They found me," she whispered as she wiped at her

mouth. "Here. I dreamed that they found me. And you." She shook her head. "It was bad."

We sat in silence for a moment, the weight of that possibility settling in the air.

Eventually, though, I couldn't stand the ache that had overtaken me, knowing she was so frightened. "They're not going to find you," I said with confidence I didn't feel. "As far as they know, you're in another country by now."

"Sure." She sniffed back tears. "But what about my mom? And Hugo? And you and your family? This is bigger than just me now."

A chill ran through me. She was right. We couldn't remain in this protective bubble forever.

"I know you're scared. We'll get through it—"

"No," she interrupted. "I should go. Being here puts you in danger. And I care about you too much—"

"I can handle myself," I assured her, gently taking the glass from her hand. "I want you here."

Her breath hitched. "You do?"

In the dim light of the moon, eyes still wet with tears, she looked so innocent. So fragile. "Yes, Mila. I want you here. We're so close to figuring this out. And until then, I will do everything I can to keep you safe."

She rested her head on my shoulder and let out a heavy breath.

"When I was a little girl and I'd have nightmares," she said, "my dad would take me outside to look at the stars. It was a reminder that all our problems were small compared to the vastness of the universe. It was comforting, you know? That realization. The perspective it gave."

"Then put your shoes on."

It was below freezing, but I'd do anything to take away the fear still gripping her.

We bundled up, and I eased into one of the Adirondack chairs in the backyard and pulled her into my lap. Together we stared out at the vast sky, drinking in the glow of the stars and the waning moon above our heads.

"I'd do this when I was on assignment overseas. I'd go out and take in the night sky. It made me feel connected to home. To my family."

We sat, curled up, for a while, keeping each other warm.

When a big yawn escaped me before I could stop it, she stood. "Thank you. Now let's get you to bed, big guy."

I hauled myself up and stretched, then shoved my hands into the pockets of my coat, wishing I'd thought to wear gloves.

As I balled them into fists, one hand wrapped around a cool metal object.

Shit.

I pulled the thumb drive out of my coat pocket.

"What's that?"

"I'd forgotten. Noah gave this to me earlier. He wouldn't tell me what it contains, but he said it would help us."

Her eyes widened as I handed it to her. "Evidence?"

"I hope so."

She punched my shoulder, her face scrunching. "You had critical evidence and forgot to tell me?"

"I'm sorry." I cringed, holding my hands up in defense. "I rushed home to tell you, but then I got distracted."

She let out a giggle and patted my chest. "It's okay. I forgive you. And for the record, the fastest way to earn forgiveness is with orgasms."

Hope bloomed in my chest. "Noted."

"Now let's go to sleep. We can look at this first thing tomorrow."

Once we were settled, her surrounded by pillows and me lying on my side, keeping my hands to myself for fear that I'd hurt her in my sleep, she eyed Ripley, who was standing sentry between us and the door, and patted the mattress.

"Come here, girl,"

Ripley cocked her head and looked at me. I'd trained her not to jump on the bed. She spent most of her days in the woods, and though I bathed her regularly, it was impossible to always keep her paws dirt-free. This was my sanctuary. Hers was the very expensive L.L. Bean orthopedic dog bed on the other side of the room.

"It's okay, girl," Mila cooed. "He's a big softie. He won't deny you. Up."

Ripley didn't need another invitation. In one smooth move, she hopped onto the bed, and after circling twice, she curled up by Mila's feet.

"Good girl. Love you, Ripley." Mila stroked her fur and smiled back at me. "She's the best dog."

I squinted at her. This was a onetime deal, and Ripley knew it. "She's all right."

"Thank you both. For making me feel less alone."

After she coaxed me closer and draped my arm over her torso, I held her as she drifted off. Damn, this felt good. Her in my bed, in my arms. But I knew better than to let myself think it would happen again.

Chapter 24
Jude

TROUBLE:

Can you pull the environmental reports for
the last five years?

LUMBERSNACK:

That's a lot of files.

TROUBLE:

I need to review them.

I've got a theory.

LUMBERSNACK:

Care to share?

TROUBLE:

No. I need to work.

LUMBERSNACK:

How about resting?

TROUBLE:

Rest is for the weak. Be a good boy and
bring me those files.

Chapter 25
Mila

I couldn't sit still. My body was pulsating with excitement. I stood and spun, realizing I'd barely left this room in two days.

Jude had dragged me to the kitchen last night and insisted I eat, then coaxed me into the shower. Then he massaged my shoulder until I fell asleep sitting up on the couch.

He carried me to bed without disturbing me, as always, but this time when I woke, he was lying next to me.

I should have been naked and orgasm-drunk with my lumbersnack. Instead, I was holed up, pulling every single dangling thread I could find on this thumb drive.

At first, I couldn't understand why the charitable donation records of a construction company would interest me. But as I clicked on files, it dawned on me. Each one was filled with several years' worth of money laundering transactions.

Including some involving Hebert Timber back when Jude's dad ran the business.

Shell corporations, offshore accounts, random real estate holdings in Quebec, sketchy charities. It was a smorgasbord of shady shit. But how did it all fit together?

One thing was certain: this was much bigger than I had imagined.

I used the restroom, then padded to the kitchen to make myself another cup of tea and find snacks.

Jude was practically perfect in all ways. Physically a specimen out of a men's fitness magazine, but with the ironic T-shirts and hipster glasses. He was kind and decent and brushed my damn hair and adored his dog. His dick was straight and thick and he knew how to use it. Truly masculine perfection.

But the man did have a flaw. A major flaw. His obsession with healthy food. Yes, I was well fed. In fact, I was slowly gaining back some of the weight I'd lost over the past year. But sometimes a girl just needed a dose of high-fructose corn syrup after a hard day.

I rooted around in the cabinets, eventually settling for fruit leather and pistachios.

Ripley appeared, tongue lolling, clearly wanting a treat.

I plucked one from the cute container on the counter, and before I even gave her the command, she sat happily, her tail thumping on the tile floor.

As she chomped on it, I let out a sigh. "Ripley girl, what is going on? What's happening on Friday the thirteenth?" I slumped against the counter. "And more importantly, *where* is it happening? And why the fuck is a real estate company involved?"

She tilted her head and hit me with those sweet doggie eyes. While I was generally anti-emotional attachment, I couldn't help but love her. When this was over, if I managed to survive it, I'd get a dog.

The problem was that I didn't want any dog. I wanted Ripley.

I stroked her fluffy ears. Leaving her would be impossible. And I didn't even want to think about leaving her owner. Nope. Wasn't doing that. Danger bang. That's all. Nothing more.

I finished my snacks and got back to work. This mess was not going to untangle itself.

Hours later, when the front door opened, I launched myself out of the makeshift office.

"Jude," I screamed, running down the hall. Ripley perked up and followed me, galloping across the living room.

He stood in the entry, his face creased with concern, as I ran at him. Without slowing, I jumped into his arms.

"Careful," he chided, holding me to his chest. "Your shoulder is finally starting to heal."

"Jude," I said, my heart pounding. "I figured it out."

He blinked at me from behind his lenses.

"The bats." I threw up my good arm, causing him to wobble. "The fucking bats." I shimmied out of his hold and danced around while he hung his coat and toed off his work boots.

"Explain."

I grasped his hand and dragged him into the spare room. There was so much to fill him in on. How could I distill years of spreadsheets into a simple explanation?

"Look." I pointed to a series of photos and newspaper clippings. "It all comes back to the bats."

He frowned. "The bats?"

Anticipation zipped through me. "Yes, the northern long-eared bat. They're endangered."

"I'm aware."

"Hugo and the Maine DEP track and study the bat habitats. It's illegal to drive on or cut on those lands."

"Yes." He dipped his chin. "This is my job, Trouble."

I took a deep breath and worked to organize my thoughts.

When I'd found some semblance of order, I cleared my throat. "It all comes back to the money. The trail. It's all here." I pointed at the stack of papers.

"I'm trying to decipher what the hell you're saying, but I'm lost." He scratched at his beard.

"They're using the bat land to traffic the drugs. That's why they haven't been caught. There's no movement, no surveillance. Nothing allowed on those lands. That's the path they're taking from Quebec."

"How?" It was a single-word question, but the answer was far more complicated.

"We already know they have law enforcement in their pocket. They must have someone in environmental control and even border agents."

"And Hugo?"

"I think he discovered that they weren't actually protecting the bats. Maybe he pushed back or refused. I don't know. But he hadn't been on the job long, and from what I could find, it looks like he'd been auditing reports from previous years."

"So the attack wasn't random?"

I shook my head. "I think he was targeted."

"Shit."

"He was only doing his job." Emotion welled inside me, my eyes filling with tears. "He loved his job. He loved being outside. Protecting nature and wildlife. Mom was so proud of him."

He grasped my hand. "I'm so sorry. But you're doing it. You're gonna get justice for him."

More than anything, I wanted him to wake up. I wanted him healthy and whole. But the chances were slim. So finding the fuckers who'd done this to him felt like my only salvation.

"The fucking FBI," I said, the sadness morphing into anger. "They never took this seriously. They told my mom he was involved in a drug deal gone wrong. My brother had nothing to do with drugs."

Emotion bubbled up, threatening to overtake me. But I choked it back. I couldn't sink into the familiar cycle of rage and grief. Not when I was so close to justice.

I pulled him over to the wall. "Here." I tapped at the massive map he'd brought home. "Before 2002, the bats were mating and nesting here." I pointed to a region outlined in yellow. "I got the records and the agreements made between the state and Hebert Timber, Gagnon Lumber, and a couple other smaller companies. When the regulations went into place. This was the area that was protected."

He nodded, head tilted, studying the map. "That makes sense. That's the most mountainous area. Near the gorge."

"Exactly. The bats nest and give birth in caves. But over time, the protected area has shifted. That was 2002. Your dad was running day-to-day operations. And this one." I spun and snatched up a printout I'd been studying. "Three years later, in 2005, this is the zone. See how the protection area has moved?"

Bringing one hand up to his chin, he adopted a traditional thinking pose while he scanned the page.

"And," I said, "that's when Huxley Construction started donating generously to bat protection efforts."

He straightened, his eyes going wide. "What?"

"Oh yes. I've got the charitable giving reports from the IRS. Charles Huxley was lieutenant governor at the time, and he advocated for the protection of native Maine wildlife species. The northern long-eared bat was classified as endangered by the state of Maine, but only threatened at the federal level."

"Is the difference important?"

I nodded. "They weren't considered endangered on that level until a few years ago, but he was leading the charge. That meant even more protection against habitat loss. Now..." I shuffled through pages until I found the one I was looking for. Then I laid it on the desk. "This is the map from 2010." Again, I'd outlined the protected area with yellow highlighter.

"Oh shit. They moved the bats."

My pulse flickered. He got it. "I think so."

He took off his glasses and cleaned them on his T-shirt. "And the road? See here." He traced his finger along what looked to be a path. "That's the old road. See how it moves along with the river?"

I nodded.

"Before the Golden Road was built in the '70s," he said, settling his glasses in place again, "there was a network of old roads. They'd been used since the 1800s. Back when lumber companies floated logs down the river or used horse-drawn trucks to transport them to the mill.

"When the Golden Road was built to accommodate all four of the big timber companies, they stopped using and maintaining those roads. They were never even paved, so it didn't matter much."

"And now?" More pieces of this puzzle were coming together.

He lifted a shoulder. "I haven't been out there in years, but I'd assume they're overgrown hiking trails."

"The one you pointed out is visible, but there are more, right? Could you add them to the map?"

He plucked a Sharpie from the penholder on the desk and traced a line along the river, then through the forest. "I'm pretty certain this is the main road. And this up here"—he continued drawing—"is not precise, but that goes west."

"To the border," we said in unison.

Straightening, I locked eyes with him, my skin breaking out in goose bumps.

I shook off the sensation and squinted at the microscopic words labeling the town the route led to. "Sainte-Louise."

"It's not a border checkpoint anymore. When the new highways were built, it all changed. But my grandpa mentioned it when he'd tell stories. Lumber came in and out of there. Canadian whiskey during prohibition too."

It was all coming together in my head. I'd heard that name many times while I was gathering evidence. Only now, though, did I realize what they'd been talking about.

"Is that where they're going on Friday the thirteenth?"

If they'd been doing this for almost twenty years, there had to be some significance here.

I turned on my heel and paced, my heart pounding and my head spinning.

"Trouble," Jude said, gently holding me by the shoulders. "This is amazing. But you need to breathe. Process. This is a lot."

He guided me to the living room and urged me to sit on the couch. Then he was gone, only to return a moment later with a glass of water.

"I'll call Parker."

"No," I said sharply, my stomach twisting into a knot. "Not until I've got it all put together. There's all kinds of stuff in there I haven't touched. For now, I'm still working out what's happening on the thirteenth." This felt too raw, too precious right now to bring in law enforcement. "I need to be totally certain."

He sat beside me and tucked my hair behind my ear. "You don't have to do all this alone, Trouble. We can help."

I nodded, my eyes unfocused. "You've been helping. I need a little more time. I promise."

"Okay." With a long exhale, he put an arm around me.

"I know you think I'm nuts," I said softly as I rested my head on his shoulder. "But there are some things I can't let go of. That I just can't forgive. I know that's a character flaw. It's why I've bounced around career-wise. It's why I don't own a home and haven't had a long-term relationship."

Ripley sat in front of me and put her head in my lap, sensing my distress.

"I'm not built like everyone else. I'm not built like you," I admitted.

I'd known it since childhood, though I'd never fully said out loud. But I trusted Jude, and although I doubted he'd understand, he was the type of person who, at the very least, listened, and it had been a long time since anyone had truly listened.

"What does that mean?" he asked.

I turned my head and gazed up at his handsome face. "Look at you. You are clearly great at adulting."

A laugh rumbled out of him, vibrating through me.

"I mean it. You own a home; it's decorated. You have a headboard and bookshelves and art hanging on the walls. You keep an animal alive and have a career."

He grunted. "I cut down trees."

"Don't minimize it. You're director of operations. You manage a big team of people. You're impressive. And you're stable. You've got a whole life."

He pulled me closer, tucking my head beneath his chin. "It may look that way on the outside, but I'll let you in on a little secret. I made my world small, and now I'm stuck in a rut because I never forced myself to stretch and grow."

"What do you mean?" I asked. It was comforting to know I wasn't the only one who felt like a fuckup all the time.

"I've never had big dreams like my brothers. I like quiet and the woods. All my life, I wanted nothing more than to continue the work my father and grandfather had done. But it's all changed. And I'm still the same. It doesn't feel right anymore."

I pulled back and put a hand on his chest. "You have to do what feels right."

He locked those dark blue eyes on mine, his jaw clenching, like he was holding something back. "I wish I knew how. But I've missed some things. I was so concerned with making my life safe and predictable that I missed out on the magic. And the thing about magic? Once it's gone, it's gone forever."

The weight of his admission hung in the air between us. Playing his words over in my mind, I sagged against him, drawing on his strength and warmth. His masculine smell, the delicious meals he made me, his sweet dog, and his comfy bed all comforted me. I'd been on my own for so long, but my life had changed so much in these last few weeks. And it was all because of Jude.

I wanted him to have everything he desired, all the magic he could wring out of life. But I feared that, like me, it would be out of his reach.

I closed my eyes, and a deep sense of peace settled in my chest. I should have been panicking and researching. But for what might have been the first time in my life, I wanted to sit still. I wanted to enjoy the magic of this moment for just a little longer.

Chapter 26
Jude

"You smell good," Mila said, resting her head on my chest. I considered pressing my lips to her crown but decided against it. We were in a strange holding pattern that included physical affection. But she'd been clear about her boundaries. And I'd been all up in my head over them.

Because Mila made me feel things and want things that were completely off-limits.

She'd fallen asleep on my chest on the couch, and holding her like that, absorbing all her anxiety and worries, had been heaven. But it was getting late.

She rubbed her eyes and straightened beside me. "How long did I nap for?"

I fought the urge to pull her back into my side. "About an hour."

"Sorry."

"I didn't mind."

We stared at one another for a moment, the air heavy between us. I wanted to touch her, kiss her, and make all her problems go away. But the last thing she needed was to be pressured. We had no idea what tomorrow would bring, so even if she wanted more, making plans was stupid.

"I've got to jump in the shower." I stood and backed away.

She was still adorably sleepy, and her hair was stuck to one side of her head. "Where are you headed?"

"The Moose," I replied. "Playing a gig."

"Oh." Her face fell in the strangest way, going from peaceful to annoyed in a flash.

"You okay?" I asked.

Was she hurt?

She shook her head. "Sure, I didn't realize you had to go out."

"Yeah, we play there about once a month. Sometimes we pick up other gigs. It's a hobby for us all, and we have several subs on standby if someone can't make it. But I committed to this a while ago."

"Okay, great." She gave me a smile, but it was forced. "I'll feed Ripley and let her out. Go do your thing." She avoided my eye as she headed toward the kitchen.

As I headed to the bathroom, she stomped around the kitchen, slamming cabinet doors.

Each loud noise worsened the dread in my gut. But I didn't have time to dissect what was going on. Not right now. I'd made a commitment, and I couldn't let the guys down.

I showered and dressed, and while I loaded my equipment into my trunk, Mila sat in the kitchen, drinking tea, staring off into space.

Part of me wanted to jump in my car and avoid the awkwardness, but guilt kept me from my cowardly escape.

She was stuck here; she had no one else to talk to. I wasn't a great talker, but at least I was someone.

"What's wrong?" I asked, walking softly into the kitchen. "You seem upset."

"I don't know." Head bowed, she worried her lower lip. "I'm mad, and I don't know why. Ugh. I sound like a toddler."

"Is it because I'm going out? If you don't feel safe here—"

She waved me off. "No. It's not that. It's just." With a huff, she scrunched her nose and closed her eyes. "Is it bad that I'm jealous?" She looked down into her mug, avoiding my eye.

Confusion swirled in my head. "Jealous? Of what?"

She stood and silently padded to the sink, where she rinsed out her mug and put it in the dishwasher. I followed her every move, at a loss.

Finally, she turned and leaned against the island. "You're you," she said, as if that explained anything, and waved her good arm, gesturing to my body. "And you're headed out to play your guitar with your beard and your glasses and all those stupid muscles."

A scoff escaped me. "Stupid muscles?"

Head tipped back, she groaned. "You know you're hot, Jude. Don't make me spell it out. I'm already humiliating myself here."

I couldn't hide the smile that split my face in half. She was jealous and being possessive. It sent a thrill through my body.

"I'm going to play guitar for a couple of hours, then come home. You know that, right?"

She let out a big sigh. "Yes, I know that. But there will be women everywhere, throwing themselves at you."

Across the granite, I covered her hand with mine. "Trouble, you've got the wrong idea. I'm not a rock star playing a sold-out stadium. It's a dive bar in rural Maine. Most of the clientele are older than my parents or grizzled loggers blowing off steam."

"Inaccurate," she quipped, pulling her hand away. "The Moose is not a dive."

"Fine," I conceded. "A fancy dive."

"No. It's a restaurant and bar trying to cultivate the street cred of a dive while being too clean and welcoming."

I bit back a laugh. "Okay, now that we have established its place in the spectrum of dining establishments, can we focus on why you're jealous? I'm sorry I'm leaving. I know you're going stir crazy, but I made a commitment."

She deflated. "God, you're so annoying. Do I really have to spell it out for you?"

It was times like these I was reminded that I had a lot to learn about women. Not one lick of this made sense to me.

"It's not about leaving the house. It's about you being all sexy Jude the Lumberjack Musician and having all these women lusting after you."

Even as dread formed in my gut, a hint of a thrill zipped through me. Had she seriously admitted that she'd be jealous of any women who might come on to me? I circled the island and stood in front of her, tipping her chin up with my fingers.

"Trouble. No one will be throwing panties at me tonight." I caressed her jawline, studying every facet of her beautiful, pouty face. "In fact, the only girl who has ever thrown panties at me was you."

"I did not." She went ramrod straight, poking a finger at my chest.

I chuckled and stepped closer, bringing my body flush with hers. "Okay, so you metaphorically threw your panties at me. Admit it, you eye fucked me so thoroughly, they probably incinerated before my set was over."

Punctuating the comment, I grabbed her ass and squeezed.

She moaned slightly, her eyes darkening but staying locked on mine.

I did not have time to bend her over this counter, but goddamn, I wanted to.

I buried my face in her neck and inhaled her honey lemon scent. "You have nothing to worry about."

With her good arm looped around my waist, she said, "I know we're not exclusive or anything." She sighed. "I could never ask that. We both want casual."

My gut clenched. She was the one who wanted casual. Me? I wanted a lot of things. Things that I did not have the emotional bandwidth to even define. But it was a fuck of a lot more than casual.

I took a step back and rested my hands on her upper arms gently, putting some space between us. "Look at me."

She complied, a mixture of defiance and vulnerability bleeding from her, making my heart seize up.

"I will not so much as look at another woman while you're sleeping in my bed." I was unlikely to ever look at another woman again, even after she was long gone, but I kept that information to myself.

"You don't have to."

"Yes I do. Even if we hadn't gotten physical, keeping you safe is my top priority. And I'm not some horn dog, for God's sake. I can keep it in my pants. Even though you called me… what was it? 'Sluttier than a pair of gray sweatpants'?"

Two red patches bloomed on her fair cheeks.

"Regardless of what you think," I went on. "I'm not. I have no intention of looking at or talking to anyone tonight. I'll play, hang with my brothers and sisters-in-law, have exactly one beer, and then come straight home to you."

She nodded, her face still red, her gaze lowered.

"And when I come home," I growled, tipping her chin up. "Then you'll get all my attention." Angling in, I captured her mouth in a rough kiss.

She kissed me back, cuffing the back of my neck, making sure I knew that she'd be waiting.

Her jealousy was hot. Totally unwarranted, but hot, nonetheless. As if I could even look at another woman. Mila occupied every one of my waking thoughts and a good percentage of my dreams. She didn't know it, but I'd be counting down the minutes until I could come back home to her.

Chapter 27
Mila

I was an independent, badass woman who never waited for a man.

Except tonight. Tonight I waited for a man.

First I paced.

Then I snacked. But a girl can only take so many kelp crispies and raw almonds before giving up. I couldn't even properly eat my feelings in this house.

Finally, I got back to work, double- and triple-checking all the information I'd gathered and organizing my evidence wall—or "murder wall," as Jude affectionately referred to it.

I couldn't afford to miss a single detail here.

But my mind kept wandering to Jude. To what songs his band was playing. To how big the crowd might have been.

And despite my efforts to keep it at bay, sadness washed over me.

Envy.

I was missing out.

I'd lived in an obsessive bubble for so long, I'd forgotten what it was like to go out and have fun. To listen to music and sip a cold beer and let go for a couple of hours. Not that I'd ever done much of it. Since childhood, I'd been focused, driven. I'd never really let anything get in the way of my goals.

Including friendships, relationships, hobbies, and fun.

I sat on the couch, hit by the weight of it all. It settled over me, pushing me into the cushions. Ripley was by my side immediately, sensing that I needed canine support. And all of a sudden, I was hit with a rush of wanting.

It wasn't specific, this type of want. It was big and unwieldy and hard to wrap my mind around. I wanted companionship *and* affection *and* sex. I wanted friends and weekend cookouts and hikes and nights out at the dive bar where I could watch a sexy guy play guitar.

I'd missed out on a whole life. First by focusing solely on my career, putting my commitment to journalism above my own fulfillment. And now, by allowing myself to be completely consumed by the search for the people who'd harmed Hugo.

No wonder it had been so easy for me to slip into the role of a fictional person, to become Amy. Mila was never a complete person to begin with.

I was dangerously close to falling into the emotional black hole that had opened up before me when Ripley perked up and wagged her tail. Head tilted, I listened closely, and sure enough, I caught the faint sound of an engine.

Like I'd been conditioned, excitement bubbled inside me.

Jude walked in, looking more handsome than when he'd

left. It was some kind of superpower that should be studied by scientists.

"Miss me, Trouble?" He set a small amp on the floor, then rested his guitar case against the wall.

My brain told me to play it cool. But I was in no emotional state to pretend.

"Yes." I strode across the room and planted a big kiss right on his lips. "I missed you a lot."

He smiled down at me, his expression a perfect mix of surprise and delight. "I missed you too. I felt guilty about going out to play without you, so I thought I might put on a little show for you here. How does that sound?"

Stunned, I stumbled back a step, nodding a little too vigorously.

"Gimme a minute."

He came back a few minutes later with a stool and one of the acoustic guitars he kept on a stand in the spare bedroom. As he settled in front of the fireplace, he gave me a shy smile.

"Sit down," he said, lowering his head and plucking a string, tuning the instrument.

The sight of him, perched on his stool, one of his long legs extended while he bit his lip and adjusted the frets, made it impossible not to swoon.

Or maybe it was the jeans, light-washed and broken in, hugging the curves of his muscular thighs. Or the maroon T-shirt that hid nothing. Whatever it was, it made me lightheaded despite the ungodly number of almonds I'd consumed earlier.

"Any requests?" His eyes sparkled, reminiscent of the way he'd looked that night on stage when I'd come home with him. The easy posture, the quiet confidence.

"Your favorites."

With a nod, he tapped one foot, then played the opening chords to "Blackbird" by the Beatles. And when he opened his mouth and the lyrics came out? A host of tingles swept through me. Holy shit. He could sing.

His voice was dark and smoky, with a hint of a rasp. Johnny Cash without the cigarettes. I couldn't tear my attention from him when he closed his eyes and the music took over, his strong fingers on the guitar, the beautiful lyrics drifting on the air.

We were alone in the living room of a small house in Northern Maine. It didn't matter. He could be singing to a sold-out crowd at Madison Square Garden and it wouldn't have been any more moving than this moment. Because he was singing to me.

He transitioned straight into Simon & Garfunkel and then some Neil Young. Just when I thought I'd melt into a puddle of goo and make a mess of his couch, he broke into "Your Body is a Wonderland" by John Mayer that then turned into an acoustic arrangement of "Baby Got Back."

An embarrassing fit of girlish giggles overtook me. He was talented and funny. He kept looking up at me and winking.

He took a break, setting his guitar on the couch. "Just need some water."

I jumped up, my heart pattering ridiculously. "I'll get it. I'm sorry I kept you playing for so long."

Lips curling up on one side, he shook his head. "I'm having fun. You like it?"

"Love it," I said, scurrying to the kitchen.

We sat for a few minutes while he drank a glass of water and I tried to get my raging hormones under control.

Was it possible to die from lust? Should I ask Willa? She was a doctor; she knew things.

"When did you start playing?" The question was lame, but most of my blood was pumping to my lady bits. If I didn't distract myself, I was liable to rip my clothes off and offer him my body. No wonder I'd lost my mind and gone home with him last year. There was no resisting this man when he had a guitar in his hands.

"Third grade." He took a big gulp of water. "The music teacher brought out recorders and made us all play them. Yes, they're the worst instrument ever, but I loved it. Took mine home for extra practice, and my mother, God love her, eagerly listened every time I wanted to perform for her. She pretended like 'Row, Row, Row Your Boat' was not ear-splitting torture."

A warmth of affection for a woman I'd never met bloomed in my chest. "That's sweet."

"After I got good enough to have a solo at the elementary school concert—we'd worked our way up to 'Old MacDonald'— my mother signed me up for piano lessons. I spent years practicing in a musty church basement, all the while shoveling snow to earn enough money for a guitar. Any spare minute I had, I'd play. When I have a guitar in my hand, I know who I am."

That statement cut through the affection like a knife through butter.

"I have no idea who I am." The confession was ill-timed word vomit, but it was true. Though it had never hit as hard as it did in this moment, after watching him do something he loved so passionately. It was a stark reminder of how much I was missing.

"You'll figure it out," he said, his expression soft. "I have faith in you."

Emotion rose up in my throat, but I choked it back. "I hope so."

"You tired?"

I shook my head. "A couple more songs?" I was being greedy, but I wanted to experience this for a bit longer.

With a nod, he picked up his guitar. He rolled his shoulders, instantly shifting back into sexy rock star Jude, and strummed. "I think this may be one of your favorites," he said.

It took five seconds for me to recognize the song. "Everlong."

Books and movies made swooning seem like this feminine, delicate experience. But when I swooned at the soul and grit that rivaled Dave Grohl, my consciousness drifted from my body. When it returned, I was reduced to nothing but need.

He stood, his fingers moving deftly, his voice intense and his forearm muscles contracting distractingly.

I couldn't feel my fingertips, and my brain was floaty and hazy, my body buzzing.

There was no escaping this. I was gone for this man, despite all the reasons I shouldn't be. No logical argument or reasonable set of facts would change the chemistry of my brain. It screamed at me to grab on to him and never let go.

When the music ended, all I could do was stare.

"How did you know?" It came out as a squeak.

"The first time you came into the dojo, you wore a Foo

Fighters shirt." He shrugged. "And 'Everlong' is one of the best love songs ever written. So I guessed. You're not the sappy type, so a hard rock ballad is definitely your style of romance."

My chest constricted painfully. How the hell could he read me so well?

One hand still on the neck of the guitar, the other arm cradling its body, he padded closer. "I know talk of the future is forbidden, but you mean a lot to me. I need you to know that. And I'll play anything you want. It killed me to see you so sad when I left. Thought this might cheer you up."

He had done a hell of a lot more than cheer me up. I stood and grasped the back of his head, slamming my lips to his. The guitar was caught between us, making me have to pop up on my toes to reach his mouth, but I didn't care.

"Take me to bed."

"Yes, ma'am."

Chapter 28
Mila

I couldn't wait another minute. All night I'd paced around in a fit of jealousy, picturing Jude on that stage, looking like a snack, with those big strong hands on his guitar.

Then he came home and played for me?

Panties? Destroyed.

Heart? Experiencing a lot of emotions I'd rather ignore at the moment.

Brain? Unable to think about anything but getting naked.

He picked me up with ease, and without breaking our kiss, I wrapped my legs around his waist. It was needy and sloppy but only made me want more.

Brow furrowed, he eased me onto the mattress. "Am I hurting you?"

I pushed up to my knees and pawed at his T-shirt. "Off," I commanded. "And then the pants."

A dark chuckle escaped him, sending a flash of need through me. "You're bossy tonight."

"Of course I am. I'm a woman with needs," I said, muscling my tank top off around my bad shoulder.

Once I'd tossed the garment to the floor, I ran my hands up his muscular chest, desperate for more physical contact. "Maybe this makes me a horny groupie, but seeing these hands on the guitar?" I grasped his wrists and pulled until he was palming my naked breasts. "A woman only has so much self-control."

"Oh, Trouble." With a growl, he took my nipple into his mouth. "You don't need self-control here. You can take whatever you want."

I pushed him away and yanked on his waistband. "In that case." I palmed his erection over the denim and gave it a squeeze. "I'll be doing just that."

With a wicked grin, he tore the jeans down. When he straightened, his cock strained against the tight fabric of his boxer briefs, the head peeking out of the top.

I licked my lips and placed a gentle kiss to the tip.

"Fuck, Trouble," he gritted out.

Peering up at him from beneath my lashes, I smiled. "Quiet. I'm taking what I want."

I yanked his boxer briefs down and gripped his length, then took him into my mouth, letting my tongue swirl around the tip. It was thick and hard and far too big for my mouth, not that I'd let that stop me.

With a lick to the underside, I inhaled deeply. Then I took him to the back of my throat. When my gag reflex kicked in, heat ignited in my belly.

He tangled his fingers in my hair, creating a charge that ran straight to my clit. Those hands. I wanted them all over me and inside me all the time.

But this wasn't about me. It was about him. And showing him how much I wanted him.

His cock surged in my hand, getting impossibly harder, proving that I wasn't the only one barely holding on.

Relaxing my jaw, I took him to the back of my throat again, using my hands to work his shaft as I found a rhythm.

Fingers twined in my hair, he was reduced to a series of grunts and gasps. Each noise inspired me to keep going, to wring every ounce of pleasure from him.

He stroked my cheek, and I looked up, only to find him fixated on me, his eyes hooded with lust. Never breaking eye contact, I stroked his cock with both my hands while circling the tip with my tongue.

"*Fuck.*" He tossed his head back, his body taut as a bowstring.

And then I was being lifted off the floor.

"Need to be inside you." With a grunt, he stepped out of his pants. Then he dragged two fingers through my soaked core.

Dazed with lust, I didn't have the wherewithal to help him as he shifted me toward the head of the bed. As he rolled on a condom, every muscle in his body was coiled with tension.

The sight had the heat in my core liquefying.

Ranging over me, careful to support his own weight, he lined himself up. Then, with a deep kiss, he pushed inside me.

I gasped, every part of me stretching to accommodate him.

"That's it," he purred. "Just breathe."

With his mouth on mine again, he moved, and as he

ghosted his lips over my jaw and to my neck, he set a slow, steady rhythm.

Eyes rolling back, I spread my legs wider, eager for all of him. This was bliss. It was perfect. It was right.

Each thrust was controlled and restrained. He was trying not to hurt me. And while the care he showed me only made my affection grow, in this moment, I needed more. I wanted him wild and frenzied.

"Jude," I whispered, taking his face in my hands. "You don't have to be careful. I won't break."

He rolled his hips, burying his face in my neck.

"Need to keep control," he said.

"Please," I begged, bucking up, seeking more friction. "You told me I could have anything I want. And I want you wild. I want you to fuck me like you need to. Give into it."

Arms locked on either side of my head, he lifted up, his eyes widening behind his glasses. "Are you sure?"

I bit his bottom lip hard and nodded, gripping his ass and tugging him closer. "Yes."

Smiling, he pulled out of me and stepped back, admiring my naked body laid out on the bed.

I writhed, needy and deprived of his touch. Finally, he clutched my ankles and dragged me to the edge.

"Is this okay?"

I nodded, clawing at his biceps, desperate for him to be inside me again.

He threw my legs over his shoulders, and in one mildly rough move, he pushed inside me. I was completely at his mercy, spread out beneath him while he owned my body. He was thrusting so deep I could feel him everywhere. It was electrifying. Normally, I hated losing control. I wasn't the kind to submit. But Jude took such care of me, making it second nature to let him own my body like this.

"God, you're gripping me so tight."

Each thrust sent me spiraling further. He bottomed out over and over again. I'd never felt so full and content.

"I need you to come, Trouble."

With my good hand, I pinched my nipple, and as if we'd choreographed it, he hit that perfect spot inside me. I cried out, my back arching and my inner walls tightening around him.

"Touch yourself. Rub that pretty little clit for me."

"I—" My breath caught. I'd always needed a little extra attention down there to finish, but touch myself while he had me like this?

It was out of my comfort zone.

"Yes. I want to watch," he growled, thrusting hard enough to hike my body an inch or two up the mattress.

Laid out under this sexy lumberjack like this was not the time to be shy, so keeping my eyes locked with his, I licked my index finger and slid my hand between us to where we were joined.

I brushed his shaft as he pulled back and thrust in again, eliciting a moan from him, then got to work lazily rubbing circles around my clit.

"Fuck, you grip my dick so perfectly," he said, thrusting even faster.

The heady sensation built, coiling and growing, his words only kicking me into a higher gear. "Watching you play with your pussy is so hot."

Eyes closed, I gave in to the pleasure, focusing on the way his thick cock dragged perfectly against my inner walls.

Awash with more desire than I'd ever known, I clenched around him.

"Eyes open," he growled. "Look at me when you come on my cock."

His eyes were molten, the muscles in his arms bulging as he held my thighs up and drove into me. The vision sent a tingling sensation through me, driving me over the edge.

I cried out as I clenched around him, my orgasm barreling through me. Full and stretched, at his mercy, I was lost. I screamed and convulsed as he pistoned into me wildly, chasing his own release.

His cock surged inside me, only amplifying the pleasure and leaving me a shaking mess.

With a groan, he collapsed, keeping his weight on my good side.

"Fuck." He rained kisses over my collarbones. "That was incredible."

I closed my eyes, savoring the feel of his warm body and the exhausted sexual satisfaction only Jude could deliver.

It had never been this good. The connection, the emotions, the intensity.

There was no doubt in my mind that this man was thoroughly ruining me.

Chapter 29
Mila

I could get used to this.

We lay tangled in the sheets, my head resting on his chest, his hand stroking my hair.

Somehow, this moment felt more intimate than any of what we'd shared.

"This is nice." He gently massaged my scalp, sending goose bumps skittering along my skin. "I wish we were in a luxury hotel in an exciting locale rather than stuck in my house."

"I don't mind being stuck with you." I nuzzled against his neck, inhaling his warm scent. "But being trapped here has its challenges. I'm used to being on the move—traveling, working, running around with a backpack and a laptop."

He let out a low rumble of understanding. "I can see that. I bet you are an incredible journalist."

"Thank you. It was always my dream. Television was hard because of the hours and the travel, but I loved producing, and I loved searching for the stories and putting the pieces together."

"Tell me about some of the places you've been."

I sighed and closed my eyes. "I loved Japan. I was only there for a few days, but I would go back in a heartbeat. The culture, the architecture, the food." I let my voice trail off. "But in reality, the job was not glamorous. Press isn't always treated well, and I was sent to some scary places as well. Syria, Afghanistan, Yemen."

"You're so brave."

My cheeks heated at that comment. "Not really. It was the job. I traveled with the crew and the talent, and it's true what they say: there's safety in numbers. Plus, we had security. But" —I shook my head—"I saw plenty of things I wish I hadn't. There are incredible journalists out there who devote their lives to reporting from war zones and shining a light on the tragedies and injustices of our world. I admire them so much, but after a few years, I knew I had to pivot to a more traditional role."

"There's no shame in that. We're allowed to grow and evolve. What I want for my life now, at thirty-four, is nothing like what I dreamed of when I was twenty-one. That doesn't make me any less brave or brilliant."

His words were simple, but they sent a shiver through me anyway.

He pulled the soft blanket up around us and gently shifted so we were even closer.

No one had ever described me as brave. Reckless? Yes. Crazy? All the time. But not brave.

"What about you?" I asked, desperate to change the subject. "Don't tell me you're one of those hard-core Mainers who's never left the state."

"God no." He scoffed. "I've traveled around the US and

Canada quite a bit. When Finn was in the Navy and stationed in Virginia, I'd drive down to visit. I've been out to Oregon a few times for timber industry stuff, and I've traveled all over the place to watch Cole play hockey. But I'd love to do more."

"What other places do you want to see?"

He ran his fingers along my spine, the move sending another shiver through me. I curled up, throwing one leg over his.

"I'd go anywhere with you."

My stomach flipped and my heart fluttered in a way I wasn't sure I should allow.

"But my dream is Hawaii."

Huh. Not what I expected. "I've never been."

"Yeah, volcanoes and beaches and giant sea turtles. It's far, but not that far, and so unique. I want to dig my toes into the sand and look out at beautiful blue water. Explore each island. Experience that kind of place."

I closed my eyes and imagined it. I'd love that too. Beach and sunshine. No worries allowed. A handsome lumberjack available for sunscreen application would make it a dream vacation.

"We should go," he said. "When this is over."

It was a wild idea. A musing, not reality. It would never happen, but we held on to the vision of it for a few minutes. Letting the suggestion hang in the air while we clung to one another. Our situation was strange and undefined and precarious. But it was a relief to allow ourselves to pretend we were normal.

I yawned, the hour finally getting to me. "I wish we

could transport ourselves to an alternate timeline. One where we're normal."

"Normal? Trouble, something tells me you've never been normal."

A huff of a laugh escaped me. "You know what I mean. A world where we could date each other."

He kissed the top of my head, a sweet gesture that only made our circumstances harder to stomach. "I'd date the shit out of you."

"I'm not even sure I know how normal dating works. I've never actually done it."

"I have. I'd teach you. We'd drink coffee, take Ripley for hikes, watch my niece Merry play soccer, probably swing by my mom's for Sunday dinners."

He pulled me closer, kissing along my jaw and earlobe.

"I'd take you out for date nights. Maybe a concert in Portland. A weekend down in Kennebunkport."

"Tell me about a date night. What would you do?" I closed my eyes so I could envision what that kind of normalcy would look like.

"Depends. There's a restaurant in Bangor my brothers love. Farm-to-table stuff. I'd dress up and—"

"A suit?"

"No. I own one suit. It's ten years old, and I wear it to funerals. I'd wear a sport coat with jeans. And my nice leather boots."

My stomach fluttered at the image I'd conjured. "Okay. I'm into that."

"And I'd bring you a plant, not flowers."

"Because flowers die?"

"No. Because I love plants. They're complex and beautiful. Like you. And every time you tend to it, I'll be on your mind. You can't forget about me if you're constantly watering the ficus I gave you. Helps my chances of scoring another date."

"Is this a good time to tell you I can't keep plants alive?"

"You'd keep my plant alive." He bit down gently on my earlobe.

"Yes. The hypothetical lumbersnack ficus. Okay, go on."

"I'd impress you by ordering good wine, and then we'd eat. I'd share with you because you'd struggle to pick just one item. Am I right? You're the type who's eager to try new things, aren't you?"

I hid my grin in my pillow. "Guilty."

"See? I told you I'm a good date. We'd drink the wine and leisurely sample delicious food. Then at dessert time, I'd order one of each, and we'd try them all. You're a sugar addict. There's no way you wouldn't want a little of everything."

I frowned up at him. "But you don't like dessert."

"For you, I'd try them all. That way, we could debate the merits of each one."

My heart thumped heavily. It was a bit scary how well he knew me already.

"On the way home, we'd take a little detour."

"Where?"

"A scenic point off 95 between Lovewell and Heartsborough. There's a small area to park there, and the view of the valley is incredible. We'd sit on my tailgate, wrapped in the blanket I'd thoughtfully packed, and look at the stars. Since I'm not a huge talker, a beautiful night sky will do some of the work for me."

"I think you're pretty good at conversation."

He shrugged. "You're easy to talk to." With a sigh, he continued on. "Then I'd take you home and walk you to your front door."

"Anything else?"

"If the vibe was good, I'd give you a good-night kiss."

A tingle zipped up my spine. "Peck or full kiss?"

"Obviously whatever the lady is comfortable with. But after a night with you, I'd probably be so pent up, I'd come in hot and have your legs wrapped around my waist and your back pressed to the front door in a matter of seconds."

My entire being heated. He was the perfect combination of crude and thoughtful. But as much as it turned me on, it also made me sad.

"How'd I do?"

I squeezed my eyes shut, wringing out every last drop of this fantasy before returning to the real world. His words had made me ache for a life where everything he described was possible. Simple pleasures, getting to know one another, leaving the house and exploring the world. Navigating life with a person at my side.

But all of that had never felt more impossible.

I choked back the heartache. "You were amazing."

He shifted and pressed his lips to mine softly. "We will get that date, Trouble."

A dull pain radiated through me. "I hope so."

Ripley wasn't ready to settle for the night, so Jude let her out once more, and the two of us went through our nighttime routines. We took turns brushing our teeth, and while he was still in the bathroom, I slipped into one of his T-shirts, pulling the collar up to my nose and inhaling deeply.

The last thing we should be doing was sleeping in the same bed like we'd gotten into the habit of. It was dangerous. But it felt so good.

He smiled as he returned, his running shorts slung low on his hips. "You wanna be the big spoon or the little spoon tonight?"

Ignoring him, I arranged the pillows to support my shoulder and climbed into bed. Willa had given me the go-ahead to sleep without the sling.

He climbed in and snuggled up next to me, careful to not bump my shoulder, then turned off the light.

"Jude?" I worried my lip.

"Yes, Trouble?"

I cleared my throat. "You know how you said we were in this together and there was nothing you wouldn't do to help me bring down the bad guys?"

He let out a big sigh, his body deflating. "Yes. I remember."

"Great. Because tomorrow, we're taking a road trip to chase down a lead."

"Where?"

"New Hampshire."

He was quiet for so long that I worried he'd fallen asleep. And as I was resigning myself to not getting a response, he gave me a squeeze and said, "As you wish, Trouble."

Chapter 30
Jude

Hours into the road trip, we finally came to a sign that read *End of the Road Farm* and turned onto a winding country road. An old white farmhouse with peeling paint stood in the distance, and in the field behind it was an array of junked-out cars. It looked like the setting of a horror movie, and not the artsy type that won Oscars. Mila had been cagey, telling me we had to talk to a source and brushing off my concerns. But now I wished that I'd pushed harder for more information.

"No," I said, stopping the car part way down the long dirt road.

"Keep driving," she said, leaning forward in her seat. "Nothing to worry about."

"No. I'm not letting you walk into a slasher movie set in Shitsville, New Hampshire."

She patted my arm dismissively. "It's fine. And this is not Shitsville. It's actually Pittsburg, New Hampshire. Did you know Pittsburg is the northernmost town in the state?

Canada is right over there." She waved ahead of us, as if the proximity to the border was a comfort.

I stopped the car, put it in park, and glared at her. "I need information. Badly. Who is this guy and why are we here?"

She rolled her eyes. "He's Dickie Perkins."

It took me a second, but recognition dawned. Dickie had been our contact at the department of fish and wildlife for decades before his retirement. "We shouldn't be here."

"Drive the car, Jude. He's a harmless civil servant, and we came all this way."

Nothing good could come of this. If Dickie was clueless to the drug trafficking, we'd get nothing out of him. But if he was involved? That could lead to a lot of trouble for us.

She grasped my hand and squeezed. "He knew Hugo. He might have information, and I need to know."

It was the shakiness of her voice that got me.

My stomach twisted with dread. "First sign of anything strange, and we're out of here."

"Deal."

With a deep breath, I put the truck in gear and rolled up to the house. From this close, it looked even more decrepit.

Mila jumped out of the front seat and was halfway up the sagging porch before I could cut the ignition.

Her knock was greeted by a muffled response from inside, then a little shuffling. When the door opened, Dickie Perkins stood before us, wheeling an oxygen tank and wearing an old bathrobe.

"Dickie," Mila said with false sincerity. "You look like shit. Can I come in?"

"Who are you and what do you want?" he asked, looking me up and down.

I'd seen this guy off and on for the last decade, but he looked a lot older and beaten down than the balding guy in a fleece vest who used to do forest walkthroughs with us.

"Just to chat." Mila walked in, skirting around him. "Nice house."

"It was my mother's," he replied dryly. "She died and left this crumbling shithole to me. But it's home."

He seemed unmoved by Mila's brash entrance, and with his hunched posture, general look of dejection, and oxygen tank, I didn't get the sense he was a threat.

"I know you," he said as I stepped inside. "A Hebert."

I nodded, keeping my shoulders back and my eyes narrowed on him.

"Oh fuck. I need a drink for this." He shuffled into the living room, which was equipped with a massive fireplace, faded floral sofas and piles of old newspapers stacked along the back wall, and took a bottle off a side table. He yanked the top off with his teeth and poured a healthy amount into a red plastic cup.

After he'd taken a swig, he surveyed me, then Mila. Finally, he opened his mouth and said, "Who the fuck are you and why are you in my house?"

Without responding, Mila slowly wandered around the room, admiring the dust-covered porcelain figurines on the mantel.

Eventually, she turned to face the old man. "Dickie," she said, her voice dripping with honey. "I need information, and I know you're my guy."

He took another gulp from his cup, attention narrowed

on her over the rim. "Jude." He shook a finger at me. "That's your name. Known your old man for decades. Total asshole, but great poker player." He laughed heartily, but it was cut off by a hacking cough. He lifted the mask that had been dangling around his neck and brought it to his face, breathing deeply. "Emphysema. It's a bitch, but my fault for not giving up my vices."

He took another hit and cleared his throat.

"How's Gus doing? Always liked him. Total opposite of your dad. Guess that's a good thing, given how things turned out."

"Focus, Dickie," Mila snapped. "We're here for information about my brother, Hugo Barrett."

"Good kid," he mused. "Smart. I trained him. Such a terrible tragedy." He shook his head. "But I took early retirement. Don't know anything about the attack."

Mila's jaw ticked, and she fisted her hands at her sides. "I'm gonna need more than that, Dickie."

With a shrug, he took another sip of liquor.

"Okay, then." Mila pushed her hair behind her ears and straightened her shoulders. "You retire at fifty-four from a job with the state. Then move to... where was it again?" She tapped her chin. "Oh yes, Macau. Where you fucked around for almost a year before fleeing some very bad people to whom you owe a lot of money. Do I have that right?"

Dickie's face paled.

"I know so much more than that. I've got the dirt on all your bad investments, the gambling debts, the multiple mortgages on this property. The identity theft and the social security fraud. Should I keep going?"

He stared at her, eyes wide and the cup in his hand trembling almost imperceptibly.

My mind was blown. Mila knew exactly what she was doing and how to get him to talk. It was impressive and also very hot. But the longer we stayed here, the more apparent it became that Dickie was involved in the trafficking ring. Which put Mila at risk.

"What happened?" she asked again.

He ducked his head and gave it a slow shake. "I was horrified by what happened."

"Which was...?" Mila asked, steepling her fingers like some kind of supervillain. "Because I've spent more than a year trying to figure out how a guy who was only doing his job gets beaten within an inch of his life and left for dead. He's not mixed up in your bullshit." Those last words were spoken with total conviction.

"I don't know," Dickie replied. "Everything's been destabilized since Mitch Hebert went to prison. People are bloodthirsty and running scared. There's pressure on both sides of the border."

Mila sauntered closer, only stopping when they were nose to nose, her face a mask of pure hatred. "I don't want vague bullshit. What happened to my brother?"

He made a choking sound and followed it up with a wheezing cough. As he reached for his mask, clearly in need of oxygen, Mila grasped his wrist and tugged on the mask herself. Damn, she was strong. He was sick, sure, but he was still a decent-sized guy. He struggled, but she kept the mask away from him.

"I'll let you fucking suffocate if you don't tell me what I want to know, you piece of shit."

He wheezed, his eyes narrowing, his face turning purple.

Just when I was sure he'd pass out from lack of oxygen, Mila dropped his hand.

He scrambled to fit the mask over his face and sucked in several deep breaths. "Okay," he wheezed. "I'll tell you everything I know. It's not much, but since you're threatening my life, I got no choice." He shuffled to the old couch and sank onto the cushion heavily.

"I loved my job. Truly. I was raised right here with a whole lot of nothing. First person in my family to go to college."

"Can it with the life story," Mila snapped.

"Job was great, but the pay was shit. Didn't matter that I got a fucking PhD while working full time for the taxpayer—"

Mila crossed her arms, being careful with her injured shoulder. "So you thought you'd become a criminal?"

"I am not a criminal," he hissed, kicking off another coughing fit. He took a few more drags on the oxygen mask.

"Make it make sense."

"I was approached by a few businesspeople. They asked if I could look the other way when it came to a few things."

"Like drug trafficking and murder?" Mila interjected.

His eyes went wide. "No. God no." He cleared his throat. "Things like ignoring signs that a closed road had been used. Moving boundaries a little to allow for access. The bats are either in caves or the tree canopy, so the roads are fine. It's common knowledge that we overregulate."

Mila only frowned.

"Then they needed me to write up a few reports."

"False reports?"

"Yeah. They needed access to the old logging road up to Sainte-Louise."

Mila darted a look my way, a flicker of triumph in her eyes.

Now we were getting somewhere.

"They'd let me know where they needed to travel, and I'd find a population of bats had shifted."

"So," Mila drawled, "you were able to shut down areas of privately owned forest to allow drug traffickers to operate with impunity?"

Dickie scoffed. "You make it sound terrible."

"It is terrible, you piece of shit," Mila corrected.

"I did my job," he argued. "I protected the wildlife. I balanced the interests of the environment and industry. It's not easy. This state was built on logging, but we can't decimate the trees and the ecosystems."

"No shit. But you could have done that job without taking kickbacks. Now start giving me names."

His gaze drifted down and to one side. "I don't know them."

"Bullshit."

"Deimos," he mumbled, still avoiding Mila's eye. "They paid consulting fees. Sometimes official payroll, sometimes unofficial. When I got into some trouble a few years ago, they stepped in and paid off some of my, uh, debts."

Mila's eyes lit up. "And who did you deal with there?"

"Couple of people. Wayne managed things for years, but he was pushed out, and then I had to talk to that little shit Denis. Fuck, he's terrible, throwing his dad's money around and making threats."

Mila hummed. "To be clear, you're referring to Denis Huxley?"

He nodded.

"Did you ever meet with his father, Charles Huxley?"

"No. But he was involved. The guy ran a construction empire and was a politician. It's not a leap to think he has his hands in lots of shady business."

"Did Denis attack Hugo?"

Dickie grimaced. "I have no idea. I doubt it. He's a dumbass, and I can't imagine he'd want to get his hands dirty. That whole mess was so terrible." Head hung, he deflated. "Hugo was a sharp kid. He loved the work and had a bright future."

Mila inhaled sharply, like she was fighting off tears.

"I trained him on the job," Dickie explained. "Counseled him about landowners and how to work with them. In our line of work, we can't be totally by the book all the time. Sometimes rules have to be bent."

"Hugo would never have bent the rules," Mila said with satisfaction.

"And that may be why he got hurt. When I had reservations, when I tried to go back to following the rules I'd been given, I was reminded of their political and economic power. They said Charles Huxley would be sure our department's funding was cut. That he'd take down the whole forest and build condos."

Mila pulled a folded map out of her bag and laid it out on the coffee table in front of Dickie, then handed him a Sharpie. "Show me," she said. "Show me how it worked."

He circled a small section. "We started here. Then I was tasked with extending some borders." He made a bigger circle. "When they wanted the road to Sainte-Louise, I had to put together a fake tracking study. According to it, the bats had moved farther north. Once that was done, we shifted the protection area."

"How did you do that?"

"Easy. Bureaucracy. I'd do my quarterly inspections, file my plans, apply for permission to find nesting areas, then fudge the data."

"Then what?"

"Occasionally I'd meet with management to confirm that all was running the way it should be. But for the most part, it was easy money. I did my part and went about my business."

Mila worried her bottom lip in thought. "Could Hugo have discovered this and tried to stop it?"

"Not sure. But my reports were good, and I filed them properly. It would take years to figure out how I'd fucked around with the data."

"Then why take him out before he completed his survey and report for the year?"

With a shrug, Dickie took another hit of oxygen.

Mila sighed, dragging her focus to me. "Who is covering for Hugo? Who took over working with your company?"

"No one," I replied. "It's been months since we've had any communication with the department."

"There's a statewide hiring freeze. Budget cuts and all that," Dickie explained.

She stood with her good hand propped on her hip and surveyed the map for a moment, then zeroed in on the older man again. "So what happens?"

"The prior year's plan remains in effect until a new survey is completed. Since Hugo was attacked last year and never filed the plan, they're likely using the last one I completed."

"So they're keeping their territory stable year after year."

He dipped his chin. "That's my guess."

Head tilted thoughtfully, Mila looked at me.

I nodded silently. The longer we stayed here, the more anxious I got. What if they were watching? Dickie was in deeper than we'd thought.

"You good now?" Dickie asked. "I answered your questions. Now get the fuck off my property."

"You're not as useless as you look." She gave him a dazzling smile. "Now, one last thing," she added, her words terse. "You will not fuck me over. You will tell no one I was here and you will not take off again. You'll stay here in case I need you."

Dickie scoffed.

"I mean it. You mess with me and you're dead. You see my handsome friend over there?" She pointed at me. "He may look like a lumberjack who dabbles in Instagram modeling, but if you so much as say one fucking word about this, you'll be in a mountain of shit with him. He's wearing a wire, recorded this entire conversation. If we take it to the feds, your former friends will find out. What do you want to bet you'd be dead in a couple of hours?"

I gave him a menacing smile, cracking my knuckles.

He practically jumped off the couch, his eyes wide and his skin pale.

As Mila turned to leave, Dickie reached for the bottle of liquor on the table. The move caused the sleeve of his robe to creep up, exposing a tattoo on his forearm. Spiny needles, a wide base. Some kind of tree or shrub. One I recognized.

I darted across the room and clutched his arm. "What is this?"

He looked up at me, lips turned down. "A tattoo."

"What does it mean?"

"It's a yew."

My brain spun with all the information about yews I possessed. Native to Maine. Poisonous if ingested. Also known as ground hemlock or the tree of the dead since they usually grew around cemeteries.

"Why?"

"All the guys involved have them. Helped us identify each other. Out in the woods, it's the only way to be sure of who the syndicate guys were."

A shiver ran down my spine. These tattoos had been popping up all over recently, and no one had figured out quite how they fit.

"Just this one?"

He nodded, smoothing his hand over it. "Yeah. On the right arm down to the wrist. Some guys have sleeves, and you gotta look for it, but this one's easy."

Mila took out her phone and snapped a photo of Dickie's forearm. Then, without another word, she strode out of his house.

I followed silently, and when we were safely inside the car, she lowered her head, her hands trembling as she wrung them in her lap.

I covered them with one of mine and squeezed. "It's okay," I said. "You were amazing."

She nodded, though weariness wafted off her and her shoulders remained slumped. "We make a good team."

With a nod, I turned around and pulled out of the horror farm.

As we headed for the highway, she finally lifted her gaze. "Thank you for doing this for me."

"Anytime, Trouble."

Chapter 31
Mila

The rain battered the windshield the whole drive home.

For the hours-long drive, I did nothing but stew in the information we'd gathered. Usually being right made me feel invincible. Chasing down leads was thrilling, energizing even. But at the moment, I was exhausted and sad. Halfway home, we stopped for snacks, and when we got situated in the car again, Jude gave me his hoodie. I wrapped it around myself like a blanket and forced my eyes closed, desperate to turn off my brain.

By the time we made it back to Lovewell, it was late and the rainy day had turned into a cool, clear evening.

Inside the front door, Jude pulled me into the hug and dropped a kiss on the top of my head.

"Go take a shower," he said.

Frowning, I looked up at him. "Why?"

"Because it's date night. While you do that, I'll fire up the pizza oven."

Slightly dazed, I showered and brushed my hair and

teeth. When I'd finished, I studied my reflection in the bathroom mirror, marveling at how much my shoulder had already healed. I still had a lot of work to do to regain my full strength, but at least I could take care of myself now. At some point, I'd get proper medical care, which would probably mean surgery and months of physical therapy. But for now, I was grateful for a functional arm.

I had no makeup, no nice clothes, and no clue what Jude meant by date night, but I couldn't help but notice how much healthier I looked. My bruises had healed, my cheeks had filled out, and the bags under my eyes were gone. I no longer looked like I was on the run from a criminal organization.

In fact, if I had access to hair products and makeup, I might even pass as the kind of woman who could be going out on a date with a handsome, sweet lumberjack who liked to serenade her with his guitar.

That realization caused a little of the heaviness of the day to lift.

But nothing could have prepared me for the sight in the kitchen.

The lights were dimmed, and candles flickered from the center of the large island. Then there was Jude. He wore a dress shirt with the sleeves rolled up and a dark blue apron as he stood on the far side of the kitchen and aggressively kneaded dough on the floured countertop.

Holy shit. I'd never imagined making pizza could be erotic. For all his modesty, it was clear that Jude was a pro. He was kneading and pulling like a chef on a TV show.

And I could not stop staring.

Because holy fucking forearms.

He put his body into it, pushing and moving with the dough.

It was mesmerizing.

He was focused and precise and had complete control. It was so Jude. Just like when he played guitar or chopped wood, he was completely in the moment.

"Hello, gorgeous." He grinned over his shoulder.

"I don't have any date clothes," I admitted, gesturing to my tank top and leggings.

"You look delicious," he said, one brow cocked and his blue eyes dark.

"Can I help?"

With a shake of his head, he turned and slid a large glass of red wine toward me. "Keep me company."

I sat on a barstool at the island and watched him as he went back to work, his shoulders bunching in a way that made my mouth water. "I want to see if I can pull some aerial photos of the spots Dickie talked about."

"No." Jude froze, this time glaring at me. "It's date night. No work talk, no investigation talk. All that responsibility will be waiting for us tomorrow. Tonight we're two people who like each other, and we're on a date."

I opened my mouth, ready to tell him that this wasn't the kind of thing we could pretend. I wasn't the type who could just turn my brain off on command.

But then he wiped his hands on a towel and snuck a few sips of my wine, and suddenly, a normal evening sounded incredible.

He'd put a record on, something instrumental and jazzy, and the fire was roaring.

While he prepped pizza, I told him about journalism

school and some of my travels, and he shared stories about growing up in the woods.

I pushed up, using my feet on the rung of the barstool, and snagged a slice of pepperoni with my good arm.

He frowned at me.

"This is good pepperoni," I said as I stole a second piece.

"It's salami," he corrected. "Genoa. And antibiotic free. Pepperoni is nothing but red dye and chemicals."

"Always so joyful." I winked.

With a grunt, he went back to carefully slicing mushrooms.

I took another slice, ripped it in half, and gave one piece to Ripley, whose tail thumped on the ground where she was seated next to me.

The warm domesticity of the moment was not lost on me. It felt dangerously normal. The kind of normal that I'd never experienced before. The kind full of affection, attraction, and the company of a man I loved talking to.

"You've never told me." I sipped my wine, relishing the way the flavor contrasted with the salty salami. "Why isn't there a Mrs. Lumbersnack?"

He looked up from his chopping and tilted his head, nonplussed.

"It's very normal to discuss romantic histories on dates." I straightened and held out one arm. "You cook. You own a cute house with art on the walls—"

"Those are framed vinyl covers," he corrected, pushing his glasses up his nose.

"It counts. You're domesticated and care for your dog. You're screaming for a wifey."

He stopped chopping completely now and hit me with a

look, a lock of hair falling into his eyes and his glasses askew. "The last thing I want is a wifey."

"But your brothers—"

"If you knew their wives and girlfriends, you'd understand that Heberts tend to favor strong women."

Head tilted, I considered that statement for a moment. "You must have a badass mom, then."

He chuckled. "You could say that."

He moved, arranging the bowls of toppings in a neat row. Then he used a weird metal thing to divide the dough into small sections, which he vigorously kneaded again.

"My dad's a piece of shit," he finally said. "You know about the criminal stuff. But he was a terrible husband and father. Left my mom after he knocked up his twenty-year-old secretary. That's Cole's mom."

"Shit."

A huff escaped him, making that tendril of hair hanging over his forehead flutter. "So my mom raised us mostly on her own—Cole included. She got a nursing degree, worked, bought a house, and kept us out of trouble. As an adult, I sometimes wonder how the hell she did it. Taking care of myself and Ripley is hard enough, but she had six of us, and she managed to juggle it all."

"She sounds awesome."

He smirked down at the dough. "She is. And she'll love you." He shook his head. "She'll want to hear all about your career and achievements, ply you with baked goods, and then break out my baby photos."

The moment the words were out, he froze. I was locked in place too. Surely he hadn't meant to say that.

Surprisingly, the thought that he wanted to introduce me to his mother made my chest warm.

But this wasn't real. It wasn't possible. No matter how much I liked him, this situation was too volatile for making plans.

"Sorry. That was weird," he admitted without looking up.

"It's okay." I gently spun my wineglass on the granite countertop. "I don't expect to meet your mother."

"No." He snapped his head up. "I want you to. When this is over."

"If it's ever over."

"*When* it's over, I promise, Debbie Hebert will be thrilled to meet the woman brave enough to take down a drug trafficking ring." He pinned me with the kind of look that left no room for questions, all intense eyes and a serious scowl.

I was strangely flattered by his confidence.

Instead of even considering the reason I'd broken out in goose bumps at that look, I ignored the confusing feelings I had for Jude and got back to my line of questioning. I was nothing if not a thorough interviewer. "I'm sure you've met nice, strong girls up here, and your brothers found love and have families."

"First of all, that's all recent." He stretched out one section of dough. "My brothers were as fucked up as I am for a long time. Being the child of a messy divorce will do that to you. Add on a criminal father, and we were all a wreck."

"What changed?"

He paused, dough stretched in midair. "Dad went to jail.

We had to face what he'd done. We lost the company and the respect of this town. It was a bit of a rebirth, really."

He gently positioned the dough on a large pizza paddle.

"When we were kids, Dad was wealthy and influential. Stayed that way until only a few years ago, actually. He was also a complete prick. I'm luckier than most of my brothers. He ignored Noah and me for the most part. We were only four when he left, and since neither of us was a super athlete, he didn't take much interest. Cole had it really bad. He was the hockey star. And Owen and Gus were downright abused for years."

"That's awful."

"My whole life, I lived with this pressure, with these expectations looming over me. I was expected to act the way a Hebert should, even if I didn't know what that meant. But when Dad went to jail, the bubble burst, and we could openly acknowledge how terrible he was."

I gave him a small smile. "And by saying it out loud, you were able to start healing."

He returned my expression, though his smile was a bright, gorgeous thing that had me squeezing my thighs together.

"Exactly. My brothers and I have had more conversations about childhood shit in the past year than in the previous thirty-three. It's been awful, but also freeing."

"Freedom looks good on you," I said with a wink.

"Hey," he teased as he pulled open the fridge and removed what looked like a log of cheese, "I'm only a guy who makes pizza."

"What's that?"

"This is fresh buffalo mozzarella." He set it on the counter and unwrapped it.

As he tore it into small chunks, I angled closer. "Can I have some?"

He held out a small piece, and when I leaned over the countertop and opened my mouth, he fed it to me, mouth quirking. His movements were slow, his fingertips grazing my lip and sending a zap of electricity through me.

I sat back and ate it, and as the flavor hit, I let out a little squeak. "That is delicious."

With a smirk, he went back to tearing the cheese.

"One time, when I was in Tuscany," I said, wiping at the corners of my mouth, "I got this mozzarella from a farmers' market that was so good I actually cried."

Jude arched a brow. "Cried?"

"Yes. I am not one of those women who pretends to be all cool and emotionless. And if you can't cry tears of joy about really good cheese, are you even living?"

He held out another piece, and I eagerly snatched it from his hand. "You know, you're full of surprises, Trouble."

"Why, thank you." I popped the mozzarella into my mouth. "And don't think you're off the hook, either. I wanna know why you haven't met a nice girl and settled down yet."

"I've met and dated a few nice girls. Women, really. And while I appreciate them in different ways, I haven't—"

I shook my head. "Wait a second. You're being too nice. Are you friends with an ex?"

"Yes," he said, as if it was the most natural thing in the world.

"One of them?"

"All of them." He rinsed his hands and wiped them on a

towel. "I've only had a few serious relationships, but of course I've remained friendly."

With a hand to my chest, I let out an exaggerated gasp.

"I'm not sure what you guys do in the city, but I was taught to treat women with respect. I even introduced Morgan to the man she's now married to."

I almost spit out my wine. "You're kidding me."

"No ma'am." He pulled a bottle of olive oil out of a cabinet. "We fizzled, but when Miles and I worked together on a logging crew and I realized how into D&D he was, I figured they'd hit it off."

"You're not into D&D?" I interrupted. "Mister graphic novel and ironic T-shirt collections?"

"I am a casual D&D fan," he clarified. "But Miles would organize games with people on the crew."

"Ah, I get it. So this Morgan girl loved D&D too, and that's a match made in nerd heaven."

"No." He shook his head as he spread cheese over the dough. "She loves fantasy books. You know, the spicy ones with dragons and shifters and stuff. Like the one Willa gave you. She was always going on about Fae and fated mates. She's imaginative and passionate, and so is he. Figured they'd be compatible."

Wow. I was floored by his thoughtful response. And his kindness toward his ex.

"And they got married?" I guessed.

He smiled. "Yes. And I officiated."

A bark of a laugh escaped me, echoing off the ceiling. "So you're a matchmaker?"

"No. But I don't just discard the people I care about.

And while I don't think I'm cut out for happily ever after, that doesn't mean I can't help out those who are."

When I didn't respond, he regarded me with curiosity.

"Lemme guess. You're a salt-of-the-earth, fire-and-brimstone kinda girl."

My heart stuttered. I felt very called out.

"Maybe," I said. "I have never had a serious relationship, and I don't like any of the guys I've casually dated in the past. And I sure as shit would never fix them up with a friend."

He nodded. "So you've never wanted a serious relationship?"

"No." I pressed my lips together and shook my head. "I can't say I've never considered it, but for most of my adult life, it hasn't seemed practical. When Hugo and I were young, our parents adored each other. I could feel the love they shared. The glances they'd give each other over the dinner table. The way Dad would randomly bring Mom flowers and how she'd make liver for dinner every Thursday because it was his favorite, even though she hated it as much as we did."

He gagged. "Even I don't eat liver."

"And that's saying something, because you're a health nut."

A scoff slipped out of him. "I believe in putting decent stuff into my body, and I happen to enjoy good food."

"Oh I know, and I'm not complaining." I stole a slice of bell pepper from the cutting board and gave his very impressive body a once-over. "But as for my parents, it couldn't last forever. Dad fought his demons for so long, but in the end, they took him."

He nodded. "Did they divorce?"

"God no. She hung on for years, after rehab failed and he drained their retirement savings." The thought made my chest ache. "It wasn't until he died that she truly understood how long he'd actually been gone. And I think that hurt more."

"I'm sure."

"But they had something beautiful, even though it didn't last. And maybe that's the best anyone can hope for."

My words hung in the air. It was depressing to think about. But maybe a little hopeful. And I'd been feeling more hope since the night I showed up here a few weeks ago than I had in years.

"Your brothers are doing great," I said, ready to move on from talk of my parents.

"Yes. But none of them got there easily. I do everything in my power to make sure they don't fuck up. And if I'd known Gus—who I'm probably closest to, even if Noah is my twin—had married Chloe when they were twenty, maybe I could have helped him figure shit out."

"You didn't know he was married?" I squeaked.

"Didn't have a clue. They got married in secret, then had a big falling out and divorced. From there, they didn't speak for twenty years."

"That's wild."

"Then she marches into the conference room the day we're closing on the sale of the business and declares she's bought the company to spite him. And now they're happily in love, and my grumpy brother is reading books about infant brain development and making googly eyes at his wife during work meetings."

"Hmm..." I said, the wine and the good company mellowing me out a bit. "So what you're saying is, even the most closed-off lumberjack has a chance?"

"Maybe." He shrugged.

"Oh, Jude. I think there's a girl out there, just waiting to knock you on your ass."

I snatched another slice of pepper, but before I could pull my arm back, he caught it and stared into my eyes.

"I've already met her." He rounded the island. "And she managed to kick my ass with only one good arm."

Chapter 32
Mila

Breathing labored and dizzy, I reveled in the rush of affection and hope and joy as he wrapped an arm around my waist and pulled me to him.

A little voice in my head whispered *love*. But I ignored it. Banished the word. This was not love. It was far too soon. And our circumstances? No this wasn't that. I didn't fall in love.

Like and lust? Those were sensations I could get behind. I liked him. A lot. He was funny and smart and good with his hands. He loved his dog and his family. And was dangerously good at Scrabble.

So it was natural. This feeling. The dizziness.

The way my heart jumped when he kissed me, or when the rough pads of his fingers stroked my cheek. It was possibility and promise rolled into a sexy package that I was powerless to resist.

"God, I can't keep my hands off you." He kneaded my breast with one hand while he used the other to tip my head up and deepen the kiss.

Reveling in his touch, I cupped the erection that was already straining against the confines of his pants. My body hummed in anticipation of the pleasure he was guaranteed to deliver.

"Fuck. Trouble." He dropped onto a stool and pulled me into his lap.

With my arms around his neck, I lined myself up and ground against him, desperate for friction. The pressure was already building inside me when he gripped my hips and pushed me down again.

I fumbled to unbutton his nice shirt, my finger shaking with a need that threatened to overwhelm me.

"Bedroom." He stood, keeping me in his arms, my legs wrapped around his waist.

I nodded, my lips on his neck, my good hand grasping at his hair.

"I need to taste you," he said as he kicked his bedroom door open. "Fuck, I'm craving it."

He eased me to my feet and pulled my tank off over my head, being sure not to hurt my shoulder.

"Sit on my face, Trouble. Ride my tongue."

My heart caught in my throat and insecurity rose inside me. I'd never been in that position before, and honestly, I wasn't sure I wanted to be. It seemed selfish almost.

He clutched my wrist, yanking me toward him. "Please. I've been fantasizing about it." With a groan, he buried his face in my neck and peppered kisses on my pulse point as he slipped his thumbs beneath the waistband of my leggings and pulled them down.

The moment I kicked them off, his hands were on my ass, pulling me closer.

"Come on," he urged. "Give me a taste."

My legs shook, anticipation winning out over apprehension. This man was begging to pleasure me. The sensation was thrilling. Like a euphoric dream I was afraid I'd wake up from before my need could be sated.

"Okay." I took a step back. "But only if you promise to be a good boy and make me come."

Eyes going wide, he shucked his shirt, and with movements as shaky as mine had felt, he removed his glasses and his pants, then lay on the bed.

For a moment, I didn't move. I was too caught up in admiring the specimen of a man laid out before me. He was broad and muscular, with dark chest hair leading down to his throbbing erection.

There was nothing I would deny this man. And as I crawled up the length of his body, kissing, licking, and biting every inch of his delicious skin, my need only intensified.

I'd only made it to his chest before he was pulling me up and positioning my aching core over his mouth.

"Hold on to the headboard," he instructed.

I barely had enough time to process his instructions before he anchored my thighs with his strong hands and got to work. This man knew exactly what I needed, lavishing my clit with attention as I adjusted to the sensation.

Eyes closed, I held on with all my strength, and when he spread my ass cheeks wide to get more access, my back bowed and a flame ignited in my core. His mouth and tongue hit all the right spots, pulling embarrassingly loud cries of pleasure from me. The angle, the intensity, and the sheer eroticism of this position sent me barreling toward an intense orgasm in record time.

As I rode him with abandon, he grunted beneath me.

My stomach lurched, and I paused, worried I'd hurt him. But as I looked down and saw the fire in his eyes as he continued to lick and suck and send bolts of pleasure through me, I realized that though I'd stopped, the rhythmic movements continued. I peered over my shoulder and gasped.

He was stroking his cock, hard and desperate, as he worked me over.

Grinning, I lifted my hips.

"Can't stop myself," he said, still stroking, his mouth brushing my pussy lips. "Watching you riding my face is so hot."

The way his strong hand worked over his length fanned the fire already burning in my belly.

"You did this." He grunted. "You make me so fucking hard I'm sure it'll kill me. Now get back on my face and come, Trouble."

I did what he asked, but I couldn't help but watch over my shoulder as he jerked his thick cock in rhythm with the movements of his tongue.

"You are so hot, fucking your hand while you lick my pussy." I moaned, eyes rolling at the pleasure engulfing me.

He sped up and doubled down, each movement oozing with intensity.

Fuck. He liked my dirty words. "Such a good boy. I want you to come while you fuck me with your tongue."

The words had barely escaped me when my orgasm swamped me. I screamed, my core clenching, my vision going dark. I gripped the headboard, my thighs shaking as he moved even faster, driving me over the edge into the kind of orgasm that bent space and time.

There was no self-doubt, no worry, no hesitancy as I rode his face and screamed, clenching and spasming as I exploded again and again.

I was riding out the last waves of my orgasm, peeking over my shoulder again, when his movements got jerky and he came in long spurts all over his stomach, making a filthy mess that somehow turned me on more.

I swung one leg over him and bent down, kissing him hard.

"I'm not sure I can walk after all that." I slumped onto the bed beside him and groped for the box of tissues on the nightstand.

He took it from me with a wicked smirk. "Then I guess I'll have to carry you to the shower."

"After that," I sighed, "I'm not sure I'll ever recover."

He rolled me over and smacked my ass hard.

"I haven't even fucked you yet, Trouble. We're just getting started."

Chapter 33
Jude

It was a foggy Sunday morning, and I was more comfortable than I'd ever been. We'd passed out after another round and leftover late-night pizza, and I'd slept like the dead.

When Ripley nudged me with her cold nose, urging me to let her out, for the third time, I rolled over, being careful not to disturb Mila, who was curled around me, naked, and checked my watch.

I blinked down at the digital display once, then again. Shit, it was already eight.

I was an early riser by nature, but the comfort of my bed and the delicious warmth of this woman had knocked me out cold.

I got up, snagged my boxer briefs from the floor, and took Ripley to the door. While I waited for her to do her business, I turned on the coffee pot and stretched. Something had shifted between Mila and me yesterday. We'd been growing closer for a while, but if I wasn't mistaken, she was finally beginning to trust me.

It felt good to have earned such a hard-won prize.

Full pot in hand, I was pouring the first cup when she screamed. My heart lurched out of my chest and I damn near dropped the scalding carafe at the sound. Without a second of hesitation, I took off, running. I found her still in bed, naked and crying and clutching her phone.

"What happened?" I whipped my head one way, then the other, searching for danger. "Are you hurt?"

She looked up at me with tears shining in her eyes. "What did you do?"

Frowning, I took a step closer.

"I logged into *WhatsApp* so I could let my mom know I'm okay. I check in with her every Sunday."

I dipped my chin. Okay. She'd mentioned they used the app to keep in touch without being traced.

"She told me that Hugo has increased neural activity."

A breath I hadn't realized I was holding whooshed out of me, and my chest expanded. "That's amazing."

"But that's not all."

She stood and walked toward me in all her naked glory, making my brain momentarily forget about comas and hospitals.

"She says that last week, Hugo was approved for transport to Mass General for care under their experimental neurology team."

I fisted my hands at my sides to keep from reaching for her. "That's great news."

Brow cocked, she studied my face for a moment. "There's more." She held up one finger and looked down at the phone. "Turns out a generous benefactor has lent my mother a penthouse apartment down the street from the hospital so she can be with Hugo every day."

My chest expanded farther, my heart thumping against my sternum. "Wonderful."

"And this generous person, want to know what his name is?" She didn't wait for me to respond before continuing. "His name is Owen Hebert." That cocked brow jumped even higher on her forehead. "Do you know him?"

My brain shorted out. She was naked, yet I was being interrogated. It made it difficult to string words together.

Head tilted, she waited, her focus remaining fixed on me. "What did you and your brother do?"

I ran my hand through my hair, collecting my thoughts. My hope had been that she wouldn't find out about this until everything was over and dealt with. But now that she knew, I'd have to fill her in.

"Owen is kind of a big deal in Boston." I sighed. "He's connected.   Like   hangs-out-with-billionaires-regularly connected. Some of whom sit on the board of that hospital."

"What did you tell him?" she gritted out. "We don't want charity—"

I grabbed her shoulder gently. "It's not charity. If not for my dad, Hugo wouldn't have been hurt. So when I told Owen, he jumped at the chance to help."

She responded by letting out a heaving sob and collapsing into my arms.

I pulled her close, conscious of her still naked state and willing my cock to behave.

"I wish I could see them," she said, her tears running down my chest. "Hug my mom and tell both of them how sorry I am. How I fucked up."

My stomach twisted. "You didn't fuck up."

"My mom gave up her life to be by his side every day. She speaks to him in French and reads novels for hours on end to stimulate his brain. She's incredible."

"You gave up your life too. And you've made big sacrifices. We're so close to finishing this. You will see them soon."

She clung to me, and I rubbed circles on her back, wishing I had the power to do more, to fix every one of her problems, to ensure that she and her family never had to worry again.

After a few moments, she took a step back. "I can't believe I'm standing here naked and sobbing on you. I'm sorry."

Affection bloomed inside me. "I don't mind."

"I'm so happy and sad at the same time. And also a little annoyed at you."

I wrapped her in my arms, resting my chin on her head. "Let's focus on the happy part. He's doing well, and he's got the best care team in the world. You single-handedly broke Dickie Perkins yesterday and have him on record admitting to a criminal conspiracy."

She looked up at me, her teary eyes shining with victory. "And Maine is a one-party consent state."

I swiped at her damp cheeks with my thumbs. "That's my girl."

After coffee, omelets, and a joint shower that went on until the water ran cold, we set up in the spare room, listening to the conversation with Dickie. Mila uploaded it to the cloud folder where she kept the research she'd share with law enforcement, and I studied the photos and maps, trying to make sense of what we'd learned. A multi-million-dollar opioid industry was dependent on the status of a bat species?

I shook my head. Only in Maine.

"We've found the route from the border at Sainte-Louise," she said. Spinning in her ergonomic chair. "And we know how they're cutting through the forest. They've got almost a hundred miles of abandoned road at their disposal. But there has to be a pickup point, right?"

I nodded.

"So the protected area ends here." She pointed to the region on the map. "That's still miles from any main road. How are they getting out of the forest and onto the highways to distribute?"

"Probably on ATVs or snow machines," I suggested.

"But wouldn't that make them obvious?"

"Yes and no. Depends on the season and the location. Some of the public trails are pretty busy."

She spun around again and straightened in the chair. "Could we go see?"

I frowned at her. "See what?"

"This area." She pointed to a piece of our territory that was northwest of town.

"Why?"

"I'm trying to understand how it all works."

I shook my head. "No. Too dangerous."

"I'm just saying drive around, get a sense. I'm not suggesting we even get out of the car."

"There's not much out there. forest and a couple of farms."

She stood and grabbed a fistful of my T-shirt. "Let's drive

by and take a look at the roads and the forest, see if anything feels off."

"Feels off?"

The way her eyes danced told me she wouldn't back down. I might as well give in now, despite how boneheaded and dangerous it could be.

"Humor me. It can't be more than thirty minutes from here, can it?"

I nodded.

She bounced on her toes. "I'll go get changed. We need warm clothes."

"Why?" Unease rolled in my gut at the calculation in her eyes. "My truck has heat."

She shook her head. "Oh no, we're taking the ATV."

Fifteen minutes later, we stood in my garage, both dressed in layers, while I filled the gas tank. This was a terrible plan.

"Are you sure you can hold on tight enough?"

The last thing I needed was to hurt her.

"Yes." She nodded like a bobblehead. "Willa says I can take breaks from the sling. And I have one good arm. How fast are you planning to drive this thing?"

"Not that fast, but there are bumps. Tree roots and stuff." Jaw tense, I pulled my glasses off and dug for the hem of one of my layers. "It's too soon. It'll be too painful for you."

She shook her head. "We're too close. And we can take it easy. Just check things out. We've got to put the missing pieces together. You said yourself—some of these are public trails. We're a couple enjoying our outdoor motorsports together." She gave me a big, cheesy smile.

I handed her a helmet. "These have microphones so we can speak to each other," I explained, pulling batteries from my pocket.

Once the batteries in both mic packs had been replaced, I pulled my own helmet on.

"You look pretty hot like this," she said, licking her lips.

"No flirting, Trouble," I said, thankful the face mask hid my smile.

"Put this on." I tapped her helmet, then swung a leg over the seat. "And hold on tight. First sign of any problems, we're out of there."

I put the coordinates into the GPS module and got her situated behind me while I waited for the route to appear. I never went up here. Near that part of our forest, there was some public land and then endless highway. I wasn't sure there was anything worth seeing. But we were too damn close to give up now.

I revved the engine and took off, keeping my speed slow and the machine as steady as I could as I steered toward the trail system. It would be a bit of a ride, but it felt good to be out in the forest, feeling the breeze, inhaling the earthy scents.

The way Mila clung to me also felt good. If I was being honest with myself, everything that involved her felt good.

When my GPS pinged, I glanced at the map. "We're approaching our area," I said. Slowing, I turned onto a dirt path only as wide as the wheelbase of the ATV. "Hang on. It might be bumpy."

The forest was thick, but the new clear signs made navigation easy. The scenery was beautiful. It brought with it a sense of vitality. We skirted a large pond, and as I sped up a little, Mila adjusted her hold on me.

"Where does this come out on the other side?" she asked through her mic.

"Let's find out."

I kicked the speed up a little more, following the GPS toward what looked like a road.

As we emerged from the forest, we found a field of baled hay and an old wooden fence with several missing posts.

A massive grain silo sat in the distance, along with several outbuildings.

"Farm," I explained.

She peered around me. "They grow grain here?"

"Yup. During World War II, Maine was called the breadbasket of New England because of all the grain it grew for the war effort. Most of these farms grow barley. It's good for livestock feed, and the really good stuff gets sold to craft brewers."

We zipped around the edges of the property toward where the trail signs pointed back to the forest. So far we'd seen nothing out of the ordinary.

But when Mila squeezed my thigh hard, my hackles rose.

"Jude, look at all those trucks."

As I turned back to the farm, several black SUVs pulled up in front of one of the old buildings.

"Just cars, Trouble," I said, shaking off the strange sensation.

"So hordes of blacked-out luxury SUVs usually congregate at rural barley farms?" she asked, her tone dripping with sarcasm. "Get closer. I wanna take a look."

"No."

She punched my shoulder hard enough to have me lurching forward. "We came all the way out here. Stay in the forest, but go around the other way. I just want to see."

Grumbling, I pulled into the forest and found a path deeper through the trees. I kept my speed slow to keep the sound of the engine subdued and so she could get a good look.

"Keep going."

The trail ended near the road fifty yards or so from the parking lot. I stopped inside the tree line, hopefully out of sight.

"They're all wearing sunglasses." Mila huffed out a laugh. "And one is wearing a suit. Loop back around. I wanna take photos of the license plates."

"You will not," I hissed. "They'll hear us snooping around. This thing is not quiet."

"Just one more loop," she pleaded. "Go really slow. If I see anything fishy, head to the forest and drive like hell."

"Fine."

Despite my better judgment, I headed back in for another loop. At the entrance, I zeroed in on a posted sign, studying the marked paths. "Let's take this blue trail, see if we can find a better angle."

I took a hard left and drove up a small hill that gave us a better vantage point while still possessing enough tree cover to provide protection.

With a gentle squeeze, she said, "Slow down."

Once I'd hit flat ground again, I reduced the speed and focused on keeping steady while she inspected the goings-on.

"I see motorcycles," she hissed. "Looks like the assholes from the Ape Hanger." Her body shifted behind me.

"Hold on. Can you pull up behind that bunch of trees and stop?"

Following her orders, I pulled behind a wide oak, but kept the engine running.

She hopped off the back and crept toward the edge of the trees, easing her phone from her pocket as she went. For several seconds, she stood still, snapping photos.

As she mounted the ATV again, she said, "I zoomed in. The black Tahoe has government plates."

"Fed?"

"I think so. And isn't it strange that small-town biker criminals and federal agents are hanging out at a random out-of-the-way farm?"

Without responding, I headed back to the main trail. When we were far enough away that I was certain they wouldn't hear the motor, I gunned it, speeding out of there like a bat out of hell. I wanted no part in whatever was happening on that farm. The ride home was bumpy, cold, and terrifying. My sole focus was getting Mila back into the safety of my house.

When the ATV was parked and we'd dismounted, I grasped the back of her jacket and shut the door, trapping her inside.

"Ow. Jude, relax."

"I will not relax," I growled, backing her against the wall. "This is officially insane. We've got the evidence, Mila. You've done an amazing job. It's over now. We call Parker and hand it all over. She's qualified to go get the bad guys."

She stomped her foot. "But we now know the feds are in on it!"

"Maybe. Even more reason to get her involved. Or maybe they're investigating."

She shot me a glare. "Don't be naïve. I knew they were dirty."

Fuck. Annoyance flared to life in my veins. I'd been in over my head since the night she walked into my house bleeding, but this was getting too close for comfort.

"Mila, I need to say something and you're gonna listen."

She was holding her helmet to her chest, her face burning with anger, her eyes murderous.

"You are reckless and impetuous and fucking incredible. I can't do this anymore. I can't let you put yourself in danger. You may not like it, but I'm in this with you now."

She nodded, her jaw still clenched tight.

"The thought of you getting hurt or being in danger is so crushing I feel like I can't breathe. Maybe this is a danger bang to you. Maybe that's all I am in your eyes." My heart clenched at the thought, but I had to say it. "But you mean something to me. You are important to me."

"Jude."

I held up a hand. "Let me finish. You owe me nothing. But like it or not, you're mine to protect."

She gasped, her eyes widening.

"And I will protect you."

She pulled her arm back and threw her helmet at me. "I don't belong to anyone. There is one thing I care about, and it's getting justice for Hugo."

Her words stung, and I took a step back, reeling from the rejection. I couldn't be the only one feeling this way. And yet...

Her eyes flared with anger. "I owe you for all you've done. And I'm so grateful, but we've got to end this."

"Stop," I said, holding up a hand. "We need to be strategic."

She put her hands on her hips, glaring at me. "You need to stop being so bossy." She was shouting now, and I couldn't stop myself from shouting back.

"Then stop almost getting yourself *killed*," I replied as I straightened again. "I need you. Your mom needs you. Hugo needs you. Stop punishing yourself and think about this. What you've done is remarkable. Let's take the next logical step."

I braced for her to find another object to hurtle at me. To yell or stomp off.

The last thing I expected was for her to burst into tears.

"Okay," she said, tears streaming down her cheeks.

This was the second time she had cried today, and it was just as painful for me as the first. Like my heart was being ripped apart. All I wanted to do was make this woman smile and laugh, and yet I caused her constant tears.

I pulled her into my body, reveling in the feeling of her being safely tucked in my arms.

"You're right," she said. "I'm so scared and so tired."

I held her tightly. "Tomorrow," I said into her hair. "I'll call Parker and set up a meeting. You can share everything, show her the maps. She'll make a plan. There's enough here for several warrants at the very least."

She nodded into my chest. "Do you really think this could be over soon?"

My heart tightened painfully. "Yes, Trouble. I know it."

Chapter 34
Mila

After a morning of anxious cuddles, Jude headed to work to inform his siblings and call Parker.

It was time. I'd done my part. Now we would hand things over to the police and the prosecutors. Parker was a good cop and had connections from her state police days. It would be okay. I kept repeating that to myself. It would be okay because it had to be okay.

My job for the morning was to finish digitizing all the evidence. I'd organize folders and ensure we included everything law enforcement needed. Then I'd make copies and save it all to a secure cloud-based drive for potential future use. This way I could hopefully help make sure the chain of custody was clear for the trials that would happen for what was likely to be the next several years.

A calm I hadn't experienced in years had set in. Maybe it was this house and the beautiful forest. Maybe it was the man who lived here. Regardless, after years of pushing, I finally felt like I could stand still for a minute. In fact, I felt like maybe I wanted to stand still.

As I crossed one more task off my list, I rolled my neck. Pain shot up my shoulder, reminding me I should put my sling back on. I'd progressed to going without it several times a day. I hated being injured, but the measurable progress helped keep me from wallowing in self-pity. And in some ways, maybe I was the tiniest bit grateful for it. After all, the injury had brought me here, to Jude, and if he hadn't insisted on working with me, I never would have made it this far.

Suddenly Ripley, who had been lying on the floor by my feet, jumped up and growled.

Startled by her abrupt change in demeanor, I stood and padded to the window where she stood at full attention, her hackles raised. I drew back the shade and scanned the yard, but found nothing out of the ordinary.

Just as I'd chalked it up to a squirrel, I caught the sound of a low rumble. With every second I stood there, it got louder until there was no denying it was the roar of motorcycle engines.

My heart took off at a sprint and panic flooded my veins. Had they found me?

Hand shaking, I closed my laptop and grabbed my phone. Then I headed for the kitchen door, where I shoved my feet into my shoes and grabbed one of Jude's jackets. Ripley remained at my side the entire time. When the noise was deafening, I crouched and peered out the window.

Sure enough three bikes were parked in the driveway, as well as a van with *Phobos Management* emblazoned on the side. The name, I was almost certain, belonged to one of the Huxley's shell companies.

My lungs seized, making it impossible to breathe. Hands

shaking, I sat on the ground, dropping my head between my knees.

They had found me. After weeks of hiding, I'd finally become hopeful that we'd make it out of this. Yet they'd tracked me down. My first thought was Jude. Was he hurt? In danger? I couldn't even contemplate it.

For so long, I'd been doing it all on my own. And that was a risk I'd been willing to take. But Jude?

I looked at Ripley, who was watching me, her big doggie eyes full of concern. With my good hand, I stroked her fur. Only then, when I focused on the softness of each strand, could I take a full breath again. My mind cleared, and instantly, I knew we had to go. I could do it. I could escape again.

They were still in the driveway, so if we slipped out the kitchen door, the woodshed would block their view.

From there, I could head into the forest. I knew the trails well after walking them with Ripley and Jude for the past few weeks. I pulled Jude's jacket tighter around me, hugged the laptop to my chest, and gently turned the doorknob.

"Okay, girl," I whispered to Ripley. "We're gonna make a run for it. Straight to the woodshed, okay?"

As I pushed the door open a crack, it squeaked slightly, but the engine noise from the driveway was surely loud enough to drown it out.

"Let me go first," I said to her.

Eyes closed, I took a deep breath. Then I slipped out the door and motioned for her to follow.

I was safely behind the woodshed when they dismounted and walked up the porch steps. There were more of them now, and a black SUV had pulled in behind the row of bikes.

When I peeked around the corner, Razor was banging on the door while a few of the other guys were circling the house.

Shit. The tree line was close, but not close enough. Probably twenty yards. But it was open grass, and they'd see me. My hands shook as I tried to find cover.

I squeezed my eyes closed and prayed for some kind of distraction.

As I scanned the woods, my gaze snagged on a dark pair of eyes at the edge of the trees. My heart stopped. Holy shit. It was a moose. A big bull, by the look of it. Frozen, we stared at one another and I swear I saw a glimmer of recognition in his massive dark eyes.

And then he was running, full speed toward the driveway, his thousand pound frame cutting intimidatingly across the grass. As he came out into the open, the telltale scar across his flank became visible.

Clive.

I let out a long breath. Maybe sharing the carrots with him wasn't a bad idea after all.

As he barreled out of my line of sight, the men broke into panicked shouts.

This was it. My only chance.

Crouching low and clutching the laptop to my chest, I ran as fast as I could down the hill toward the tree line. Halfway there, I glanced over my shoulder. Several guys had taken off on their bikes while others were still stomping around the front of the house.

Even a big tough biker was terrified of a giant bull moose, and with good reason.

As I got close to the edge of the forest, I waved at Ripley. Like the incredible companion she was, she darted down the path.

I could hear shouts and crashing noises from the front of the house. It sounded like Clive had knocked over the row of bikes parked out front and was causing all kinds of mayhem.

Relief washed over me as I crouched behind a fallen oak. We'd gotten out.

That put me into overdrive. I took off, stumbling down the path, avoiding the main trail to the state park and veering off toward the mountains. They'd be less likely to look for me in these dense woods. Ripley followed, quietly traversing the rough terrain with a lot more ease.

I tripped a few times but didn't fall and didn't reinjure my arm—a small miracle, I was sure. Thank fuck I'd grabbed Jude's jacket. The chilly air stung my face as I ran.

Stopping to catch my breath under a thick canopy of trees, I dropped to my knees and let out the sob I'd been holding on to.

They'd found me.

There was a good chance this was the end.

I had to warn Jude. Signals were weak out here, but I'd have to take a shot.

TROUBLE:

Guys showed up at the house. I ran out the back with Ripley and the laptop. In the woods now. Warn your family. Call Parker.

When my phone vibrated in my hand immediately, I

sent up a silent thanks to the entities listening but declined the call. I couldn't risk talking on the phone right now.

LUMBERSNACK:

What the hell is going on? Are you safe?

TROUBLE:

Yes. Hiding out in the woods. warn everyone!

LUMBERSNACK:

Okay. Where are you? I'll come get you.

TROUBLE:

I stayed off the main trail and went up toward Mountain Spring.

LUMBERSNACK:

Drop a pin, find cover, and stay warm. I'm leaving now.

TROUBLE:

Don't worry about me. Protect your family and call Parker.

LUMBERSNACK:

You are my family. I'm coming for you.

I made my way farther into the densest part of the forest in this area and found a small copse of downed trees that provided a decent wind break. Once I ensured the ground was dry, I sat. I'd barely gotten settled when Ripley curled up next to me on the hard ground and put her head on my lap.

With a deep breath in, I dropped a pin. Then I hugged my knees to my chest, wrapping Jude's coat around me while Ripley huddled next to me for warmth.

This was my fault. I'd gotten too comfortable. I'd been

playing Scrabble and eating pizza while my brother was in a hospital bed. I'd let my guard down and let Jude in. And now he was in the crosshairs too.

My feelings for him were mixed up with a dangerous cocktail of guilt and uncertainty. As much as we'd fantasized about riding off into the sunset together, or at least lounging on a Hawaiian beach together, that was not going to happen.

And I had to prepare myself for that.

By the time he arrived on an ATV that looked like a tiny pickup truck, I was a sobbing, freezing mess.

"It's okay." He pulled me close and held me for a long moment, letting me cry into his chest. "You're safe."

"But we're not. They know, and they went into your house. There's no way they didn't find the evidence wall, and now everyone is in danger."

"Shh." He opened the ATV's tailgate and patted the bed, and Ripley jumped in. "We're gonna be okay. Parker's on it. My brothers are on it. You and me? We're getting out of here."

My heart stuttered. "There's nowhere we can go where they won't find us," I hiccupped. "I'm as good as dead, and we've lost the element of surprise."

"Trouble," Jude said, cupping my cheeks and staring deep into my eyes. "We're in this together. Until the end. And I will not let anything happen to you. Now get in. We've got a flight to catch."

Chapter 35
Mila

Jude drove through a section of the woods I'd never seen before. The whole way, as we jumped over tree roots and drove through streams and over rocks, I sat stiffly beside him.

Ripley was in the back, unbothered by the terrain.

"Where are we?" I asked.

"Almost to work. Gus will drive us to the lake."

"The lake?" I shouted over the roar of the engine.

"Yeah," he hollered in response. "We're lucky Finn hasn't taken the pontoons off the plane."

I had no idea what he was talking about, but I wasn't going to bother asking. I was just glad he was here. This situation was far bigger than I could handle on my own.

We pulled up to Hebert Timber headquarters, and without slowing, Jude drove straight into a massive garage bay. A large, intimidating guy stood inside with his arms crossed and his feet planted shoulder-width apart. He was thick and tall and wore a flannel shirt. That, when combined with his dark beard, gave him a Paul Bunyan vibe.

Jude killed the engine and hopped out. "Gus."

Ah, Gus. The oldest. I'd heard about him. The family resemblance was there. The same blue eyes and the same broad shoulders.

I climbed out, only then noticing a large van parked in the next bay.

Gus gave me a polite nod, then turned back to his brother. "Got everything you asked for." His voice was a low rumble, like he didn't use it a whole lot. "You should be set for a bit while things calm down."

He pulled Jude into a hug and clapped him on the back.

"We'll be okay here. Won't we, girl?" Gus bent down and rubbed Ripley's ears.

Frowning, I locked eyes with Jude.

"She's gotta stay here," he said, putting his arm around me. "Gus will take good care of her."

The thought of leaving Ripley, the dog who had probably saved my life today, made me dizzy.

Gus stood and held out a hand the size of a bear paw to me. "Thank you. You've done so much."

I took it, at a loss for what he was referencing. "Me?" I squeaked.

"Parker's upstairs with my wife, going through your files. Thinks she can get a judge to issue warrants in a few days. We may finally see these guys taken down."

I let out a breath I didn't know I was holding. The past few hours had been a blur.

Jude stepped up beside me. "Mila is brilliant," he said, giving me a squeeze, "but we've gotta run."

"Hop in," Gus said. "Stay in the back. We don't want you to be seen."

Confused as hell, I moved on autopilot, following Jude to the van and letting him help me into the back. Ripley joined us, sticking close to me. Inside, there were giant backpacks, water jugs, and several other random items.

"Where are we going?" I asked as Jude held a granola bar out to me.

"Off grid for a bit." He wrapped his arms around Ripley and buried his face in her fur. "I love you, girl," he whispered. "You did good today. We're so proud. Uncle Gus is making you a big steak tonight. And we'll be home soon."

Ripley put her head on his lap, eyes fixed on his face, and let him stroke her fur.

The ride to Lake Millinocket was bumpy but blessedly short. Gus drove down the service road, and as he approached the flight dock, he glanced at us in the rearview mirror.

"Stay in the van," he said. "Finn is going through his preflight checklist."

I peered around the driver's seat and surveyed the area.

At the end of the wide dock, a plane on pontoons floated in the water. A man who might have been even taller than Gus walked around the aircraft with a clipboard and a flashlight. He wore a flight suit and was rocking an impressive man bun.

This was all too much. "Jude," I whispered, sitting back, "I'm scared."

He scooted over, pulling me into his chest. "I'm scared too. But we've got this. You and I will be safe, and my family will handle everything here."

"Won't they follow us?" I looked around, searching for black SUVs or motorcycles. I didn't know the area well, but beyond the small park, there was a church steeple and what looked like a main street filled with shops. This was hardly lying low.

"Where we're going, they can't follow." He stroked my cheek. "I've got you. I promise you. I'll keep you safe."

I opened my mouth, my first instinct to argue. Instead, I leaned in, kissing him softly. His presence was grounding, his voice soothing. His words made me believe that maybe this was possible, despite the constant stream of doubts.

The back doors opened, startling me. Then Gus appeared, the pilot at his side.

"I'm Finn," he said with what I can only describe as a devastating smile.

Jesus, what was with this family? They possessed some tall, strong lumberjack genes.

"Here." He threw two dark hoodies and baseball caps at us. "Put these on and stay here. Gus and I will load the supplies, then I'll need to recheck weight."

He and Gus grabbed the backpacks, plastic totes, and water jugs, lifting them as if they weighed nothing, and headed off. Two trips later, the van was cleared out.

When he'd finished his weight check, Finn returned, wearing a broad smile. "Okay, lovebirds, Marge is ready for you."

Once we'd donned our hoodies and ball caps, we jogged down the dock, waving to Gus and Ripley. When we reached the aircraft, Finn lifted me up into the side door like I was a child.

"Headset is on your seat. Sit in the middle. We've got to stay balanced," he said as Jude swung himself into the passenger seat and slid his headset on like a pro.

Feeling like a deer in headlights, I dropped into the seat.

Finn gave me a big smile. "Just sit tight and enjoy the ride. People pay big money for these views." With that, he shut the tiny door and walked around the plane, giving it one more inspection.

He climbed in, started the engine, and toggled all kinds of switches. He followed that up with pressing a series of buttons. I sat frozen in my seat, focused solely on breathing.

I'd flown in more than one small plane and had experienced a few very bumpy flights, so this wasn't new to me, but the shock of the day had officially swamped me, making it difficult to digest any of this.

"Ready?" Finn asked through his headset as the sound of the propeller became deafening.

Jude gave him a thumbs-up, so I did the same, and then we were off, gliding over the water as we picked up speed.

The nose lifted, and my stomach clenched in response. In seconds, we'd accelerated further, and the next thing I knew, we were in the air.

As Finn circled around the lake, I took in the view. Gus stood on the edge of the dock, waving. Ripley stood beside him, her nose in the air.

The sight of her made my heart pang. I already missed her.

Within minutes we were out of town, soaring over the endless miles of forest. The sky was bright blue, and beyond the green ocean of pines, wild foliage grew. Thousands of trees and leaves in every shade of red, yellow, and orange dispersed throughout the dense canopy.

We soared and swooped across mountains and rivers,

with nothing but vast wilderness spread out in front of us. It was breathtaking.

After forty minutes, we began to descend. It was a bit nerve-racking, given the size of some of the trees, but Finn seemed completely at ease.

He banked right, and a large, glittering lake came into view. The water was bright blue, and a dock that looked newly built stood out against the wild backdrop. It was alone out here. There wasn't a house, a road, or a boat to be seen.

Finn circled twice before reducing speed and touching down with precision on the glassy surface. We taxied a bit to reduce speed before he steered toward the dock.

When we were close, Jude climbed out and stood on the wing of the plane. And when we approached the dock, he jumped onto its wooden boards. While he tied off, Finn flipped all his switches and read his instruments.

"Where are we?" I asked as Jude opened the door and hit me with a devastating smile.

"Paradise." Finn's grin looked so much like his brother's. "Also known as Big Eagle Lake."

Jude helped me down, then went straight to the cargo hold and began unloading. I followed, grabbing one of the backpacks as he picked up a gas can and a large axe. We piled the supplies on the dock, and when it looked like we had everything, Finn handed Jude a clunky satphone.

"It's charged. Should be good for a week. As agreed, check in at eight every morning. We'll give you updates then."

With a nod, Jude clipped the phone to his belt. "Thanks."

Finn, hands on his hips, turned to me. "You're in good hands. No one knows the woods like Jude."

"Will you come pick us up?" I asked.

How long were we expected to stay here? It was beautiful, but the weather had taken a turn lately. It was already freezing, and the nights would be almost frigid. While I was no stranger to roughing it, I certainly wasn't used to being completely alone in the woods.

"When you're ready," he said. "Call me anytime."

He gave us a salute and then swung his giant frame back into the cockpit.

Jude waited for his signal, then untied the line. Then Finn was off, zipping across the water before taking flight. Leaving us alone in the wilderness.

It was then that I officially couldn't take it anymore. I was scared and tired and hungry.

"What the fuck is going on?" I shouted, the words echoing off the nearby trees.

Jude, who'd picked up a gas tank, set it down again.

"Tell me the truth. I'm freaking the fuck out over here. You rescued me from bad guys in the woods and then threw me on a plane, and now we're in the middle of bumfuck nowhere. Are we even in America right now?"

"Yes. We are in the state of Maine," he replied far too calmly. "This lake is on the Gagnons' land. It's remote, without any proper roads."

He pointed at a shed at the end of the dock.

"For years they would camp up here. They'd keep emergency supplies in the shed. Now that they're all married with kids, they prefer the small cabin they recently built."

"Apparently Finn was planning to fly Henri and Alice

out here for a night, so the plane was ready. According to him, they come out here about this time every fall to celebrate some anniversary. So he checked in with them and brought us instead. My brothers gathered supplies, and Chloe and Parker are working through all the evidence you put on the drive."

He hefted a pack onto his back, then picked up the axe and the gas can again.

"Let's take some of this stuff inside. It's a short walk up this path." He gestured ahead. "We'll get you warm and fed and talk about everything."

With a nod, I shouldered the other large backpack. Instantly, my shoulder screamed.

Jude reached for it, but rather than passing it over, I adjusted it so it was balanced evenly, then picked up a tote bag and a water jug. My shoulder was fucked, and there was no going back now.

Silently, we walked up the dock and around the shed. Sure enough, about fifty yards from the shore was a small cabin. Made of dark wood with a green metal roof and two small windows in front, it looked like something out of a fairy tale.

It was one large room, with a small kitchenette equipped with a tiny table and two chairs, a large wood stove, and a queen-size bed.

A small loveseat sat in the middle of the space, facing the oversized back window.

A small bookshelf was filled with dogeared paperbacks, and pretty landscape paintings hung on the walls. There were lacy curtains and candles on the table. It was quaint and new and so much more than I expected.

"There's a bathroom through there," he said, pointing to a narrow door next to the kitchen. "Pump shower and a cassette toilet."

I dropped the backpack, rubbing my shoulder. "This is nice."

He nodded. "Told ya. It's the Gagnons' little escape. They come out here for romantic trips."

I couldn't help but smile. That was strangely sweet.

"I turned the electricity on. They've got solar and a battery bank, so the lights should work. The fridge takes a while to get cold, though. Water heater takes even longer."

He hefted a cooler onto the countertop and began unpacking bags.

"How long?" I dropped onto the small couch, massaging my aching shoulder. "How long do we need to stay here?"

He took the satphone off his belt and placed it in the middle of the table.

"Not sure. Probably a couple of days. It's not so bad."

"It's not that. I'm worried about everyone." Dread formed in my gut like a lead ball. "And my mom and Hugo."

He waved a hand. "Parker talked to the Boston police. They will have a detail at the hospital and with your mother."

My heart lodged itself in my throat. "How?"

With a shrug, he set a roll of paper towels and olive oil in a cabinet. "I told you. Owen knows people."

I stood, desperate to move. Otherwise my anxiety would overwhelm me. I unpacked sheets and towels, several sets of warm clothes, and plenty of food. The cooler was stocked with steaks and a bottle of champagne. Clearly Henri and Alice had big plans for the evening.

Jude led me out the door and around the back to a tiny woodshed and a small firepit made of large stones. He brought an armload of wood inside and got the stove lit.

"You rest," he said. "I'll finish setting up and make food."

"Have you been here before?" I asked, a tiny twinge of jealousy catching in my throat. Had Jude brought dates up here for romantic rendezvous?

"Never," he said. "Finn told me about it."

"You seem to know what to do."

He shrugged. "I've spent a lot of time in the woods. Usually in outposts and camps that are half as nice as this. But in the end, they're all pretty much the same. It's not a big deal."

It felt like a big deal as I watched him get the stove going, unpack groceries, and make the bed with fresh sheets and a fluffy blanket.

For so long I'd been alone. When the shit hit the fan, I had no one but myself. But now, I had Jude and his family and, hopefully, the police on my side. That knowledge made this whole ordeal a little less terrifying.

Later that night, after feasting on Henri and Alice's chocolate covered strawberries and cuddled up under several layers of blankets, my fear began to fade.

"Thank you," I said, burying my face in his chest.

"I told you I'd do anything to protect you." He tucked my hair behind my ear. "And I meant it. You are brave and passionate and infuriatingly reckless. But you're mine. And no one hurts my girl."

That single word hung in the air. *Mine.*

It felt like too much and too little at the same time. My

pulse quickened. What did that admission mean? And was I ready for it?

Before I could spiral out, Jude kissed my forehead and pulled the blanket up. "Stop overthinking, Trouble. I'll spare you the time. You are mine. We'll get out of this, and afterward, I'll do anything and everything you want."

Eyes closed, I let the warmth of his body and his words comfort me, praying with everything I had that he was right.

Chapter 36
Jude

I left Mila fast asleep in the cabin and went outside to take stock. This was an incredible spot. If only we weren't hiding from murderous criminals, it would make for a cozy, romantic getaway.

I didn't spend much time thinking about romance. Never had. But with Mila, I was beginning to crave it. Traveling with her, laughing and spending nights wrapped around one another. All of it.

But today was not the day for dreaming. Right now I had to stay focused and keep her safe.

I turned on my satphone and strolled to the end of the dock to ensure I got the best reception. Then I dialed Gus. Hopefully he would have good news.

"Jude. We're working on it," he said in lieu of a greeting.

"What's happening?" It was chilly, and the sun was only barely above the horizon.

"Parker is digging in, making calls to state police and FBI contacts."

I clenched my fist. Making calls was not going to cut it. It was the eleventh of October. If Mila was right, something big was going down in two days. We couldn't risk it.

"The district attorney's office has a team working on it too. They're putting a case together to get some of the higher-ups."

"Huxley?"

"Unsurprisingly, bringing down Huxley is going to take a lot of political juice, but warrants for some of the lower-level players should be issued later today, and they plan to move right away. Possibly tonight or tomorrow morning."

Eyes closed, I pinched the bridge of my nose. This was progress, yes, but it wasn't enough. I wanted every thug that had come to my house behind bars and every higher-up who'd ever even considered harming a hair on Mila's head in jail.

"If they rush, this could all fall apart. You know that."

I did. But Mila had served this up on a silver platter for them.

Once we'd ended the call, I picked up a big rock from the shore and threw it as far as I could, desperate to work through the frustration and fear building up inside me. I wanted to be better. Hell, I should be better.

At the sound of the splash, several birds flew out of one of the towering trees. Great, I was even pissing off the wildlife.

I trudged back to the cabin, focused on digging out the instant coffee packets I'd seen. They could be expired for all I cared. *Cabin* was a generous word for this tiny structure. But it was cozy and warm and new.

I thought of the Gagnons—the family my father had taught us to hate—and sighed. Yet another thing he'd been wrong about. They weren't the enemy. They were good people who cared deeply about the forest and the town.

They were all settled down too. They'd celebrated marriages and children and all sorts of milestones. In addition to being blissfully happy, several of them were probably pretty exhausted. Hence the need for a hidden forest getaway.

Anger continued to bubble up inside me as I strode down the dock. After working so hard for so long, being out of the loop felt like torture. I trusted Parker and I trusted my family. But given what we were up against, I needed to be more involved.

As I stepped off the dock and around the shed, I saw her.

She was out by the woodpile, dressed in sweats and my flannel shirt, watching me.

I couldn't help but smile. She was so damn beautiful.

And she was mine.

There was no use fighting it or pretending otherwise.

Mine.

That word, as incredible as it was, instantly sent me spiraling.

What if I couldn't protect her? What if I couldn't be the man she needed me to be?

She jogged over to me and launched herself into my arms, vanquishing my self-doubt. I held her tight and buried my nose in her hair.

"I woke up and got scared," she said into my chest.

Pulling her closer, I closed my eyes and soaked in the feel of her body against mine.

"I can't believe I said that," she mumbled.

"Why?"

"Because I don't say things like that. I never admit weakness."

I angled back and tucked a short strand of dark hair behind her ear. "It's not weak. It's honest. And sometimes the bravest thing you can do is be honest."

She opened her mouth and then closed it again, her eyes searching mine.

There was a lot to say here. More than I could probably articulate.

But the weariness that had weighed on me even moments ago was gone. "I'm scared too," I said. "But you make me brave, Trouble. You inspire me."

"I feel so guilty dragging you into my mess."

I kissed the top of her head. "Most days I don't feel much. I do the things I have to do and try to enjoy my life. But for so long, there wasn't a single thing that could tear me out of bed in the morning. Nothing that felt like fire shooting through my veins."

I took a breath. It was time to be brave.

My heart pounded in my ears as I willed myself to say the words. "But now I've got something. There's one thing in my life these days that lights me up. You."

She gasped, her muscles contracting in surprise.

"When I'm with you, I'm hit with emotions I never thought I was capable of, and I want things I didn't even realize existed. You woke me up, Trouble. I'm here because I believe in you and I'm in love with you."

She pulled back, eyes wide and lips parted in surprise.

"You love me?" she whispered.

Face breaking into what I could only imagine was a ridiculous smile, I nodded. "Yes. I know it's fast and crazy and we're out in the middle of the woods, but I have no interest in hiding it. You make me want to be honest and wild."

"I like you wild." She gave me a much more subdued smile as she pulled me down for a kiss.

I cupped her face, lingering in the moment. I needed the contact, the connection with her.

"I think I love you too," she said as we finally pulled back.

"You think?"

She wrapped her arms around herself and shivered. "Yes. I think. I might be more certain if there was coffee." She gave me a wink.

I picked her up and threw her over my shoulder, then jogged to the cabin.

"I'll brew you the best wilderness coffee of your life, Trouble."

Chapter 37
Jude

The supplies for Henri and Alice's romantic getaway were more than sufficient. Perhaps the rose petals were a bit much, but as I was quickly entering my romantic sap era, I decided that maybe it was kind of adorable. By day two, we were starting to get bored waiting for updates.

We sipped coffee at the outdoor fire pit and hiked in search of the perfect marshmallow roasting sticks so we could roast the pink marshmallows we'd found in one of the gear bags.

"Figures you'd be a great marshmallow roaster." Mila licked a glob of the sticky substance off her fingers. "You've got the perfect slow rotation for equal browning."

I admired my creation. Yes, it was just lightly browned, the sugar oozing and crusting on the outside.

"While you stick yours in the fire and char 'em beyond recognition."

She shrugged, putting another on her stick. "I stand by my methods. Delicious and efficient."

She leaned against me on the log that had been cut to provide a bench, and I wrapped one arm around her, inhaling the fresh mountain air.

"I've spent my whole life chasing adventure," she said. "Yet now that I'm living the plot of a heist movie, I want to be normal."

I wasn't sure how to respond. There were plenty of parts of my old, boring life that I enjoyed, but I'd be lying if I said I wanted to go back to that. Because every moment with Mila was better than even the best alone. Every one was worth the risk, the fear, and the danger.

"I can't even think about it. I'm too scared. Let's pretend to be normal people."

I kissed the top of her head. "Okay, Trouble. So we're here on a romantic weekend date."

"You flew me out on a floatplane for a date?"

With a chuckle, I gave her a squeeze. "Anything for my girl."

"Okay." She sank into me, her body relaxing. "Tell me more."

"I'd cook for you, take you on hikes, and then wrap you in the down comforter and go down on you for hours."

She shivered, her eyes dancing in the glow of the campfire. "I love the sound of that."

"If I really wanted to pull out all the stops, I'd gas up the ATV in the shed and take you out to the wildflower meadow."

"What's that?"

"Back in the '70s, there was a massive wildfire. Took out hundreds of acres of forest. They aren't always a bad thing. Fires clear forests and provide an ecological reset. They also release a lot of seeds that grow and scatter and flourish in the nutrient-dense soil."

She hummed. "I had no idea."

"We have photos in the office. I'll show you sometime. Fireweed comes first, and then other species. Eventually shrubs and saplings. But sometimes, when an area burns, wildflowers take over. It's called a superbloom."

"Superbloom? I love that." She turned, her hair tickling my cheek, and peered up at me.

"The area is called Sinistre Nord. We own part of it, but it's mostly state land."

She frowned, considering the words. "That means the disaster in the north, right?"

"Yeah, something like that. My grandfather used to talk about it all the time."

"And it's all wildflowers?"

"No, a lot of the forest has grown back since then, but one meadow that abuts a lake is still a rolling sea of flowers."

"Another lake?"

I pressed my lips to her head. "Yeah, another one of those inaccessible Maine gems. We'll go soon. I promise."

She sat up straight, her body tensing, as if her consciousness had gone elsewhere.

"Mila?" I sat up too. "You okay?"

She shook her head. "Sorry. I just... I think I've heard that phrase before. Sinistre Nord," she said slowly. "But I'm tired and stressed. I'm probably imagining things."

"It's called ecological succession," I explained. "Growth and evolution after devastation."

"So the forest grows back?" She looked up at me, her

expression suddenly filled with fear. As if she was no longer talking about flowers.

I kissed her softly. "Not just that. It grows back stronger and healthier. Battle-tested, rising from the ashes. But different."

"So it looks different? Maybe different from the old maps and photos?"

I shrugged. "Probably."

Eyes flaring, she cupped my chin and brought her lips to mine.

"When will this end?" She sighed.

I looped my arm around her waist. "Soon. We'll come back from this. Stronger and better than ever. Because you, like my beloved forest, are pure wild."

She shifted and straddled me, grinding against my already hard cock. I pulled her close and peppered kisses down her jawline. She said nothing, yet her body begged me for distraction and comfort.

Right now, there was little I could do to better our situation. But I could give her this.

I ran my hands up her thighs as she ground down against my lap. My desires burned through me, making me wonder if I could last. The stress of the last few days and the quiet tranquility of the woods made me crave her even more.

She kissed me wildly, needing this as much as I did. She needed to get out of her own head, to let herself feel something other than fear.

"Do you want to go inside?" I asked as I unhooked the clasp of her bra.

She shook her head as I cupped her breasts, gasping. "Jude."

Her breathy voice sent blood rushing to my groin.

I pushed her to standing, assessing my options. It was cold, but we were both burning up. It only took me a moment to find a suitable place and back her up to a large pine tree. "Hold on."

I placed her hands on the tree trunk and dropped to my knees behind her, slowly easing her leggings down. She shivered as I pulled them down, inch by inch, peppering her skin with kisses.

She looked devastatingly sexy, her hair wild, her baggy sweatshirt giving me a peek of her ass, as she looked over her shoulder, licking her lips.

I got her leggings down to her ankles and guided her feet apart before trailing my fingers over her ass crack toward her pussy.

"Dripping." With a groan, I leaned in to taste her.

"Jude." She sighed, tilting her hips to give better access.

I slipped a finger inside, and she instantly clenched around it. "You need this?"

She nodded, her legs shaky.

"You need to come?"

"Yes. So badly."

While I finger-fucked her, I slid my free hand up her thigh and gave her a light swat.

She cried out, and her channel tensed around my finger again.

I rocketed to my feet and pushed my sweats down to release my aching cock. The need to bury myself inside her was overwhelming.

"Shit, I don't have a condom."

"I don't care. I've been tested."

My cock surged at the idea of sliding in bare. Filling her up and watching it drip out of her pussy. Fuck, I'd never had that particular fantasy, but now it was all I needed.

"So have I. Nothing on my end. Are you on birth control?"

"No."

Oh shit.

"Pull out." She commanded.

"That's not 100 percent effective," I reasoned. If I'd learned one thing in high school health class, it was condoms or nothing—no sex. Every time. But Mila made me want to bend the rules and get a little crazy.

"I'll take the chance." She arched back against me.

I slipped a second finger inside her, making her gasp, trying to block out the impact that statement had on me. The thought of taking her bare, the thought of potentially creating a child with her. It was more than I could ever hope for.

"I need your cock now."

It was risky, but I couldn't help myself.

Pulling her hips back, I lined myself up, and with my eyes closed, focused on every sensation, I thrust inside her bare.

"God, Mila." My body trembled, my nerve endings lighting up as I adjusted to the perfection that was her wet heat. "You feel so good."

In response, she moaned and rolled her hips.

Fuck, I had to move. Gripping her hips hard, I thrust into her, setting a rhythm. "Fucking you bare against a tree may be my new favorite thing."

"Harder," she cried, her nails digging into the bark. "Please."

I wouldn't deny her, but I was barely hanging on. Desperate for distraction and eager to get her as close to her release as I was, I spanked her again, a bit harder.

When she clenched around my cock, I almost passed out.

"You like that?" I said, giving her another spank.

"Yeah," she whimpered, head dropped to one side.

"Good." Another swat. "Tell me, Mila," I said, leaning back to assess the red mark I'd left on her ass. It was just visible in the firelight. "Who do you belong to?"

"You." She threw her head back and screamed. "I belong to you."

"Good girl."

As if spurred on by my praise, she thrust against me, her breathing growing more ragged.

I focused on deep, hard thrusts, soaking in the way her moans echoed off the trees.

"That's it." I groaned, fucking her faster. "You're so close I can feel it."

Soon she was crying out and pulsing around me. I spanked her again, hard, and she unraveled, her body quaking and nonsensical words spilling from her mouth.

I grit my teeth, intent on letting her ride out her orgasm. It was a miracle I didn't lose control, but as she came down, I pulled out and spilled myself all over her ass cheeks, a thrill coursing through me at the sight of my seed dripping down her still pink skin.

I'd never seen anything sexier in my life.

After cleaning her up and helping her back into her pants, I pulled her into my lap, burying my face in her hair.

"I love the woods," she said, as I peppered her face with kisses.

"You just like getting fucked up against a tree," I teased.

She cocked a brow. "Can we do it again sometime?"

"Of course. That's a white pine. But we should try out other species too."

"For science." She smirked.

"Yes. I mean, what if you come harder against a maple?"

She giggled. "Or a birch."

"Yes, Trouble." I tipped her chin up and stole a kiss. "We have a lot of research to do."

Chapter 38
Mila

The phone rang when we were eating the steaks Henri and Alice had packed. We'd skipped the champagne, too keyed up from our outdoor fuck-fest and the anxiety of waiting for news. We'd hiked and had a rock skipping competition in the lake to help pass the time.

If I wasn't so damn terrified, it would have been fun. Though it seemed impossible that anything could be hotter than Jude making pizza or chopping wood, the man here in his natural element absolutely was.

"What's happening?" I asked, looking out the window into the dark wilderness.

"This is Parker Gagnon. I'm sitting here with Agent Bryce Portnoy of the FBI and Sergeant Williams of the Maine State Police."

I let out an exhale, my shoulders sinking in relief. "Okay."

"Jude's family is here too. Ms. LeBlanc and Mr. Hebert."

"We're happy to report that through joint cooperation,

we've secured several arrest warrants. They'll be executed overnight."

"That's great news," Jude said.

As much as I wanted to be excited, apprehension still swirled in my stomach. "Did you arrest Charles Huxley?"

"At this time, there is no plan to seek his arrest," she said, her voice monotone and official.

"What the fuck?" I snapped.

Jude squeezed my good shoulder, but I pulled it away.

"Ms. Barrett, Sergeant Williams here." He cleared his throat. "Please understand there are nuances to this investigation."

Parker piped up. "We expect that several of the perpetrators, including those who broke into your home, will be in custody by tomorrow."

"We picked up someone who goes by the name Razor yesterday. He was driving while intoxicated in Heartsborough and provided some very helpful information to supplement your work," Sergeant Williams said.

I bit back a sardonic laugh. That wasn't surprising. Razor was not known for his discretion or his loyalty. But even he wasn't close enough to the top to be all that useful.

"This is Agent Bryce Portnoy with the FBI, assistant director of the Portland field office," a third voice said. "I want you to know that law enforcement has this well in hand. Great civilian work, of course. But..."

I froze as he continued to speak. That voice. Nasal and a bit high-pitched for a man. I'd never met him, but my hands shook and bile rose in my throat. It was familiar and not particularly comforting.

With a concerned frown, Jude squeezed my hand.

"You okay?" he whispered.

I nodded as I scanned the small cabin, looking for paper. Eventually, I settled for a piece of paper towel and a pencil that was perched on the windowsill. As they spoke, I furiously scribbled notes.

"Can you repeat that?" I asked sweetly, trying to get every detail down.

He obliged, though his tone remained borderline condescending.

"What are you doing about the shipment?" I asked. "Friday the thirteenth is tomorrow."

"We have no intel to confirm that a shipment of anything is coming," Portnoy continued.

Dread washed over me. "There was an exchange planned," I explained. "Drugs, guns, cash. They spoke in code, but I heard it with my own ears."

"Sources on the inside indicate they may have been spooked."

My stomach churned. No way. They'd been planning this for months. The Jason talk, the random mentions of the date, and discussions regarding meetings and shipments. This was too big. At the poker game, the number fifty million had been thrown around.

And his voice. It had set off an alarm bell in my brain. I couldn't parse out why. But I had the laptop and my phone. If I could keep this guy talking, maybe I'd figure it out.

Silently, I pointed at Jude's blue backpack, and he brought it over to me.

"How many warrants, Agent Portnoy?" I asked as I tapped on the icon for the voice recording app.

"Seven," Parker replied, her tone once again subdued.

Fuck, I needed him to speak.

"And more coming," Portnoy added. "At the bureau, we build our cases methodically."

That was bullshit. Only seven? "The conspiracy chart I provided had thirty-one players on it, going from top to bottom."

"You can't expect us to go out and arrest thirty-one people based solely on your hunches." His tone was dismissive.

While I gritted my teeth to hold back a retort, Jude clenched his fists.

I shook my head, warning him to let it go, then tapped the red button on my screen so I could record the sound of the FBI agent's voice.

"I provided evidence," I clarified. "And I understand the process and the fourth amendment considerations. But if only seven people are out, that leaves the other twenty-six to continue on with tomorrow's plan."

"There is no tomorrow," Bryce insisted. "We have no solid intel."

A chill ran down my spine. There was definitely a tomorrow. And it was something big. Arresting Razor would not change that. Men like Charles Huxley worked with precision. They would have planned for all kinds of scenarios. They would have backups.

"You did good, Mila," Parker said. "They're running scared. This is how we build cases. The wheels are in motion and justice will prevail."

As much as I wanted to believe her, my gut was telling me this wasn't over yet.

Parker, her tone a little more easy, said, "You can come home soon."

"As soon as possible," Portnoy cut in. "We need to question you. We can send a plane—"

"No." I needed more time to think. "We will call Finn and arrange a ride home. It's already dark here."

After another few minutes of conversation, we hung up. The minute the connection was severed, I pulled my laptop out of the backpack. "Where is the battery bank?"

Jude hopped to his feet. "On it."

We set up the computer and the phone on the small table and plugged both in. Then I played a recording from the poker game. Then another. I'd collected so many over the last year.

As the men on the recording talked about Friday the thirteenth while glasses and poker chips clinked in the background, I closed my eyes, taking myself back to that smoky room, envisioning the faces at the poker table, remembering the drink orders I'd filled.

After only minutes, I was overwhelmed with impatience. I stood and paced the small space, running my hands through my hair.

"It's still happening tomorrow," I said. "I know it in my bones."

"Let's call Parker."

I held up my hand, then turned to cross the room again. "Don't. She'll think I'm crazy. I need to think."

At the window, I spun around, only to find Jude blocking my path. He pulled me into his chest and pressed his lips to my crown. "Whatever it is, you will figure it out. You are brilliant."

His words ignited a tiny spark of hope in my chest.

I eased out of his hold. "Can we look at the maps of the restricted bat territory again?"

"Sure."

The laptop screen wasn't big, but we studied the map section by section, reviewing the most recent restrictions.

"Where was the fire?" I asked. "The Sinistre Nord."

Jude took off his glasses and used the hem of his shirt to clean them, shaking his head. "It's hard to say, looking at this map. But it was in the northern section of our land, bordering the state section."

"Is any of that area included in what's closed now?"

Squinting, he zoomed out, then in again.

"Possibly. The fire happened before I was born, but I do know it destroyed the old river road." He traced his finger along the river. "It ran right here."

"And that's one of the roads we suspect they're using now?"

"It would make the most sense, seeing as it's a direct shot to Sainte-Louise," he said. "Let's look at one of the big aerial maps."

He toggled around in my folders until he located it.

Once it had loaded, we studied it silently.

"Look," I said when I caught sight of the river trail. The more I thought about it, the more it made sense. "If you head west, you hit the border, where we know they're crossing to avoid detection." I traced my finger down the map on the screen, scrolling down. "And if you follow the river trail."

"Fuck." Jude roughed a hand down his face. "That's Pine Hollow Farm."

We looked at one another. Midway between the border

and the farm where we'd seen the SUVs was what we were looking for. The spot that had slowly been added to the bat protection zone.

"So the big road had been cleared, and then a fire took out the old-growth trees."

"Yes."

"And it's deep in the protection zone where no one would be allowed to drive?" I arched a brow. "This is the spot." I tapped the screen. "They created a network of roads and trails to transport drugs and God knows what else from Canada. The fire cleared a lot of the land, making more room for roads and potentially more."

Jude hummed. "So you're saying—"

"There's got to be a hub here. It's smack-dab in the middle of the protection zone. It's difficult to get to, and there are no caves anywhere. Look at the topography."

The light of the computer screen reflected off his lenses as he studied the map. "Yeah, definitely no caves for bats to nest."

"Exactly. So of all the hundreds of acres, this is the spot they wanted to protect. And we know why. It's a convenient midway point between the two destinations, and mother nature did some of the work by clearing the forest."

Sitting back, Jude frowned at me. "Why haven't the police or the FBI found it?"

"They're still under the impression that there are no roads there." I wiggled in my seat. There was more to it, but that was my gut instinct. "It's been two days. They aren't wasting resources by sending people hours into the woods. Not yet, at least."

"How far away is it?" I tapped the screen.

"On the ATV?"

I nodded.

He shook his head. "Far. If the trails are dry, maybe two or three hours?"

"Do we have enough gas to get there?"

"We have two full cans. So yes, we definitely have enough to get there. But we don't have enough to get back."

I considered his words as I studied the map again. If something was going down, this was where it would happen.

"What do we do?"

I thought about being chased by Razor and the other flunkies. I thought about poor Hugo in a coma in Boston and Jude's family being haunted for years.

And I knew what I had to do.

"I'm going there tomorrow," I said.

He lurched up in his seat. "*No.*"

I held up a hand. "I'm asking you to come with me. It's dumb and dangerous, but if we give up now, they may get away with this completely. I'll spend the rest of my life running and sleeping with one eye open."

"But—"

I squeezed his hands. "Jude, I love you and I want a future with you."

His dark blue eyes widened.

"But there is no future unless we end this."

"Together?" he asked, the single-word response surprising me.

I nodded. "Together. But..." I blew out a breath. "We may get killed in the process."

"I'm willing to risk it. I swore to protect you no matter the cost, and I will."

We needed a plan, some more time reviewing maps, and a way to get photos or videos that would send these fuckers away for good. "Are there any guns here?"

"There's a hunting rifle in the shed. It probably needs to be cleaned."

"Do you hunt?"

He shook his head. "There are bears out here. They mostly stay away, but it's better to be safe."

"Can you shoot?"

He scoffed. "A bear? Yeah, if I had to."

"How about people?"

His face paled. My sweet lumberjack was a lover, not a fighter. "If I have to."

I pushed up onto my tiptoes and kissed him. "Good. Make sure the ATV is gassed up and good to go. I've got to pull up some maps and make a plan."

"You sure we shouldn't get reinforcements first? The two of us can't take on a whole trafficking ring by ourselves."

He was right, of course. We couldn't take them all down, so we'd have to go undetected and observe. We'd only intervene if absolutely necessary. Based on the way he'd described the land, there were plenty of potential approaches and ample forest to keep us out of sight.

"I'm a woman. Which means I'm perpetually underestimated. And we're gonna take advantage of that." I stood. "Now let's get to work. This criminal enterprise isn't going to take itself down."

He wrapped an arm around me, squeezing my ass hard. "I fucking love you, Trouble."

Chapter 39
Jude

Insanity.

Outright insanity.

But she had asked me to help her.

She wasn't running off, trying to do it all on her own. I loved this woman and she loved me enough to let me in. To allow me to make this fight—her fight—mine too.

And damn if that didn't make my heart swell.

We'd spent the night plotting a course to the site and locating as many potential trails and roads to and from the area as we could.

If there was any chance in hell I could protect her, I would. Or I'd die trying.

Because Mila was my person.

It was stupid of me to fight it.

It was a certainty.

An eventuality.

We fell into bed in the middle of the night, and I watched over her as she tossed and turned.

Early in the morning, I crept out of the cabin. When I

got to the end of the dock, I turned on the satphone. I needed to talk to someone. Someone who would get it. Who understood what I was doing.

"You okay?" Gus asked, his voice hoarse.

"Sorry it's so early."

"Nah. No problem. Simone and I are snuggling on the porch while Chloe sleeps."

I smiled, thinking of my infant niece and how much my oldest brother had changed recently. It gave me hope that someday I could have those things too. I'd learned more about myself in the last few weeks than I had in the last few years. Mila pushed me and made me brave, and every day with her made me want more.

"Is something wrong? I thought you guys were going to fly home later today."

"Change of plans," I said, quickly catching him up.

"Fuck." He growled into the phone. "Parker is good at her job. She's got connections and resources. There is no way she missed this."

I'd thought the same thing. We trusted her. Though she had been kidnapped and shot at by our fucking father a few years ago, I couldn't imagine her willingly putting us in danger. She'd been helpful in the process of bringing this drug ring down, even if it was taking far too fucking long.

"Maybe they can't tell you guys," he reasoned. "Maybe the mission is top secret or some shit. They could be taking them down right now."

"I hope so. Regardless, we have to check. We have to know."

Dread settled in my stomach. This was a suicide mission. How could Mila and I—on a twenty-year-old ATV with one rusty rifle—fend off a sophisticated drug trafficking operation?

"Can you get proof undetected? You know the woods better than anyone."

Coming from Gus, that was high praise. The simple words gave me a much-needed confidence boost. "Yes. I think I can."

"Do you have supplies?"

I'd cleaned and oiled the old rifle stored in the shed, and I'd found one box of ammo. It was something, but nowhere near adequate protection.

We'd charged up the electronics and packed the laptop safely, and we had both phones ready for photos and videos. I'd also included flashlights, water, matches, and emergency blankets in case we got lost or stranded.

"Sort of," I admitted. "She figured it out: where they're coming and going, how they're getting around, and specifically, where the meetup point is."

"I wish you could wait."

"I can't. Something big is happening. If we don't go now, we'll lose our chance. And this is my fight now. I love Mila. I'm not letting her do this alone."

I could admit now that I'd been in love with Mila since the night she walked into my house, battered and bleeding, and I'd made sure to tell her, both with words and actions. But I hadn't said it out loud to anyone else. Doing so now felt liberating.

"I understand."

"You do?" I expected logical Gus to fight me, to argue that it was too soon. That I didn't know her.

"Of course I do. She's your person. You'd fight dragons for her."

I shook my head. This was a surreal conversation. "I would."

"Then I understand. I think it's insane and dangerous, and I'll be fucking terrified until you check in to tell me you're okay. But I get it."

My dad had been a nonfactor in my life for years, even when I worked for him. Gus had always stepped in to fill the void. His acknowledgment cemented my determination. This was my fight.

"She changed me," I admitted.

"The best ones always do."

"I was content—"

"Contentment is bullshit," he snapped. "It's a cop-out. You deserve more, Jude. You deserve risk and adventure and a love so intense you can't sleep at night."

The baby cried out softly, and his voice got muffled as he soothed her.

"Love is an adventure," he said a moment later, his words clear again. "Trusting your heart to someone else is one of the most dangerous things we will ever do in this life, but it's by far the best one. So I get it."

"Thank you." He was right. Loving Mila felt a hell of a lot scarier than bad guys with guns. But together we could withstand any challenge.

"You do what you need to do. Stay out of the way and then call me. If you need me to send Finn, I will. Or I can drive out myself in one of the big trucks. Did you charge the satphone?"

"Yes."

"Okay. Love you, brother. Don't fucking die."

"Don't plan on it." With a shake of my head, I ended the call. Then I turned back to the cabin and took a mental snapshot of this place. With any luck, Mila and I would return under better circumstances one day. With any luck, this would be a wild story we could tell our grandkids decades from now.

But first we had to survive the day.

Chapter 40
Mila

We dressed and packed up in silence, splitting a mug of instant coffee and a protein bar before loading our gear and the extra can of gas on the back of the ATV. There were no helmets, so our knit hats would have to do as protection from the elements. Speaking was impossible with the noise of the engine and the cold air whooshing past us. I was bundled up in almost every piece of clothing that had been packed for me. Jude was just as layered up. Freezing and exhausted, we made our way through the deep woods.

We stopped a couple of times for water and bathroom breaks and to stretch. Jude oriented himself with photos of the maps on his phone. We had no GPS out here, but he seemed to know exactly where we were going.

My shoulder ached fiercely as I clung to him, worrying I was wrong. Doubt had begun to seep in sometime in the middle of the night. And in the light of day, I was questioning everything. Had I missed important details? Was I drawing the wrong conclusions?

Jude pulled to the side of a wide gravel road and killed the engine. Then he hopped off and unlatched the gas can.

I stood to stretch as he topped off the tank.

"We're on the river road." He explained as he screwed the cap onto the can. "This is the border of the bat protection zone. Once we leave it, who knows what we'll find."

I blew out a long breath. This was it. We were going into enemy territory.

"Or," he said with a small shrug. "We can take this east, meet the Golden Road and make it to one of our camps."

He was giving me an out. A chance to change my mind.

While I appreciated it, it wasn't happening.

"We've come this far," I said.

He strapped the gas can back onto the ATV and stalked toward me, his eyes full of a mix of determination and dedication. As he approached, he pulled me into his arms and kissed the top of my head.

"I love you, Trouble."

"Love you too," I said, reveling in his warmth.

"Just like we planned, I'm going to circle around the old roads, see the condition. We do not get off the ATV unless we know it's safe. We're safer on this than we are on foot."

I nodded, hit with a flood of memories of being chased through the woods.

"We stick together."

"We go in together and we come out together," I said, pulling him down for a kiss, trying to fake confidence.

We got our phones out and powered them on. Once we'd double-checked that they were on silent—not that it was likely we'd have a signal, but one could never be too careful— we stashed them in zippered pockets so they'd be handy.

Jude would drive, and I would take as many photos as I could. The plan was to only get close enough to get the evidence we needed.

Back on the ATV, he revved the engine and patted my leg. Then we took off again, totally in the dark about what we might find.

We drove on narrow trails that were far more overgrown than any we'd been on yet. Jude had to navigate slowly around bulging tree roots and other debris as we made our way through. The canopy was so thick it blocked out almost all the sunlight, even though it was almost mid-day. About thirty minutes from the main road, as we approached what looked like a clearing, the sun started to peek through. But as we crested a small hill, it became clear that what we'd discovered was not a clearing at all.

Jude killed the engine and stared. In front of us was a road. An honest-to-goodness road. Wide, graded, and packed tight with gravel.

"This is not supposed to be here," he said, scanning the forest around us. "Are we in the right place?"

From our position on higher ground, we could see that the road extended far into the distance.

"And is that a roof?" he asked, digging out the binoculars.

He pointed at a piece of what had to be metal glinting in the sunlight.

"Fuck," he said, holding the binoculars out to me. "It's definitely metal."

I grabbed them and adjusted until I could clearly see the building ahead.

"Our outbuildings don't look like that," he explained. "We mostly build pole barns. For other structures, we use corrugated metal for roofing. Noisy but sturdy. Lightweight and easy to replace when necessary."

"Can we get closer?"

He nodded and adjusted his hat. He'd just put his hands on the handlebars, ready to fire the ATV up, when he straightened and once again scanned our surroundings. "Do you hear that?"

I froze, head tilted, straining to pick up what he'd heard. Within seconds the sounds got louder. Engines.

Jude pulled the ATV off the road, and we crouched behind a copse of trees, looking down the hill.

Pickup trucks. Four of them.

"What the fuck?" Jude hissed beside me.

I grabbed the binoculars I'd looped around my neck and focused on the vehicles as the last one passed.

"The license plate is blue and white."

"Quebec," he said under his breath.

"And the bed is packed and covered with a green tarp that's tied town tightly."

He nodded.

"Let's follow them." I popped up.

Jude stood more slowly. "How the hell are they driving trucks through here? This doesn't make sense. Did you recognize anyone?"

I shook my head. "Just random men. They had hats on." It was freezing, after all.

He turned the engine over and straddled the ATV. "Stay here. I want to see where this road leads."

"No." I stomped up to the vehicle. "In together and out together."

"Fine." He dipped his chin. "Hop on. We'll go down the

road and then turn into the woods if we hear or see anything. Just hold on and be ready to take photos."

I wrapped my arms around him, the adrenaline coursing through me blocking out any pain in my bad shoulder. We were so close.

Jude drove slowly down the hill toward the damn near immaculate road. The parade of trucks had barely kicked up any dust. The forest was thick and untouched here, which was far different from many of the other areas we'd explored. But straight through the middle was this pristine road. And I knew exactly where it led.

About half a mile down, the road widened, revealing scrub and small, skinny trees scattered throughout the landscape. This must be where the fire had burned. It made sense that plant life was still growing back.

It made even more sense when we came around a rocky ledge and found a massive warehouse-style building smack-dab in the middle of it.

A dozen or so vehicles were parked around the large brown structure, and a massive garage bay was open. I couldn't make out the details of anything inside, but people were moving in and out. On one side, several motorcycles were lined up.

Jude immediately veered off the road, having to travel pretty far to find adequate tree cover.

"That's it," I said. The vindication that hit me was all-consuming. This was the spot we'd mapped. It made sense. The nerve center of an operation no one had been able to track for years.

No connecting roads, with only one way back and forth between the border and the farm.

And by the looks of it, several dozen people.

"We need to get closer," I urged Jude.

He shook his head. "No. It's not safe. They're armed."

"I can't see anything from this far away."

He shook his head. "No."

A zap of annoyance ran up my spine. "We can't get good photos from this distance. I didn't exactly pack my paparazzi lens. get a bit closer," I begged. "Cut through the woods if you have to."

I stood on the back of the ATV, neck craned for a better look. We were so damn close.

"Fine, but stay low. If I get a bad feeling, we're out of here."

Without hesitation, I dropped back onto the seat and held on tight.

He drove through the woods, keeping his distance. Though between the vehicles and machinery around the building, I couldn't imagine they could hear us. The path to the facility was bumpy and slow. Remaining hidden meant it wasn't possible to look for the smoothest route. The skinny trees were not great coverage, but there were several boulders and bigger trees to hide behind as we got farther off the road. I had my phone out, taking video as we drove toward the building.

Bumping and creeping through the woods, the tires spitting mud and sticks in every direction, we made our way. But I needed to get closer.

I tapped his shoulder and brought my lips to his ear. "We need to go on foot."

He shook his head and continued on. But as we came to

several large rock clusters and wild tree roots growing around them, it became necessary.

We left the ATV behind a boulder and hiked through the rough terrain, crouching low as the noises got louder.

On the far side of the building, several large machines sat. Big digger-type things that I couldn't name to save my life.

What I did recognize was the Deimos Construction logos plastered all over them. I snapped several photos. Then, feeling bolder, I pulled my hat down, tucking my hair in. Then, with Jude right behind me, I headed toward where the trucks were parked. If I could get close enough to get photos of the license plates, that would suffice.

Before we were close enough to make them out, a clicking sound nearby startled me.

I froze and snapped my head up, finding myself looking down the barrel of a revolver. Above us, a large man with a long, grizzled beard loomed.

"*C'est quoi cette merde?*" he said, looking us up and down.

What the fuck? indeed. This was not part of the plan.

"Get up," he said, his accent thick. "Hands up."

Jude tried to step in front of me, but the man pointed the gun straight at me until he got out of the way.

Shaking, mind spinning, I did my best to focus on breathing evenly. I had to keep my wits about me if we had any hope of getting out of this situation.

Jude had strapped the rifle to his back when we abandoned the ATV, but there was no way he'd get it and get the safety off before this man fired.

Beard guy yelled out, and another guy came running over, this one a bit younger.

"*Va cherer Denis,*" Grizzly Adams shouted.

The younger guy nodded and darted towards the building to get *Denis*. I prayed it was a kindly old man who would let us go and not Denis Huxley, indicted arsonist and attempted murderer. Because not only would he recognize me immediately, but he was a known loose cannon with terrible judgment. Not my first choice for counterpart of a backwoods negotiation.

The mountain of a man kept the gun trained on me as he gestured for Jude to pass over the rifle.

With shaky hands, Jude took it off his shoulder and handed it to him.

"Who are you?" the man sneered with a thick Quebecois accent.

"Hikers," I replied. "*Nous sommes en randonnee.* We're just on a hike," I said with a shrug.

Brow cocked, he gestured for us to turn and walk toward the open road. As we reached the tree line, I hesitated. But when he poked Jude in the back with the gun, I came to terms with my lack of options and continued moving.

No sooner had we made it to the road than Denis Huxley himself strode our way, a gun in his belt and a wide smile on his face.

"You've got to be shitting me," he said, the grin making him look even more rat-like. "Another fucking Hebert? God, I cannot escape you people. You never stop causing fucking problems."

He ran a hand through his greasy hair.

"Can't wait to kill that bitch, Victoria."

Jude stiffened beside me.

"The rest of your family too. I told my dad a decade ago that it was time to get rid of your old man, but he had a soft spot for him. Fuck of a lot of good that did us." He shook his head and kicked at the dirt. "He should be here soon. Betting he'll agree to let me shoot you pretty easily. Don't think he'll make that mistake a second time."

I opened my mouth to try and reason with him, but before I could, a commotion at the building had all of us focusing on it.

Several dark SUVs came in from the other side of the road.

Including one with *Lovewell PD* on the side.

Relief washed over me. *Oh, thank God.*

"*Flics!*" Several men shouted the French slang word for police, running to their trucks.

Denis turned as several more vehicles arrived and police in riot gear exited quickly.

Jude grabbed my hand and tugged, and we broke into a run, headed for the woods.

"Get them," Denis yelled, pointing his gun at us.

Jude pulled me down to the ground as a shot ricocheted off a tree nearby. Other shots rang out, echoing off the trunks around us. Shouting too. A man yelled instructions into some type of sound system as we continued to run.

Men spilled out of the warehouse, some getting in trucks and peeling out, gravel flying. Others shot at the police cars.

"On that ledge," a deep voice yelled. The command was quickly followed by a spray of dirt nearby. Then a round of shots was fired in our direction. Jude pushed me ahead of him, shielding me as we ran toward where we had left the ATV.

The men chasing us were on our heels as I stumbled over roots and rocks. Fuck. I wasn't sure I was fast enough to outrun them.

A large, thundering crack stopped me in my tracks. I snapped my head up as a large tree branch fell.

Jude pulled my arm, but before he could get me out of the way, the branch slammed into my hip, throwing me several feet.

I landed on the rocky earth, and pain erupted, lighting up my entire left side. Though I was no longer on my feet, I was still moving. It took a moment to orient myself. Only then did I realize I was slipping. I reached out, grasping for saplings, tree roots, anything to stop the fall. It was no use. I continued to fall, only stopping when the back of my head made contact with a hard surface. My vision went blurry, and I could no longer see or hear Jude.

There was screaming and shooting and the occasional screech of tires, but no Jude.

There was pain and dizziness, but I'd lost his comforting touch.

"Mila," a voice called out. "Are you okay?"

A man stood over me.

Not Jude.

He wore a vest, and there was a shiny badge hanging around his neck.

"Mila, it's Special Agent Portnoy," he said. "Can you get up?"

I opened my mouth to respond, but pain ricocheted through my head.

He was FBI. That made sense. They really had shown up. My intel was right all along.

But where was Jude?

"Let me help you." He held out a hand. "I'll get you to safety. You're okay now."

With a slight nod that made my head spin, I reached for his hand and tried to sit up.

As I was working up the strength to pull myself to standing, my hand still locked in his, the sleeve of his uniform shirt shifted.

On his wrist, wrapping around the outside of his right hand, was a tattoo. Thick trunk, spiny branches.

A yew.

Chapter 41
Jude

I wiped the dirt from my stinging eyes. Where the fuck was Mila? The noise had escalated to a roar, with shrieking tires and shots ringing through the trees.

My head was fuzzy and a searing pain tore through my thigh. I pressed a hand to the injury, and when I discovered the blood, my heart dropped.

My jeans were torn. All I could see was blood and dirt.

But none of that mattered. Mila was all I cared about. I had to find her. Protect her.

I got to my feet and grasped a sapling to steady myself. I scanned the area for Mila, somewhat relieved to see law enforcement flooding the clearing. There were people everywhere. I limped toward the action, calling her name as I maneuvered down the small embankment toward where the trucks were parked.

She had to be here. She had to be okay. I wouldn't entertain any other option. I would find her and I would get her out safely.

The police were so busy slapping cuffs on the men who

hadn't run and chasing those who had that they paid me no mind as I limped toward the action.

I was cresting a small hill when I saw her. She held her shoulder as she walked quickly toward the building with a man wearing a vest and a badge.

I let out a sigh of relief. Good.

I picked up my pace, practically jogging, ignoring the unbearable pain. She was safe. I just needed to get to her.

As they turned a fraction, I recognized the man she was with. Portnoy.

Even better. I didn't like the guy, but surely he'd keep her safe.

I slowed to an awkward walk and stumbled out of the way of trucks speeding from the scene. I rounded the building in the same place where Mila had a moment ago, finding several men on the loading dock. They were hefting massive rubber totes into a truck.

And the director of the FBI field office in Portland was standing right alongside them.

My stomach dropped.

The hand Portnoy had on Mila's shoulder was not protective like I'd thought. No, he was pushing her toward the building.

I took off running again.

"Mila," I shouted.

She turned, her face etched in pain, scratched and dirty and drawn.

"Jude, no," she cried, violently shaking her head.

Portnoy jerked her shoulder, causing her to cry out, and pointed his weapon at me.

On instinct, I threw my hands up.

"Bryce," I said, trying to keep my tone neutral. "Great bust, man. But Mila and I need to get out of here."

He laughed. "No. She's getting in the truck." He nodded toward where the men were furiously packing boxes. "I've been looking for this bitch for more than a year." He grabbed her by the hair, and she let out a cry. "You have caused me so many fucking problems. But don't worry. We won't make the same mistake we did with your brother. You'll actually be dead by the time we're done with you."

His expression was cocky, his body language overly confident. It was the look of someone who knew they'd already won. Like a lifelong bureaucrat, the kind of bland guy no one suspects. For years, we'd cooperated with him, trusted him to protect us, and he'd been a criminal all along?

Bile crept up my throat as Mila and I locked eyes. I had no weapon, no training, and a pretty severely wounded leg. But I'd be damned if he hurt a hair on my girl's head.

Silently, she pleaded with me, giving her head a small shake. She didn't want me to get hurt. I understood that. But given the stakes, there was no other choice.

Portnoy was preoccupied with the packing of the truck as I crept forward slowly, closing the distance between us. He had the gun in one hand, but his finger wasn't on the trigger.

He didn't regard me as a threat. Perfect.

I looked at Mila again, lifting my chin, signaling to the gun. Her eyes widened, as if she understood what I'd discovered. I raised my eyebrows. His hold on her was no longer painful. He assumed she'd go along with his demands. God, was he wrong.

My girl was not great at following directions.

When I was a few yards away, I gave her the signal.

As she grabbed his arm and forced it up so the gun was pointed at the sky, I ran at full speed, crouching down and leading with my shoulder.

When my body made contact, a shot went off, but I was too adrenalized to let it slow me down. As we fell to the ground, I threw punch after punch and took my fair share too as we grappled for control.

Mila was screaming, and more shots rang out, but I was completely focused on a single goal. Pounding this fucker into the ground so he could never hurt anyone again.

I'd never been a fighter. I was the calm guy who de-escalated. But the rage firing in my veins knew no end. He'd pointed a gun at Mila. He'd threatened her and my family. This was fucking over. I'd be certain of it. If I ended up in jail because of that, it would be worth it.

I was stronger, but he had more training, landing several blows and reaching for the gun that lay a few feet from us. Twisting my hips, I managed to get an arm free. I grabbed him by the hair and hit him square in the face before he could get it.

A smallish black boot appeared in my periphery, stepping on the weapon.

"Bryce." The voice was feminine and familiar.

Taking what felt like my first breath in minutes, I looked up. Parker stood above us, in a vest, with her badge around her neck, gun pointed directly at us. Despite the melee, she looked nonplussed.

"Fuck off, Harding," he hissed.

"It's Gagnon now." The words were followed by the telltale click of a safety being released. "Get your dirty ass up."

Ignoring her, he threw an arm around my neck and cocked his fist back.

"I will shoot you, asshole. You know how accurate I am."

With a palm to his face, I shoved him off me. As I was backing away, Mila rushed to my side, collapsing into my arms.

"You're not going to shoot me," Portnoy sneered. "You're a nobody rent-a-cop now. I'm gonna get in my truck and drive to the border, and you're not going to stop me."

Parker barked out a laugh. "Funny. Now get up. I want to slap the handcuffs on you myself."

"You never were good at this job," he blustered. "We both know this case is full of massive holes. So you can either let me go now or watch me walk out of a courtroom in a year or two when all this bullshit evidence blows up in your face."

Mila stiffened next to me, and I held her close.

"Put your hands up," Parker said, taking a step closer without lowering her weapon. "God, you're insufferable. Guess I should have learned my lesson back when you were the world's shittiest boyfriend. Now you've upped the ante and had to be a dirty criminal too."

"Fuck you," he spat.

"Nah, I'm good. And trust me, when my head hits the pillow every night from now on, I'll sleep well knowing how they treat cops in prison." She smirked. "Now get up. If I shoot you in the head, it'll mean more paperwork for me."

I pulled Mila's shaking body close. She was crying, her hands twisted in the fabric of my jacket. But she was safe. That was all that mattered.

Parker lifted the radio strapped to her shoulder without

taking her gun off Portnoy. "Bring my Tahoe around. I've got a VIP criminal here who needs a ride to the station."

It was satisfying, watching Parker cuff Portnoy and shove him by the head into her vehicle while gleefully reading him his Miranda rights. But the sensation paled in comparison to having my girl in my arms. She might have been a bit bruised, but she was okay.

"You need a medic," Parker said, nodding at my leg. "You got shot."

Frowning, I looked down at my bloodstained jeans. Maybe it was the adrenaline or the relief of knowing Mila was safe, but I had barely felt anything. I touched the area, and it burned. Shit, I guess I really had been shot.

Mila gasped and pulled away, clapping her hands to her mouth as her eyes filled with tears again. "Oh my God. Let's get you to the hospital."

"I'll have someone take you straight away. We'll be here cleaning up this mess for a while," Parker said, radioing one of her deputies.

With my arm around Mila again, I limped around the side of the building to where the police were taking photos and loading dozens of people into cars.

The warehouse was even bigger up close, and it was filled with giant pallets wrapped in plastic. "You know," Parker mused, "I expected the shitload of drugs. The illegal weapons are just icing on the cake. The ATF guys are gonna have a field day when they get here."

She opened the back door of a black SUV. "Office Fielder here will stabilize the wound and then get you to the hospital."

"Thank you." I nodded at Parker as Mila tried to force me into the vehicle.

The last thing I wanted was to let go of her. Fielder was a good guy and I trusted him, but all I wanted was to go home and take my girl with me.

"Looks like you got grazed," he said, applying a clotting agent to the wound once he and Mila had finally talked me into climbing in. "You did good, son. Heard you charged at a gunman like a crazed bull."

I laughed, though the pain that rocketed through me had me biting back the sound. Now that the adrenaline was wearing off, I was fading fast.

Once he'd bandaged the wound, he closed the door and rounded the hood.

Tucked safely in the back of the car, I closed my eyes. It was over. Mila was safe.

"I love you," she whispered, her head on my chest. "But did you seriously run at a guy with a gun? That was really stupid, you know."

"It was teamwork," I said. "You grabbed his arms so he couldn't shoot me."

"You saved me."

I kissed the top of her head. "We saved each other, Trouble."

Chapter 42
Mila

We spent the night at the hospital. Jude got stitches and a heavy dose of antibiotics, and when we were finally left alone, I curled up in the bed next to him. We were filthy and exhausted, but for the first time in hours, I could finally draw a full breath.

The bullet had grazed his thigh, causing minimal damage. But he'd need to rest for a while and would likely need a little physical therapy.

Curled up on his chest, I tried to wrap my mind around the events of the day. I'd thought of nothing but this trafficking ring and avenging my brother for so long. I'd lived as Amy. I'd quit my job and given up my entire life. And as good as it felt to see all those guys arrested, to know that I'd done my part to take them down, there was still a gnawing emptiness in my gut.

Because now I had to rebuild. Start from scratch. And I wasn't sure I knew how.

"Rest, Trouble," Jude murmured, pulling me against his chest. We were not supposed to be wedged in this hospital bed together, and the nurses would probably yell at me when they came back to check his vitals in an hour, but I couldn't stand even a few inches of distance. He'd been shot trying to help me.

"I can't. My brain is going too fast."

"Let me help you slow it down." He kissed me softly.

Instantly, I melted into him. Okay, that was a bit better.

"The timing is terrible and doing this in a hospital is even worse." He shook his head. "But now that this is over, or at least over for now, I want you to know I love you."

A lightness I wasn't sure I was capable of feeling at the moment fluttered through me. "I love you too."

"I know you've probably got a lot of exciting things out there waiting for you, but I'd love to be a part of it."

Heart clenching, I buried my face in his neck. "I want that too," I said against his skin. "In every other aspect of my life, I'm lost. But the one thing I know for certain is that I want to be with you." Heat pricked at the backs of my eyes. "The possibilities are overwhelming. I can't even begin to figure out what comes next. But you are the best person I've ever met. Regardless of all of it, I want to be by your side."

He held me for a moment, the two of us silent, both processing my admission. This felt good. Vulnerability, honesty. I'd never been comfortable with either, but Jude was worth it.

"We have time to figure it all out," he whispered. "You were so brave. So amazing. Let yourself recover. Then we can write our next chapter."

"I don't know what I want the next chapter to include," I admitted. "Aside from you and Ripley."

"That sounds like a good start. First, let's try being

normal, like we planned. I'll take you out to dinner, and we can go for hikes with Ripley. From there, we can take that vacation we were talking about."

I smiled at the thought of sand in my toes.

We fell asleep making mundane plans for when he was released and we'd both healed. We'd paint the bedroom, and he would teach me how to work the pizza oven. Then there were the endless Scrabble rematches and some nights volunteering to babysit his nieces and nephew.

As I drifted off to sleep against his strong chest, all I could think was how perfect it all sounded.

GUS MET US THE NEXT MORNING, HANDLING THE discharge paperwork and tearing up when he saw his baby brother in a hospital bed.

"Fuck, Jude." He shook his head.

"Any news?"

"Lots of arrests. Charles Huxley took off. They think he's headed to the Cayman Islands, but Parker has a team from the ATF hunting him down."

Of course she did.

"The town is in an uproar. It's wild out there. Everyone is so worried about you. How are you guys feeling?"

"Tired," Jude said, shooting me a wink. "Can't wait to get home."

The nurse rolled a wheelchair into the room and motioned for Jude to get into it.

"Do you really think you need that?" Gus picked up the crutch his brother had been using.

"I got shot," Jude huffed.

"The doctor said *grazed*," Gus replied, arching a brow. "Pretty sure that's different." He ruffled Jude's hair affectionately. "I'm not gonna start going easy on you now, little brother. Plus Mom is going to fuss all over you when we get to her house."

Jude frowned. "Mom's house?"

"We've all been summoned. She's got to feed you and see for herself that you're okay. No use fighting it."

With a chuckle, Jude shook his head. "Sorry." He pushed my hair behind my ear. "My family can be a lot, and it looks like you're meeting my mom today."

After loading up in the car and driving the forty minutes back to Lovewell, I was starving and in desperate need of a shower.

I knew so much about Jude and had heard all about his large, boisterous family, but aside from that first night, I hadn't actually met any of them but Willa. With every mile we traveled, my stomach twisted tighter and worries consumed me.

Would they resent me for putting him in danger? How could I look his mother in the eye, knowing it was my fault her son had been shot?

Turned out there was no point worrying. Gus hadn't even put his truck in park before people were spilling out of the house. They were hugging and crying and telling me the names of all the various kids who were running around.

There were others too. Parker and her husband, who was holding a little girl, and more of their family members. Parker's brothers-in-law, maybe.

I couldn't keep track. And honestly, the someone I was most interested in seeing wasn't even human.

At least fifteen people had come out of the house when Ripley finally bounded down the front steps. She stopped right in front of Jude, sniffing his crutch and instantly sensing his injury. He bent at the waist and buried his face in her fur, hugging her fiercely.

When he straightened, I dropped to my knees and did the same. "You are such a good girl," I said as she licked my face. "I missed you so much."

Jude's mom, who insisted I call her Debbie, hugged me several times, getting teary and thanking me for saving her precious boy.

I explained gently that it was the other way around, but she wouldn't hear it.

Inside, I felt as if I'd found myself on the set of a heart-warming movie. The home was neat and filled with food and kids. Every person in attendance was happy and kind and determined to feed me. The love that filled this place to the brim made my heart ache for my own little family. I missed my mom and Hugo so much.

Once we got settled at Jude's, I'd talk to him about borrowing his truck so I could drive down to Boston this week.

Debbie led me to the couch, carrying a slice of pie the size of my head in one hand. She'd urged me onto the cushion and forced the plate into my hand when Willa sat next to me, giving my knee a reassuring pat.

"You doing okay?"

I nodded, taking a big bite. Shit, this was good pie.

"You're madly in love with him, aren't you?" she asked,

following my gaze to where Jude sat across the room, babbling to his niece Tess.

I shrugged and stuffed another bite of pie into my mouth. "It's okay. The Hebert boys are an irresistible bunch."

"Truth." A woman with a dark ponytail joined us. She'd been introduced as Victoria, Noah's girlfriend. "We all knew he was hung up on you," she said. "The mystery woman."

"I was pretty much gone when he played the guitar for me," I admitted, feeling like I was being granted admission into some kind of sisterhood.

Victoria fanned herself and Willa pumped her first. "Good work, Jude."

For a moment, I was entranced by the bearded man in glasses across the room. He looked tired, but so, so happy as his brothers gathered around him.

"What are your plans?" Willa asked. "Are you staying?"

"Yes, I was wondering too," Victoria said, her expression eager. "And if you have free time, I'm always looking for volunteers at the food bank."

I looked between them, at a loss for how to respond.

"Do you know how to knit?"

"Ladies." Alice Gagnon appeared, giving me a big smile. "Don't overwhelm her." She sat in the chair beside the couch and crossed her legs. "Mila, sweetie, when you're healed, I want you to come and talk to my students about journalism. Tell them all about your exciting career."

"Maybe leave out the getting shot at part," Willa said.

"That's my favorite part." Parker sauntered up with a baby on her hip and a beer in her hand. "When I go to career day, I always bring a sidearm."

Alice rolled her eyes. "Ignore Chief Gagnon. She'll be

gloating about arresting her crappy ex-boyfriend for the next decade."

Parker tipped her imaginary hat at me. "I owe you, Mila. Cuffing that fucker will go down as one of the greatest moments of my life."

Willa raised her wineglass and Parker clinked her beer against it.

"How did you know to come?" I asked Parker. "When we spoke on the phone?"

She shifted the baby and took a long sip of beer. "I wasn't being totally transparent that day on the phone because I suspected a law enforcement leak. Never thought it would be Bryce, though." She chuckled. "He's always been an uptight by-the-book asshole, but I guess even those types can go rogue. Also," she sighed, "Gus called me. Told me what you two were planning."

I looked over at Gus, who had his arm around his wife, a petite redhead, and had a sleeping baby on his shoulder.

"I knew your instincts were good," Parker continued. "And when Gus told me about the location you suspected, it made sense. Had the state police on standby, and it turned out to be a bigger bust than we ever could have imagined."

Victoria leaned forward. "Did you seize a lot of drugs?"

"Yes. Millions of dollars' worth." Parker nodded. "And weapons and cash. Turns out it wasn't just drugs they were running, but illegal weapons. We stopped a lot of bad shit from ending up on the street today. And the dominoes will keep falling. This is big."

Relief washed over me. I was bone-tired, but the knowledge that people were safer because of what we'd done gave me a surge of energy.

"We could not have done this without you," Parker admitted. "We were so stuck for so long."

Willa stood abruptly. "Everyone," she said.

Slowly, people stopped talking and turned toward us. "I'd like to propose a toast to Mila and Jude."

Jude shuffled over and Victoria and made space for him. He eased onto the couch and put his arm around me. "To the bravest woman I've ever met," he said, his eyes shining.

"And the lumberjack she dragged along for the ride," one of the brothers shouted.

The room erupted in laughter.

Without giving myself a chance to second-guess the move, I kissed him chastely on the lips. Even though it lasted mere seconds, heat crept into my cheeks as I pulled back.

"I'm thinking a summer wedding," Debbie trilled, clapping her hands.

My heart may have lurched, but I didn't have even the smallest inclination to backpedal or run.

"Mom, give them some space."

I snuggled into Jude's chest, soaking in the warmth and safety of his hold as his family bickered good-naturedly around us.

As the night went on, plans were made for Thanksgiving, the Gagnons challenged the Heberts to more wood chopping, and I played peek-a-boo with some really cute kids.

I had no job, no home, and no direction. I had no idea what my next chapter would look like, but I was certain it would start here, in Lovewell, with my sweet lumberjack.

Epilogue
Mila

Four Months Later...

The tranquil turquoise water was mesmerizing.

Side by side, Jude and I lay in beach loungers. His hair was ruffled, his shirt tossed over a nearby chair, his skin a warm tan. We'd woken up this morning for a kayaking tour where we'd seen turtles the size of small cars. And now we were in a shaded cabana on the beach, soaking up all the beauty of this place.

Jude had made good on his promise to take me away, whisking me out of an iced-over Maine for an incredible two-week vacation.

We were safe. My brain knew that, but my nervous system was still catching up. After the arrests, I'd spent months working with law enforcement while making frequent trips to Boston to see my mother and Hugo.

Hugging her after more than a year of very little contact was one of the best moments of my life.

And Hugo? For so long I worried I'd lost him forever. I spent hours talking to him, telling him every detail of what had happened, watching on the monitors as his brain activity increased at the sound of my voice.

The specialists had made incredible progress. He'd even opened his eyes briefly a few times and would sometimes squeeze my mother's hand while she spoke to him.

The doctors said the changes were miraculous. They were doing more tests and trying multiple types of stimulation they believed would continue to heal his brain.

Every report gave me hope. I would do anything to get him back. To give him back the life that had been stolen from him.

Jude shifted in his chair, giving me a big, sleepy smile. "You okay?"

I nodded. "I love it here. It's so peaceful."

"Then I'll bring you back every year, Trouble. It can be our special place."

He dragged me off my lounger and onto his, pulling me on top of him and kissing me, his fingers playing with the sides of my bikini bottoms.

"Being here with you is bliss." I kissed him again, then settled against his warm chest.

This had been a trip of a lifetime. We'd started on the big island, hiking volcanoes and snorkeling with manta rays. Every experience was more special with Jude by my side. Seeing his excitement and wonder only intensified my own. He'd even nerded out over the tree species, asking the park rangers endless questions. It was adorable.

For a relationship forged in danger and very strange circumstances, we were really enjoying the "normal honeymoon" as we were calling this period. We reveled in doing mundane tasks and running errands together.

He took me for breakfast at the diner, over to his mom's for Sunday dinner, and to all his favorite spots. After our vacation ended, he was set on teaching me how to ski.

And we still played Scrabble. Curled up under my favorite blanket, with Ripley by our side.

I had no idea what I'd do with my life once the dust settled for good. The investigation was ongoing, and I'd given dozens of hours of interviews to every possible law enforcement agency and prosecutor. While I was content to stay in Lovewell and wake up next to Jude every day, at some point, I'd have to get back to work.

But I'd changed. Like Jude had said, I'd been through the fire. My regrowth may look different, but I'd be stronger for the pain I'd been through.

While the old Mila would have jumped on the next journalism job as a means to run away from all that had happened in the past year, the new version of me embraced the opportunity to settle and recalibrate.

Sitting on a beach in Maui on top of my hot lumberjack boyfriend was not a bad way to do it.

We'd had lunch on the beach and were debating whether we should go for a swim or head back to our villa and get naked when my phone rang.

Things had been blissfully silent since we'd left. Jude had lectured Parker and forced her to promise that she wouldn't bother me with case details. He wanted me to relax.

But I'd refused to turn my phone off completely.

And when I fished my phone out of my bag, my heart stuttered.

It was my mom.

"Mom?" My throat was thick, making it hard to speak. "Is everything okay?"

She sobbed, and my stomach plummeted. I couldn't form the words to ask about Hugo, but I feared the worst.

"He's awake," she got out between hiccupping sobs.

"What?" I was on my feet in seconds, Jude by my side, leaning close to the phone. "He woke up?"

"Yes. He can only speak a few words, but he's awake. The doctors are doing tests and taking measurements. But he recognized me. I held his face in my hands and kissed my son."

I had so many questions. There was so much to do.

"Mila, the doctor came in. I'll call you back."

When the call disconnected, all I could do was stand in place, in shock. If Jude hadn't been holding me up, I probably would have collapsed.

"He's awake." The whispered words had barely passed my lips when I burst into tears of my own.

Jude held me while I shook. Relief and sadness and joy tore through my body. Awake.

I had no idea what the future would hold for him, but he was still here with us.

"Come on." Jude scooped up my bag, then lifted me off my feet. "We've got to pack."

"But—"

"We've got to get to Boston."

I nodded, arms looped around his neck. He was right. I

needed to see my brother. I wasn't sure how we'd get there, but at this point, I was willing to swim.

While I packed, Jude called Owen, who helped us find flights. Apparently one of his billionaire friends had a jet on Oahu and could give us a ride to San Francisco, where we could jump on a red-eye to the East Coast.

"Trouble," Jude said, zipping his suitcase. "Pants."

I looked down at the leggings he'd laid out for me on the bed, still standing in my undies, losing my mind. Thank God for this man. With ease, he got us checked out of the hotel and over to the airstrip.

As we soared over the blue Pacific, I took my first full breath.

Awake.

It felt like a dream. As did the sweet lumberjack currently sitting next to me.

"I hope I have time to shower. I want to look good when I meet my future brother-in-law for the first time."

I put my head on his shoulder. "You look great."

"No comment about the future brother-in-law thing?" he teased, holding a hand to my forehead as if checking for a fever.

I surveyed him, so full of love and hope and certainty that I could not have made it through the last several months without him, and shrugged. "I'd marry the shit out of you."

His eyes bulged. "Seriously?"

"Yes. But not yet. I've got to make you work for it."

I was rewarded with the most beautiful smile. "I wouldn't want it any other way, Trouble."

Want more Jude & Mila?
Click HERE to read the Bonus Scene!
Warning: it will make you laugh, cry and swoon!

THE MAINE LUMBERJACKS SERIES IS NOW COMPLETE! Thank you for joining me on this journey to Lovewell. **All five books are available on Amazon and Free to read in Kindle Unlimited.**

Bonus Chapter

Want more Jude, Mila & Ripley?
Scan HERE To Read It!
Warning: it will make you laugh, cry and swoon!

Acknowledgments

Thank you for taking this trip to Lovewell with me! This is my 16th full length novel, and one that is so near and dear to my heart. I can't believe that, after nine books, Lovewell has it's HEA. I've spent the past three years living in this world and creating these characters. Thank you for joining me on this journey.

Like all my books, it would not have been possible without the support of several talented and dedicated people.

Morgan Leigh, I asked for help, and you jumped in with both feet, quickly becoming the MVP in my life and the person who keeps me organized and on track. I treasure your friendship and your positive attitude. No one is more willing and more capable of learning new things than you are, and I am pinching myself that I get to call you mine.

Erica Walsh, thank you for being my friend and cheerleader for all these years. From cover design to finding photos and editing blurbs, you are truly in my corner every single day. We have cried and laughed and yelled together over the past four years, and I am a better person and writer because of you.

Beth, thank you for your thorough editing. I am amazed by your patience, professionalism, and kindness. Your careful work has helped bring these characters to life, and I am truly in your debt.

To my oldest friend, the indomitable Caroline, thank you for igniting my love of romance by introducing me to Jane Austen (and Colin Firth in a wet shirt) at the tender age of fifteen. My entire romantic worldview has been shaped by our shared love of happy endings and your friendship for these last twenty-seven (!!!) years is a true gift.

Becca, thank you for your professionalism and excitement about this series. You and the Author Agency have been such wonderful partners throughout this process.

Catherine, getting to know you has been one of the highlights of my year. Thank you for your marketing expertise, your passion for books, and your invaluable TikTok wisdom.

Sue, thank you for the gorgeous cover. You took a simple idea and elevated it with your immense talent. I am so grateful to get to work with you.

To my hype teams, thank you from the bottom of my heart for loving these books and this crazy world I've created. Most days, I pinch myself that I'm surrounded by such an amazing group of positive, kickass people.

Thank you to my mother, who always pushed me to do my best and believed in me even when I did not. I am the kind of person who decides to write books in my nonexistent free time because of you.

Thank you to my family for being hilarious, loving, and silly. To my children, G & T, you push me, challenge me, and surprise me every day. Being your mom is my life's greatest adventure. Thank you for never going easy on me. To G, my mini-me, you are my #1 fan and I can't wait to share my author journey with you as you grow. And T, thank you for kicking ass in Kindergarten, so I had the mental and physical space to write this book.

And finally, I'd like to thank Taylor Alison Swift. For getting me through not only the production of this book, but through all of my life's challenges for the past decade. You have taught me, and countless others, how to harness my creativity and, most importantly, how to invest in my potential. Your work has made me a better mom, writer, entrepreneur, and person. Thank you.

Also by Daphne Elliot

LOVEWELL

The Lovewell Lumberjacks Series

Wood You Be Mine?

Wood You Marry Me?

Wood You Rather?

Wood Riddance

The Maine Lumberjacks Series

Caught in the Axe

Pain in the Axe

Axe-identally Married

Axe Backwards

Axe-ing for Trouble

THE MOM COMS

Mother Hater

Also by Daphne Elliot

About the Author

In High School, Daphne Elliot was voted "most likely to become a romance novelist." After spending the last decade as a corporate lawyer, she has finally embraced her destiny. Her small town steamy novels are filled with flirty banter, sexy hijinks, and lots and lots of heart.

Where to Find Daphne

daphneelliotauthor@gmail.com

Stay in touch with Daphne:
Subscribe to Daphne's Newsletter
Join Daphne's Reader Group
Follow Daphne on TikTok
Like Daphne on Facebook
Follow Daphne on Instagram
Hang with Daphne on GoodReads
Follow Daphne on Amazon

www.ingramcontent.com/pod-product-compliance
Lightning Source LLC
Chambersburg PA
CBHW070157310726
48976CB00001B/129